INTRINSICAL

INTRINSICAL

Amber,
It was great meeting
You at B.E.A. I hope you enjoy
Intrinsical!

_LW_

LANI WOODLAND

PENDRELL PUBLISHING

For Mom and Dad

Who taught me that anything was possible if you have enough hope and work hard enough for it.

PROLOGUE

My shadow stretched out in front of me, making my small build and slight frame seem almost tall—willowy even. It had an air of grace about it that I envied, and made me feel more elegant than the boarding school uniform-wearing sixteen year old I was.

The humid summer swelter had not yet surrendered to the much more bearable temperatures of fall. A gust of wind momentarily stirred the air, giving me a respite from the suffocating heat as my shirt billowed out around me. I could feel the sturdy beads of my necklace warm against my skin, reflecting the bright sunlight onto the wall of the campus library in a shower of amber sparkles.

I decided to seek solace from the heat in the shade of a tall tree. Dropping to the well-manicured grass at its base, I slouched against the scratchy bark that pricked my scalp and snared my mocha-colored hair. A lone white cloud hung in the sky, thin and shredded around the edges, losing a battle against the summer's unyielding heat.

Out of the corner of my eye, I noticed something slide past me. Curious, I turned to find something shimmering in the air, almost like a fine mist—but it was unlike any mist I had ever seen. Instead of a transparent white, it was a deep charcoal gray, almost black. It brought to mind a dark rain cloud, one that promised a terrible storm. The mist radiated coldness. "Cold" wasn't the right word though. It was . . . chilling, and not the good air-conditioned kind. Its chill ran down my spine and the warm sweat that had beaded on my skin now turned icy.

The fog hung in the air for a moment, its whirling tendrils frothing, churning, and folding in on themselves. I shuddered as the writhing patch of darkness glided a few feet off the ground. It seemed to move with purpose as it swirled around the students who were loitering around campus.

"What *is* that?" I asked myself, speaking aloud. I blinked and rubbed my eyes, sure I was imagining it. But I wasn't; it was still there.

My stomach sunk as I watched the fog. It couldn't be a ghost. Could it? My grandmother's descriptions of some of the ghosts she had encountered trickled through my mind. But I was different than other women in my family; I couldn't see them. Had genetics caught up to me at long last?

The mist wound around one student, then another, releasing each before moving on, still searching. Then, abruptly, it paused, circling tightly around a boy with sable brown hair.

His friends surrounded him but no one seemed to notice the blanket of vapor that now enveloped him. Some-one must have told a joke, because he threw his head back in a laugh, a sound that rang through the air like a velvety melody. With the speed of a whip slicing through the air, a tendril of darkness slid inside his open mouth. My own mouth went suddenly dry. I felt sick, as if I had swallowed it myself.

The boy's eyes instantly went wide and his hands went

reflexively to his neck. He leaned forward, gasping for air as if the darkness were squeezing his airway shut.

I jumped to my feet and felt myself take a step forward.

Eyes bulging wide, he kept one hand clasped at his throat while his other hand waved desperately in the air, signaling for somebody to step in and help him. "Brent? Brent!" I heard one of his friends shout.

I didn't even realize my feet were running toward him, pushing authoritatively through the immobile, gaping crowd. One friend pounded him on the back before I shoved him out of the way.

I kneeled in front of a complete stranger, as if somehow I had the power to save him. I knew the basics of CPR, and although I had never done it, I now steeled myself to try, fumbling for the information I had once learned. Tears streamed down my face and I took his hand in mine. "Hey!" I shouted. His brown eyes met my hazel ones and I could see he knew what was happening, knew he was moments from death. He stared back at me, and in his expression I could see he was pleading desperately for help. I was sure that the horror I saw in his eyes was mirrored in my own.

Dropping his hand and rising to my feet I circled behind him and wrapped my arms around his body. Leaning in close to his ear I promised, "You are going to be okay!" My shaking hands clasped together as they found the correct placement. I repeated again, "You will be okay." It was a promise to myself as much as to him.

Leaning forward, my hair, tears, and necklace fell in a silky puddle across his cheek. I could feel the warmth from his skin on my face, and my heart started beating faster at what I was about to do. The air around me shifted as I thrust my hands under his ribs. With a violent blast, the intruder that had entered his body withdrew. The freezing vapor encircled us both before vanishing with an anguished scream. Brent instantly took a deep, painful-sounding breath, and began coughing as soon as the fresh air filled his starved lungs. He turned toward me and his eyes locked with mine.

"Breathe with me," I instructed, trying to help his ragged breathing normalize. Slowly, the panicked look in his eyes quieted but his hand clutched mine as if it alone were tethering him to life.

I knew there were people around me, that someone was recording the whole thing on their phone. I was even aware of some of them trying to get our attention, but I couldn't make out anything they said. I didn't care about any of it; all that mattered was that he was alive.

A pair of hands grabbed me forcefully from behind, moving me out of the way. The movement broke our eye contact and I lost my grip on Brent's hand. The world tumbled back to life around me, and now I could make out the conversations that were happening in the crowd. I could see the larger group of onlookers frantically rehashing what they had just seen.

I didn't care. None of it mattered.

He was still watching me, but the nurse slid between us, checking his pulse and making sure he was okay. The crowd began to thin as everyone realized the action was over and lost interest. His friends stood off to the side waiting for him, shuffling around nervously. I dug my shoe into the grass, trying to fade into the background, unsure if I should stay. Shaking my head, I tried to clear away the intensity of the moment.

"I need you to come to my office, just to be sure," I heard the nurse instruct him as he stood with a slight balance check. Looking up, I watched him nod, but he wasn't looking at her, he was looking at me. When he turned to walk toward the infirmary, I followed for a few steps before I stopped myself. *What was I doing?* He didn't need me anymore. Instead, I headed towards my dorm.

I had only taken perhaps three steps when someone caught my wrist. I knew it was him before I even turned around. I looked back, blinking stupidly, wondering if this was even real. I could feel the strong pulse from his fingers that slid down to my hand. Boldly, he lifted my hand and placed it on his chest over the steady thumping of his heart. I stifled a gasp as I felt my own heart shift to beat in rhythm with his.

"You saved my life," he stated in a raspy voice. "I'm in your debt." Despite the twinkle in his eye, there was a weight to his words that made me shiver. He opened his mouth to say more, but the nurse, a formidable woman, caught hold of his elbow and steered him towards her office.

I stared after him until the reality of what had happened hit me and my whole body began to tremble. His near death hadn't been an accident; something— a ghost? —had tried to kill him, and only I had been able to see it. Panic spiraled through me. I spun on my heel and dashed toward my room, grateful every step for the heat of the day.

CHAPTER 1

The next afternoon by the pool, I angled my lounge chair to give me the best view of Brent. He was taking a lifeguard training course, treading water while holding what looked like a smooth, black brick above his head. I bit my lip as he sank lower in the water.

Cherie, my best friend, sitting beside me nudged me with her elbow. "Yara, he isn't going to die just because you take your eyes off him."

"I know that." I sighed, shifting my gaze toward her.

"You're going to have a permanent image of him burned into your retinas if you keep staring at him so hard."

I laughed. "Not a bad way to go blind."

She shook her head. "You've got it bad."

I nodded, glad the heat had already flushed my cheeks so no one could see my blush. "I know." My eyes slid back toward Brent.

"You're hopeless." There was no judgment, only amusement in her voice.

My book— well, my celebrity magazine carefully folded inside an SAT prep manual— was propped on my stomach so it looked like I was reading and not staring at Brent. I wasn't sure how long I had been watching him when Cherie left to go swim with Steve, Brent's best friend and potentially Cherie's next boyfriend.

Clearing my thoughts of Brent, I put on my sunglasses and admired our new boarding school's beautiful glass pool house. An enormous clock hung on the largest wall, a focal point that drew the eye toward its iron hands. Though beautiful and elegant, it wasn't enough to keep my attention for more than a couple of seconds. My eyes kept flitting back to the largest of the two swimming pools where Brent and the other trainees were swimming laps.

I still had a hard time believing that Cherie and I were really students at Pendrell, the elite and— until yesterday— all-boys prep school. Classes hadn't started yet. We were on campus doing the whole "Welcome to your new school thing" and getting settled into our dorm room before the school year began.

I closed my eyes and enjoyed feeling the sun on my skin. There was a slight breeze courtesy of the open retractable roof. I inhaled the warm end-of-summer air, relaxing and feeling all my worries float away. The school seemed so peaceful, and I had a hard time believing Brent had almost been killed in front of my eyes the day before. I tried to swallow down the image of what had tried to hurt him. I didn't want it to be real. I wanted nothing to do with ghosts and spirits, especially ones that appeared as sinister patches of storm clouds, trying to kill people. They belonged in the world I had rejected.

I heard Cherie's familiar laugh and looked up to watch as she playfully splashed Steve. She had met him last night at our first dinner in the cafeteria where he had accompanied Brent over to meet me officially. Cherie had tossed her blonde hair, batted her eyelashes and convinced Steve and Brent to eat dinner with us. In the course of that meal, Steve and Cherie realized they were into each other.

With the two of them controlling most of the conversation, Brent and I had barely spoken last night— although, whenever I had glanced in his direction, I caught him watching me too. I was hoping that seeing me today would help him realize that he desperately wanted to ask me to the dance tonight. Now that there was a gorgeous guy I was interested in, it was the part of the school's orientation I was most looking forward to.

On the stone table beside my chair sat an open package of my favorite candy. I fished out a handful and sorted out the greens into my discard pile before popping the rest into my mouth. My older brother Kevin used to eat the greens, but he wasn't around to do that anymore, so now they'd just end up in the trash.

I turned my attention back to Brent, who stood on the side of the pool shaking the excess water out of his dark brown hair. His slow stretch emphasized his cut chest and caused a group of girls to fan themselves and call out to him. My eyes narrowed at his admirers when he rewarded them with a smile, starting a chorus of flirty giggles.

A flash of something I didn't want to name pulsed through me, and I clenched my jaw as I turned away from Brent to start reading my magazine. I was soon lost in the trashy details of some actor's life when a shadow appeared at the foot of my chair, blocking the sun.

I looked up into Brent's eyes and my mouth suddenly went dry, my stomach tightened, and my brain turned to applesauce.

"Hey there," he said, drying his hair with a towel, being careful not to drip on me as he sat at the end of my chair. He flashed me an easy grin and ran his fingers through his hair leaving the tousled locks artfully disarrayed.

I smiled, closing my book and placing it in my lap while

trying to ignore my racing pulse. "What's up?"

"Nothing really." He paused before leaning close to me. "About yesterday, what you did."

I bit my lip and felt my throat constrict. "Yeah?"

He scratched a spot on his neck and looked back toward Steve in the pool. "Never mind."

Tension that had started to build inside me unwound and I breathed deeply. I reached out and grabbed a red candy. "Help yourself to the greens if you want."

"Thanks, they're my favorite." He popped a few into his mouth and chewed. An odd feeling of satisfaction swept over me knowing the greens weren't going to waste. Brent folded his towel as he swallowed. "So, are you liking Pendrell so far?"

"Yep. The student body is great." It wasn't until I had said the word "body'" that I realized my eyes had been studying his chest and I quickly looked away. He suppressed a chuckle, and I knew, mortified, that he had noticed.

Trying to make my voice not shake, I corrected, "I mean, everyone is so nice." I nervously pushed my sunglasses high up on my nose. "How do you like it?" I asked back, trying to redirect the conversation to avoid any further humiliation.

"I really enjoy the student body here as well," he said while eyeing me. "It got a lot better looking this year." I lowered my glasses and gave him the evil eye as I thought about his group of giggly admirers. "Why did you come here?"

"I was considering going for a swim. I've heard the pool's a great place for that."

He sighed in exasperation. "No, why did you come to Pendrell?"

"It was this or Brazil. Besides, Cherie really wanted to come." My fingers began gathering my hair into a ponytail.

His eyebrow raised in curiosity. "Brazil?"

"It's where I was born. My dad was transferred to the States when I was really young, but now the company has called him back. My parents agreed that I could stay here and finish high school."

"So how did you end up at a stuffy private school?"

"I was dragged into it by Cherie. She really wanted to come here for, uh . . . personal reasons," I edited carefully, "and since I'm a Legacy kid and could get in easily, she begged me to come with her."

"A Legacy kid, huh? So who was it?"

"My great-great-grandfather taught here way back in the day. And my great-grandfather and my grandpa were students here."

That was my official story, the one that was polished and edited enough not to invite questions that probed into areas that I really didn't want to dig into.

"Okay, so that's your story, but why did Cherie want to come here so badly?"

I cringed internally and hoped it didn't show. "She's sort of a . . . history buff."

"History? Our history department really isn't that strong. Wouldn't she be better off at . . ." he trailed off as he noticed my cheeks flush. He looked confused for a moment and then I could almost see a few pieces of information click together in his head. "Wait a minute. She wouldn't happen to be interested in the Pendrell Curse, would she?"

I tried not to deflate into my chair like a saggy, popped balloon. "She might have mentioned it."

Brent made a sound that was a mixture of coughing and clearing his throat. "Are you serious?" The corners of his mouth drooped slightly. "*You* don't believe the stories about ghosts and curses, do you?"

The black mist from yesterday flashed in my mind. I swallowed before answering, choosing my words carefully. "Of course I don't believe in curses," I said, with a hasty wave of my hand.

He brought his fingers to his mouth and started gnawing on one of his nails. His eyes narrowed, pupils hardening with a cold glint, and he dropped his hand in his lap. "So she's not planning on investigating the curse, is she?"

"Nope," I lied with a gulp, my blood running cold. "Do people do that a lot around here or something?"

"Yes." He paused for a second and I thought I heard his teeth grinding.

Brent looked away, leaning back from me and shaking his head, lips pursed. The conversation stalled and a series of possible questions ran through my mind. I asked the first fully formed one I could grasp. "So, have you been training to be a lifeguard long?"

Brent's eyes found mine again. "It's my first year, but I've always loved the water."

"Me, too, usually." I stopped short of explaining that my recurring nightmare had recently made me wary of water.

A wicked smile spread across his face. "Well then, let's get you in!" He scooped me up, letting my disguised magazine clunk onto the wet cement.

"Put me down!" He only held me tighter. My heart thudded in my chest, and it wasn't just the fear of being tossed in. He ran to the edge of the pool and with a glint in his eye, cannon balled us both into the water.

We were a tangle of arms and legs, trying to find the surface. My eyes opened and widened when nothing in the pool was what I had expected. The water that had appeared so clear and blue from the surface was shadowy and dark.

Suddenly it felt like the water was crushing in on me, pushing me down. I couldn't see Brent; I was alone and I was stuck, sinking. In a panic, my limbs struggled to propel me to the surface as my lungs burned inside my chest, threatening to burst.

It didn't make a difference. I had almost given up hope when I felt strong hands grab me under my arms. I opened my eyes and saw Brent next to me, the water now bright and clear again. My frantic swimming strokes subsided as he pulled me to the surface, where I took in a huge breath of air.

"You looked like you freaked out there for a second. Are you okay?" Brent asked, concerned.

Still panting for air, I nodded. Carefully, as if helping a child, he lifted me to the safety of the ladder and I pulled myself up and sat right on the edge of the pool with my feet dangling in. I was trembling soul deep, shaken by my underwater experience; it reminded me starkly of my nightmare. Gripping the edge of the pool, I hung my head and breathed deeply, fighting to stave off the panic that threatened to resurface at this realization.

"I should apologize but I won't because I'm not sorry in the least, Yara," Brent admitted with a half-checked smirk as he treaded water in front of me.

"I gathered that," I said with a weak grin.

He smiled widely, making whatever anxiety I had completely vanish. I noticed Cherie watching me. She raised an eyebrow that wordlessly asked if I wanted her to come over. I shook my head slightly and she nodded in understanding. The truth was I now felt fine, only slightly foolish for overreacting. I was lost in my thoughts when Brent splashed me.

"Hey! I wouldn't push your luck." I wagged my finger

at him in warning.

"What? You're already drenched!"

"It's the principle of the matter." I laughed, kicking my feet to splash his face.

"Oh! Is that how we're playing it?" With that he grabbed my leg and pulled me back in, dunking me under the water. I peeked into the depths of the pool to make sure my imagination wasn't playing tricks on me again. It wasn't; the sun dappled brightly through the clear water. Brent's chiseled calves kicked in front of me and I playfully grabbed his ankle, pulling hard enough to submerge him as I resurfaced with an evil laugh. I was about to make my getaway when his strong hands caught my waist, sliding his arms around me and holding me tight. Part of me wanted to enjoy the warmth that flooded through my body by being in his embrace, but I didn't want this to be too easy for him. Instead, I elbowed him softly enough not to hurt, but hard enough to surprise him, so I could make my escape.

"Not so fast!" He reached for me and missed.

Then reality sounded through the air like a steam engine's whistle as it pulls into the station— only in our case, it was the whistle being blown by Brent's instructor. "Brent! Break's over," he called from the water's edge.

"Yes, sir." He swam to the side and climbed up the ladder before asking, "See you tonight at the dance?"

I glanced at him over my shoulder with my best coquettish smile, and called, "Maybe."

I didn't get to notice his reaction or his reply because I submerged myself, totally overjoyed that he had brought up the dance. If I needed proof that Brent was into me, I now had it; that was definitely flirting.

When I resurfaced, Cherie and Steve were standing by our lounge chairs. I walked over to them, ringing out my wet sarong.

"We're going to go for a walk. Want to come?" Steve asked a bit too politely.

I didn't want to feel like a third wheel, so I shook my head. "I think I'll go home and shower. You guys have fun."

I made my way to my dorm, while sweat mingled with the chlorinated water dripping from my body. Thoughts I had been trying to keep at bay while with Brent refused to shrink back to the recesses of my mind. First I had seen a cloud of mist trying to strangle someone, then the pool turned my reoccurring nightmare into a near reality. With both of those happening within twenty-four hours of my arrival, I was beginning to seriously question my decision to come here. Maybe I should have listened when my grandma tried to persuade me not to enroll at Pendrell. I had a feeling that the past I was trying to put behind me wasn't going to go quietly.

CHAPTER 2

After a thorough scrubbing, I stepped out of the shower still sopping wet. I pulled my terrycloth robe around me and shuffled contentedly to my room. Cherie still wasn't back. Though a mirror image, her side of the room couldn't have been more different from mine. Discarded swimsuits and accessories were strewn across her unmade bed and makeup littered her desktop. Clothes hung out of the open drawers of her dresser, and her closet couldn't quite close because of the pile of shoes in the way. Her walls were covered with posters of indie bands that I had only heard of because of her. My bed was tight enough to bounce a quarter off of it, my books and CDs arranged alphabetically, and my clothes organized by color. A corkboard with carefully arranged snapshots and reminder notes hung above my bed.

Drips of water puddled onto the cheap, tight-knit carpet as I combed out my tangled hair. The fading light of day tumbled through our lone window, diffusing our room with golden hues. Once my hair was snarl-free, I leaned on the small ledge of the window, watching a game of flag football below. Something moved behind me. I spun around, finding nothing; the room was perfectly still, like it was holding its breath. My eyes were drawn to the carpet near the door, where the individual water droplets from my hair were pooling together, forming a single unit, creating a recognizable shape. A footprint. A second, then a third footprint appeared, and only clamping my lips closed kept the shriek tunneling up my throat from escaping. Someone or something was walking across the room toward me.

The temperature in the room plummeted, and I pulled my robe tightly around me, my breath forming a frosty mist. That's when the smell caught my attention. Chlorine. The room reeked of it so strongly my eyes watered, its chemical taste basting my tongue. I wiped the tears with my sweaty palms, swallowing shallowly.

My heart pounded a warning in my chest and the blood drained from my face as the room grew dimmer. Feeling unsteady on my feet, I took a step back and leaned against the window, pressing my bare hand against the glass. Its arctic cold almost burned my skin. The scream I had been repressing made its way out in the form of a whimper and I fell against my desk, my hand skidding across my jewelry box and pencil sharpener. The door swung open, and I twisted toward it just as Cherie floated into the room. She sat down on her bed with a dazed, dreamy look on her face.

I glanced at the carpet and found the floor dry and the footprints gone. The light had returned to normal, the chlorine smelled had vanished, and even my hand didn't hurt anymore. Everything was completely normal. Everything but me. Pulling my robe even tighter around me, I dropped into my desk chair, my leg shaking.

I couldn't deny it; that was definitely a spirit. My second encounter with a ghost. No one had warned me it would be so terrifying. I was on the verge of telling Cherie everything when my hand traced the scar above my left eye. I'd gotten it in second grade, courtesy of a rock thrown by a classmate who insisted *Vovó*, my grandma hadn't seen his mother's spirit. It had been the first in a long line of similar encounters, but it was the only one that had left a physical scar. As for emotional scars, there were too many to count.

I knew Cherie would believe me, but still I hesitated. Everything hinged on this choice, whether or not to admit I could see ghosts like *Vovó*. Names I'd heard her called still echoed in my ears: crazy, witch, insane. So did all the useless arguments I had used to defend her, until one day I finally stopped, realizing they never fixed anything.

In Brazil, her gift of seeing and talking to ghosts was accepted-appreciated, even. There, she was a respected woman, revered for her knowledge of herbs and spirit lore. But here in the United States, in my neighborhood, she had become a community joke. She stayed with us every summer and each time I had to endure the looks and insults slung at her. They didn't bother her, but they bothered me. I didn't want that to be my future.

I didn't want to be an *Acordera*, a Waker, someone who could communicate with ghosts. All I wanted to be was a normal sixteen year old. My fingernails dug into the palms of my hands as I stared at the smudge of my handprint on the window's glass, and realized that I could never be that now.

Cherie looked at me for a moment. "Are you okay?"

"No," I admitted honestly. "Something really strange . . ." I trailed off, trying to decide if I wanted to reveal what had just happened. I still hadn't even told her about the mist I had seen attack Brent. If I made this confession, everything would change; there would be no going back.

"The weirdest thing . . ." I started again, but then my courage failed.

Cherie watched expectantly, waiting for me to finish the sentence I had left hanging there like a pair of long johns on a clothesline.

Finally, she tried to tactfully change the conversation. "Speaking of strange and weird, did you see our P.E. clothes? I'm thinking they might be the embodiment of the Pendrell Curse, like their entire purpose is to . . ."

I nodded, not really paying attention to her, concentrating instead on my own troubled thoughts.

"Yara, are you listening to me?" I looked at Cherie and mumbled an apology, having missed most of what she had said. "I'm eager for a ghost hunt," Cherie said. My stomach lurched. "I have some plans to get things rolling for tomorrow. Are you game?"

"Aren't I always?" I asked, trying to unclench my fists. Cherie had spent time over the years talking with my grandma and had picked up what she considered to be hot tips about finding out if a place was really haunted. It has always been fun to be part of her paranormal adventures, to get swept up in her enthusiasm, but now— well, everything was different.

"You almost look scared," Cherie said, noting the frown on my face.

I didn't want to admit that I was.

*   *   *   *

While I blow-dried and curled my hair, Cherie headed for the shower. I flipped the radio on to a jazz station and let the silky tones flood the room. Humming and scat-singing along, I slid on my favorite pair of jeans and my plum-colored silk tank top, then topped it off with my new jean jacket. After clasping on the necklace my grandma had given me before I started school, I examined myself in the mirror and grinned.

When Cherie walked in, I was quick to change the music to a more neutral station. She grumbled under her breath about my lack of musical taste as she picked out her outfit. Once she was dressed, she spritzed herself with her favorite perfume, a mixture of rose and iris that she had worn since middle school. Cherie called it her signature scent. And truly it was. I swear, even from the grave I'd smell it and know it was her. After passing each other's inspection, Cherie and I headed toward the dance.

Cherie did most of the talking as we walked, which was good, because I could barely pay enough attention to respond with the appropriate uh-huhs. Already on edge, I kept feeling like I was being watched, maybe even followed. There were no sounds of footsteps, no movement around me that didn't belong, at least not that I could see. And yet the prickling on my neck made me paranoid. I kept checking over my shoulder and knew I wasn't imagining the way the light bent and darkened on the path behind me.

The wind carried the smell of chlorine past me and I froze, grabbing Cherie's hand for support. "Do you smell that?"

"What?" Cherie asked, sniffing the air.

"Chlorine?"

Cherie shook her head and I dropped her hand, not sure if I was relieved or worried.

The Victorian lamppost above poured light around us and I reached out my hand, letting my fingers bump across its ribbed post.

I tried to sound casual as I asked, "Do you feel like we're being followed?"

She glanced behind her. "No. Do you?"

I resisted the urge to lie. "Yeah . . . maybe."

"I don't see anything." Cherie shifted her weight and began tapping her foot. "I know something's up. What is it?"

"Would you still be my friend if I turned into my grandma?" I bit my lip, not able to look at her. I tried to picture myself living like *Vovó*, walking through forests scouring for herbs, speaking with spirits no one else could see, delivering messages from beyond the grave. I shuddered.

Cherie's eyes sparkled as she stepped closer to me. "What happened?"

Not ready to have this discussion, I backpedaled. "Nothing happened. I was just wondering."

Cherie snorted. "I'm letting this slide for now. But I'm warning you, we are finishing this conversation."

"Okay," I agreed, knowing I really didn't have a choice.

* * * *

As we passed under a banner welcoming us to the Back to School Dance, a spinning globe of flashing colored lights drew our eyes upward to the ceiling covered with blue and white balloons.

"Great turn out," I yelled over the music as we pushed our way through the throngs of people.

"I know," Cherie said, practically shouting. She grabbed my hand and led me into the middle of the fray. A sort of frantic, contagious energy was pulsing from the dance floor and Cherie and I were swept up in it.

When the pace of the music slowed, I almost groaned in protest before heading to the back wall, or as I called it, "Loser Row." But Cherie nudged me, and my head shot up, following her nod toward the entrance. Brent was weaving his way across the dance floor toward us. His brown eyes were focused on me and shining in what I hoped was anticipation.

"Wanna dance?" He asked.

"I guess you'll do. All the cute guys are already taken," I answered with a grin.

"You wound me with your callousness," he sighed dramatically, taking me in his arms.

"I do have a black belt in demolishing overstuffed egos."

He laughed as he tugged me closer, his hands firm on my waist.

I fought back a smile, my fingers playing with the hair curled at the base of his neck. "So how did you end up at Pendrell?"

"Family school. Grandpa, my dad, my brother all went here."

"Any of your siblings at school now?"

Brent's body was suddenly tense. "No, it's just me now. Do you have any siblings?"

"I have an older sister, Melanie, in college. And an older brother, Kevin, who died about two years ago." I took a deep breath. "Although, technically, I'm now older than he ever was."

I waited for the obligatory apology but Brent didn't offer one. Instead he locked eyes with me and said, "That's rough." He sucked in some air. "I've been through that myself. It was my brother, Neal."

Going through a tragedy leaves an impression on people's souls. Once you've had a loss, you learn to deal with it and move on, but you carry that hurt with you always. Staring at Brent, I recognized his pain. It was so transparent, I was surprised I hadn't noticed it before.

"Want to talk about it?" I asked gently.

He smirked at me. "I appreciate the offer, but I'm a guy. We don't do that." My nose scrunched up in confusion. "We don't discuss our feelings."

"That's a relief; I don't want to talk about it either."

The corner of Brent's lips curled into a smile that matched my own. We had stopped dancing, standing instead in each others arms in the middle of the dance floor, sharing each others heartache without words.

I didn't dance with Brent again, but after the evening wound down, he found me standing with Cherie and Steve and walked us back to our dorm. Brent and I strolled along a few feet apart and I let my arms swing freely by my side in case he chose to reach out and grab my hand. He didn't.

He cleared his throat. "Will you walk with me for a while?"

I nodded, chewing the inside of my cheek. He reached out and took hold of my elbow, leading me away from the dorms, across campus. He stopped by the cafeteria and charmed a peach for each of us out of the cleaning lady. We ate our fruit while we walked, lessening the need to talk. The sticky fruit juice clung to my fingers and I tried to lick it away while Brent navigated us through a grove of avocado trees into a well-manicured garden. In the middle of a square of lawn sat a white gazebo and an elegant fountain; flowers and shrubs lined the edges. A stone path wound its way through the grass. Strings of white lights strung from Victorian lampposts lit up the entire area, dispelling the darkness inside the ring of oak and avocado trees that lined the garden.

"It's beautiful." I was stunned that such a location existed inside the wild of the groves.

"You like it?" It was a rhetorical question, but I nodded anyway. "It's the Headmaster's Garden, where he entertains guests."

"And all Headmaster Farnsworth's important guests hike through the grove?" I asked with a knowing grin.

"No, the exit over there—" He pointed across from where we stood. "—leads to a private road that would take you to the guest quarters."

"Let me guess. We aren't supposed to be here?"

He laughed a quiet but nervous laugh. "Uh . . . not exactly. But we should be okay."

"I wasn't worried."

Shyly he took hold of my hand, leading me toward the gazebo. We sat next to each other on the smooth wooden bench inside it, our fingers still intertwined. We each faced forward, but I was very aware of his strong presence beside me.

"I wanted to thank you for yesterday."

"You're welcome, but I didn't really do anything," I said, focusing on our hands, not daring to look at Brent.

"But you did."

I didn't know how to respond and an awkward silence spread around us. My fingers fiddled with a button on my jacket as I searched for something to say.

He took a deep breath like he was about to make an important announcement when a rustling in the trees brought us both to our feet, spinning toward the sound. Squinting into the darkness, I thought I made out a shape in the shadows.

"Anyone there?" Brent called, sliding his arm around my waist protectively, bringing me against his chest. We stood silently staring into the groves, but nothing was moving. It was as silent and still as a graveyard.

Brent seemed concerned when he turned toward me. "We'd better go back." I nodded and we left, hand in hand. Glancing back, I saw a dark figure moving across the garden. I tried to convince myself I was only imagining the chlorinated smell that followed me home.

CHAPTER 3

The next morning at breakfast, after loading up our plates to their maximum capacity, Cherie and I sat down next to a large window that offered a hillside view of Corona, California, and it amazed me how beautiful it was from a distance. Pendrell's campus was located off a small and winding road that cut through the fifteen or so acres of school-owned groves. The orange and avocado trees that covered the surrounding hills in dark green vegetation seemed to separate us from the rest of the world.

Cherie pulled out the schedule of events for the day. "We have the campus tour this morning."

"Should be thrilling." My voice dripped with sarcasm like the syrup leaking from my pancakes.

"I know. But before that, we can go on our ghosting expedition," Cherie promised enthusiastically.

"And how much trouble are we going to get in if we get caught?" I asked, fully aware that most of Cherie's grand schemes included breaking at least a few rules.

Cherie paused before answering, a little too angelically, "Not too much." Somehow I didn't believe her. "After that we get our schedules, books, et cetera," Cherie said between bites of a blueberry muffin. "Then we have an hour for lunch and some free time.

Free time, I thought to myself with a smile. I considered a couple of ways I'd like to use my free time and my eyes wandered around the room searching for Brent. Not seeing him, I swallowed down my disappointment with another bite of pancake.

As soon as my plate was empty, Cherie stood up, eyes full of anticipation. "Alright, let's go."

I followed her out into the foyer, taking a left instead of the right that would have led us back to our dorm. We walked through the covered breezeways, then cut across the lush lawns and around the Spanish Revival-style buildings. Cherie navigated us through several paths and one very long steep set of stairs, which in turn led through a stand of fragrant eucalyptus trees. Our journey continued as we passed through a wall of ivy, a field of wildflower weeds so tall they almost stretched above my head, and on through a maze of denser trees that had grown so wild they created a thick barricade, almost impossible to get through.

Finally, hot and sweaty, we ended up in front of a rather dilapidated brick building. It was so worn down that piles of broken bricks and charred boards were strewn among the tall thorny weeds surrounding it.

The fact that the interior had been burned out was evident by the black fringes framing the broken windows. More recently, vandals and partiers had left it pretty much trashed. I could tell by the many cigarette butts littering the ground that Pendrell's no smoking policy wasn't enforced here.

I tucked a piece of hair behind my ear. "Where are we, exactly?"

Cherie's bottom lip protruded in a pout. "Didn't you listen to me at all last week?" Not waiting for my reply she added, "This is the old sports house, more importantly, home of the original pool."

"Did you bring our swimsuits?"

She gestured toward the building, her nostrils flaring. "It happens to be the most haunted place on campus. The book says it's basically been left undisturbed." Cherie walked toward the crumbling building and looked through one of the cracked windows. I came up next to her and peered in as well.

The lobby looked to have originally been done in dark woods though they were now scarred black, burned and heat-blistered. Protruding into the foyer was the curved cylinder of a revolving door, wrapped in the same wood paneling that decorated the walls. The stainless steel moldings arched out sinuously into the room above the door, their dull metallic sheen now tinged blue. The fire had left behind only charred remains now littered with the trash and debris of decades of neglect.

Cherie grunted as she tried the door handle forcefully, but it was locked tight. "I figured it would be, but I thought I'd still give it a try," she said as she eyed the window hopefully. I shuddered as I pictured one of us trying to shimmy through the pointed shards of glass glistening in the sun like cold, cruel sentinels. Cherie shook her head and stepped on an empty beer can, crushing it.

"I think the pool's closed today," I joked. "Something about not having a lifeguard on duty."

Cherie gave a polite laugh, her eyes still surveying the entry options. "They closed it about sixty years ago."

"I would have guessed it was longer than that," I said, kicking away a pile of cigarette butts. "I'm surprised they left it here. It's sort of a blemish on the beautiful grounds, don't you think?"

"Yeah, but it works out lucky for us."

"Okay, so what's your plan to get inside?"

Cherie's mouth turned up into a grin. "I just figured it out." She hurried past me to the opposite side of the building.

I turned and followed her toward a tall tree that came within inches of a second story window.

I nodded in appreciation. "Great plan."

Since elementary school, I had loved climbing trees, monkey bars, or anything else, and I prided myself with the fact I was good at it too. Cherie had found many uses for my ability over the years.

I was almost disappointed that the tree was such an easy climb thanks to all of the thick branches along the trunk. It only took a minute to climb my way up to the second floor, and as I peeked through the leafy covering, I knew that Cherie wasn't the first one to think of using the tree to get inside. Unlike the window below us, this one was cleaned of any shards of glass.

Cherie stretched from the limb to the window, then made her way carefully inside. Broken glass crunched beneath her feet as she landed and started walking around.

I tried to avoid stepping on glass as I climbed in, but it was impossible; it was everywhere. The floor was absolutely disgusting, littered just like the ground outside, with old magazines, pizza boxes, aluminum cans, and cigarette butts.

The corners of Cherie's mouth sagged as she led the way toward the pool, the passage growing continually darker. Upon entering the pool room, I was surprised to find the light just as dim. Even though there were plenty of windows, they were covered in a layer of grime that didn't let in much light. The thick, tile-covered walls seemed impervious to the morning sun; the room felt positively freezing. Shivering, I rubbed my arms with my hands, trying to warm myself. Goosebumps surfaced along my skin.

I turned to look at Cherie who was standing with her arms stretched out in the air, head held triumphant, taking it all in. Then she turned and with a slight bow to me, her hands together in praying position, she said, "And that is how it is done, Grasshopper."

I laughed at her excitement as I studied the room. We stood on the mezzanine level overlooking the room. Stairs led down to the head of the pool, where a dangerous-looking diving board still stood, protruding out over the empty basin of tiled cement.

"Why haven't they restored it?" I asked, more curious than I wanted to admit.

"Not sure," Cherie admitted, happy to see my interest piqued. "I think they were scared," Cherie said as her voice dramatically dropped to a foreboding whisper.

I scratched my head. "Scared?"

"Of the place being cursed or haunted."

"Oh."

The musty air felt so palpable I could almost taste it. I worked my tongue across the roof of my mouth as if trying to get the moldy tang off my taste buds. I took a cleansing breath, only to find the air thick, old, and unsatisfying to my lungs, my inhalation ending in a dry cough.

Whatever history this room had, it made my skin crawl. It wasn't just the poor lighting, dusty air and debris-littered floor. Something horrible had happened here, and had left its residue behind. It seemed to rise from the bottom of the tiled pool and leak from the ceiling, clinging to the walls and binding itself like some parasite into any host it could ensnare. I imagined its cold fingers rooting inside me, spreading throughout, and leaving traces of itself embedded in my soul.

Unconsciously, I dusted myself off in an attempt to loosen the imaginary grip as I walked carefully down the stairs to the main floor. Cherie had already made her way down and was now walking around the old-fashioned pool chairs and touching the once white tiles on the wall.

"Amazing," she muttered as she pulled her hand back and looked at it. I stretched my hand out and touched the wall, too, to see what was so amazing. It was wet, but otherwise seemed normal. Cherie smiled at me like we had just shared a momentous experience. I tried to hide how underwhelmed I was by a wet wall and plopped down on one of the ancient chairs, drying my hand on my uniform, watching while Cherie roamed around.

"Come look at this!" She called out, and I dutifully joined her at the edge of the pool where she knelt, peering down over one of the sides.

"Do you see that?" She asked, her voice full of satisfaction. "It's wet, just like the wall."

"Uh-huh," I replied, noncommittally. "And condensation is interesting because . . ."

"It's not just condensation!" She took a deep breath. "It's interesting because I read about it, but it's so much cooler to actually see it. No matter how hard they try or what they do, this whole level is always wet. I wish I could get down to the bottom of the pool. I want to feel it with my own hands," she said peering back at the dark depths below us.

"You want us to go down there?" I whined like a six year old. Since the pool had no shallow end, I wondered if she was expecting us to jump. I was also worried that even if we made it down unscathed that we wouldn't find a way back out, expert climbing skills or not.

Cherie made a disappointed face at me. "Luckily for

you, there doesn't seem to be a way down," she said, obviously disgruntled about it. "Would you like to know why it's always wet here?" I shrugged my shoulders indifferently so she answered, "Because people died here. And it's commonly believed that the moisture is drawn out and left behind by the presence of the wandering spirits."

"It does have an ominous vibe, doesn't it?" I conceded trying to keep my goosebumps at bay.

Cherie was excited that she finally had my attention. "It does! The spirits still roam in this room," she added dramatically gesturing around us.

"So who died here?" I asked, slightly amused by her enthusiasm.

"A couple of students, about sixty years ago."

"How many is a couple?" I questioned, folding my arms around my chest, feeling cold again.

"The accounts vary. Some stories say there were two; others say three boys were here that night, but one survived. It's hard to tell because the school tried to hush it up."

"Why?"

Cherie rolled her eyes. "Don't you have any imagination?"

I shrugged to answer that I didn't. Cherie gave me a look to let me know she pitied my closed-mindedness.

"Obviously, they didn't want to tarnish the name of the school, and they didn't want to be blamed."

"Okay. But how did they die?"

"They drowned rather tragically," Cherie said as she continued examining the room.

"Isn't every death considered tragic?"

"Yes, but a lot of this one was preventable."

"How?"

"The school designed this room not only for a pool, but

for a gym, too. So they had a retractable gym floor built over the pool." Cherie walked around the pool and sat down on the edge of the diving board. She turned toward me and motioned me toward her.

I shook my head. "Uh . . . Cherie, I hardly think that's safe. It could seriously give out at any minute."

"Scaredy-cat."

"Stick and stones," I said, not budging an inch. I took a moment to inspect the ground with new interest but saw no evidence of the retracting floor. "So, where's this floor now?"

Cherie pointed to a wide band of paneling against the opposite wall. "It slides out from over there. They had been having technical difficulties with the floor for over a month, and the building was closed for repairs the night of the fire. From what the investigators could tell, there was a group of friends here after hours who became trapped under the floor when it closed. They figured the same faulty wiring that was playing havoc with the floor started the fire. None of them made it out. And the weird thing: the only key was in the headmaster's office. The official report declared it a tragic accident. But I'll bet there was some foul play involved—murder, or maybe suicide." Cherie seemed too pleased by the idea of intentional homicide.

My case of the creeps returned in full force. Was I standing where people had been murdered? I had been where people had died before, but never where someone had been murdered. "Why would do you think that?"

"Because it's haunted," she answered simply.

A sickening image of students trapped in the water, pounding on the floor above them, flashed before my eyes. I could feel the blood drain from my face and a chill run down my spine. Ghost stories sounded fine at home, coming from my family, but standing here in this freezing, dark room it was terrifying.

Perhaps I shouldn't have shown any interest whatsoever, because it only seemed to encourage Cherie more, and her voice raced to share her wealth of knowledge. "There are several accounts of people who have seen wet footprints all around the pool, even though the pool had been empty at the time. And here's the best part; there have been accounts of the footprints even being seen in our room!"

Oh crap! Instantly the hair on the back of my neck stood up as images of the footprints on our dorm floor played in my mind. I broke out in a cold sweat. "Footprints?"

She nodded with a smile. "Yes."

I gulped hard. Trying to be casual I confessed, "I saw some footprints after my shower last night."

Cherie's lips pouted and she straightened her shoulders. "That isn't possible. I haven't felt any ghostly activity in our room."

It was hard to stifle the laugh forming inside me. Cherie had no paranormal radar whatsoever, but I didn't have the heart to tell her. Not ready to delve into the awakening of my ghost-seeing abilities, I decided to calmly shift the conversation. "Cherie, why would the footprints be in our room?" In the back of my head I remembered how Cherie had specifically requested it.

Her smile vanished and she blinked at me with an all too-innocent blank face. "What was that?"

"Why are there ghosts' footprints in our room?"

"Um . . . because it's where two of the students lived. Pendrell legend suggests they went back to their room after the accident, not knowing they had died." Even as she told me her dark tale, her eyes danced in anticipation; I could practically feel the excitement growing inside her.

I looked at Cherie aghast. "Cherie, why would you actually choose to live in, not visit, but live in a haunted room where a confused ghost might put us in danger. I know *Vovó* warned you they can be the most dangerous."

Cherie looked absolutely crestfallen. Worse— she looked hurt. I still thought that I was right, but I felt a twinge of guilt at having hurt my friend. But after seeing Brent attacked and having a ghost in my room, Vovó's warnings all seemed a lot more important now.

We stared at each other for a moment, not sure what to say. Eventually Cherie shrugged. "I hadn't really thought of it that way," she said. "Sorry. I mean, I've never been successful before so I didn't even think about the fact it could be dangerous. I just— "

I interrupted her, trying to repair some of the damage I had done. "No, you're right," I lied. "It'll probably all turn out to be smoke and mirrors like every other place you've investigated."

"Exactly." Cherie smiled wide and I could tell our small spat was mended. Our fights never lasted long because we couldn't stand being mad at each other.

My next question slipped out against my better judgment. "Did you ever read anything about a black mist on campus?" I held my breath, waiting for the answer.

Cherie cocked her head, thinking. "No. Why?"

I exhaled slowly. "No reason."

Cherie raised her eyebrow but then looked at her watch and cursed quietly to herself. "We're going to be late," she said, grabbing my hand and dragging me back toward the window. We climbed back down the tree, Cherie complaining to me the whole way about not having enough time to see everything she had wanted to see. Personally, I couldn't relate; I had seen enough.

It was a relief to be out in the fresh air again, walking among the birch trees, feeling the warmth of the sun on my face. Still, no matter how hard I tried, I couldn't forget the unsettling feeling of the room and a foreboding feeling that everything that had happened to me here all led back to the people who died in that pool.

* * * *

By the time our tour ended, lunch was almost over and my stomach grumbled hungrily. After procuring my grilled cheese sandwich and tomato soup, I followed Cherie to a table where Brent and Steve were already sitting. Being near Brent made my heart beat a little faster than normal, and it kicked into overdrive when he scooted his chair closer, so our legs touched, soft as a whisper.

"We're going to the pool after lunch," Steve said. "Do you guys want to come?"

Not another trip to that creepy place, I thought with a sigh.

"We've already been this morning." Cherie spread her napkin carefully across her lap. "Of course, you probably mean the swimming pool with water in it, right?"

Hope entered my heart as I remembered there was a normal pool, ghost-free and full of non-haunted water, making the invitation much more appealing. But then I remembered what happened yesterday and I began shaking my leg under the table.

"Of course. Water usually helps with the swimming." Brent's tone was one someone would use on a confused child.

Cherie paused dramatically with an impish grin. "We checked out the original swimming pool, the one that's locked, off limits, and supposedly haunted."

Understanding flickered across their faces, and I think

the phrase "off limits" especially caught their interest. Giving up all pretenses, Cherie eagerly told them of our morning adventure.

"You guys did that without us?" Steve complained. "We would have gone with you."

Cherie dabbed the corners of her mouth with her napkin. "Honestly, I didn't think you'd be interested."

I doubted Steve was upset about missing the pool; I think it had more to do with missing time with my best friend.

"How did you even know about it?" Steve asked.

Cherie smiled demurely. "I did my homework before I came to school."

"We've been down there before. I mean, everyone goes there at least once, sees it isn't that big of a deal, and leaves. There's no reason to go back—unless, of course, you believe in ghost stories." Steve's expression turned serious when he saw the looks on our faces. "Do you believe in the ghost stories?"

"No, of course not. It was just for fun," I said before Cherie could answer. I knew for a fact that ghosts were real, but I had learned not to go around telling people that. Even without looking, I could feel Cherie's heated glare and I determinedly avoided her gaze.

"So, do you guys have any other big plans as far as checking out old school rumors?" Steve asked, his crystal blue eyes watching Cherie.

"Well I thought about looking into the Pendrell curse," Cherie announced, sipping the soup from her spoon.

Brent scoffed. "You really believe in the curse?"

"Don't you? I mean you almost died, and with it being so close to the end of the second year, isn't it almost time?" Cherie asked.

"I was choking— it wasn't suicide," Brent said, narrowing his eyes.

"I was meaning to ask you about that. What were you choking on? I asked around, no one knows what happened." Brent didn't answer, but the muscle of his jaw clenched. "I know they're all found to be suicides. But maybe they're not. Maybe they're accidents or maybe even murders!" Cherie held up her spoon to emphasize her point. "That makes more sense than the brightest, most popular students of this school killing themselves every two years, doesn't it?"

"Look," Brent said, his voice chilly, "you just started here. You don't know what you're talking about."

Steve tapped Brent on the back. "Yeah. It was usually about midterms or finals and everyone who knows the person who . . . dies agrees that they hadn't been acting like themselves. They all had majorly traumatic breakdowns. Too much pressure. There's no mystery."

"Maybe." Cherie leaned in, lowering her voice, her blue eyes wide with enthusiasm. "I'll let you know what I find out at our next investigation."

"When?" Steve asked. Even though I doubted he believed in ghosts, he wasn't about to let that stop him from any activity Cherie was involved in.

"I haven't decided that yet. It didn't sound like you'd be interested."

"We wouldn't miss it."

"Yes, we would." Brent slammed one hand down on the table while his other one crumpled his napkin and tossed it on his plate. He pushed his chair away from the table and jerked up. "I've got to go."

"Brent?" I asked as he turned to go.

"I'll catch up with you later." He gave me a tight smile that didn't go further than his lips. I stared after him, wondering what exactly had happened.

* * * *

After lunch, I was in the library, picking up the textbooks I needed for my classes. I had already double checked my list to make sure I hadn't forgotten anything, so I arranged my books by size and hefted them into my arms, trying to balance the unsteady stack.

"I thought I might find you here." I glanced around my book tower and found Brent smiling at me.

"Hey," I said. "You okay?"

Brent raised a fingernail to his teeth, then shook his head and dropped his hand. "Yeah."

"Really? Or do you just not want to talk about it?" I adjusted the top book with the tip of my chin.

"Need a hand with those?"

I nodded and he took all but two from my arms. "I guess that means you don't want to talk about it." He didn't say anything just tucked my books under one of his arms. "You just seemed ticked or something when Cherie started talking about the curse."

He gritted his teeth. "What is wrong with your friend, anyway?"

"What do you mean?" I followed him into the library's elevator and pushed the button for the first floor. He didn't answer, he just stared straight ahead, and I shuffled my feet in the awkward silence until the doors of the elevator slid open with a slight squeak that echoed across the deserted floor.

"Well it isn't exactly normal to take such a morbid interest in people's deaths," he said finally. We walked toward the nearest study area, with two arm chairs, a table, and a sofa illuminated by a large stained glass window. Blue, red, and green rainbows danced across the table.

~ 37 ~

"That's not it. She wants to help, she wants to—"

"Solve the big mystery? Why do the over-worked, under-praised students of the most elite prep school on the West Coast kill themselves? The answer is in the question." Brent dropped my heavy stack of books on the table and sagged into one of the chairs.

"It's more than that. Cherie has this need to prove there is life after death, that the universe is bigger than science can explain." I took a deep breath. "She had just started dating my brother right before he died." I waited for Brent to respond in some way, but he didn't. "His death really rattled her. Ever since then she's been obsessed." I didn't mention that even Cherie's popularity at our old school hadn't stopped people talking about her.

"Why Pendrell?"

"You have ghost stories, curses, the best education, and it's close to home. How could she not choose to come here? It has everything she wants."

"Well, tell her to back off. Every year some stupid person brings up the curse and—"

"She isn't stupid." My hands clenched my books tightly, digging them painfully into my chest.

Brent gave me a level stare to let me know he didn't agree.

"She isn't stupid," I repeated. "I mean, this place is downright creepy sometimes. You can feel that, right?"

"Creepy?"

I focused on the stained glass window, noting the graceful design of the roses. "Yeah."

Brent rested his elbows on the table leaning toward me. "Like footprints in her room, dark, ghostly presences, and a feeling like someone is following her."

My tongue felt numb, and my fingers tingled. "Exactly.

That is exactly what she saw," I lied. I knew I was being a coward, but I still wasn't ready to admit it was me who had experienced these things. Brent wasn't like the kids I had fought with as a child. The muscles in my shoulders relaxed. "How did you know?"

"Because it's in every piece of trash book that is out there about the supposed curse."

I felt like I had been blindsided by a semi. "But she did see it."

"Then you're right; she isn't stupid," Brent agreed. "She's crazy!"

A sensitive internal trigger fired a series of disjointed but powerful images behind my eyes: Grandma talking to nothing but the air in public places, the pointing and taunts that followed. Only in this case he'd called Cherie crazy. Only it wasn't really her; it was me. That nagging fear that had worried me since childhood became a reality: I had just been called crazy. The room spun for a moment and I figuratively felt myself join the ranks of my lineage. Had each of them had someone they cared for flippantly dismiss them the way Brent had just dismissed me? Apparently, Brent was no different than the other close-minded people who had ridiculed my Grandma, and now me.

"She isn't crazy either," I said through clenched teeth, my fingers clamping tighter on my book.

"If it looks like it should be in a straight jacket and it talks like it should—"

I really hadn't planned to do it but before my brain had a chance to veto the idea, I chucked my five-pound calculus book at him. It soared through the air and clocked him right in the temple. There was the loud thud of the book making contact with his cranium, and then a clatter as the book bounced off the table and landed on the floor. It was probably the most effective and satisfying use the book would get all year.

He rubbed his head while glaring and swearing at me. I hesitated before retrieving my textbooks and stalking off without a word.

Chapter 4

Kicking hard, I struggled to swim up toward the air that my lungs were burning to breathe. My legs flailed and my hands clawed, but the tightening crush of water told me I was still sinking. With a sickening realization, I knew it was my gown that held me captive. Frantically I tried to free myself from the confused tangle my dress had become, but my panicked fingers were unable to undo a single button.

My knotted hair and ripped dress swirled around me like a beautiful ethereal dream, hypnotizing me, twirling in the water with enticing promises of what awaited me once I surrendered to my inevitable fate. I'm drowning; I accepted it as the hazy black edges of my vision started to spread into the center of my sight. My eyes were drifting closed in defeat when I saw him, swimming toward me and I fervently wished he had been a few moments earlier, because I knew he was already too late.

I sat up in bed in a cold sweat, my heart racing, my fingers clutching my sheets in panic. Even though it had been nothing more than a nightmare, my lungs still greedily gulped up air as if it had been real; it felt far too real. For the last month I had the same dream several times a week, every detail nearly identical.

This repeated experience was disturbing, eerie even. I

had only had such vivid dreams once before. I pushed that memory aside reassuring myself it wasn't the same thing. My hands instantly cradled the necklace my family had sent me from Brazil. They said Grandma had picked it out from her local feira market. If she were here, she'd remind me that dreams, especially recurring dreams, were not to be ignored. Her superstitious nature had taught me that, "Dreams are the universe's way of trying to tell us something." Of course she had been against me coming to Pendrell, warning me that my grandfather had left believing there was something evil happening at this school. I had been so determined to not live in Brazil that I hadn't listened.

This train of thought didn't help lessen my nerves. I closed my eyes and tried to go back to sleep but all I could see were the horribly realistic images from my nightmare. Finally I decided to concentrate on the one aspect that wasn't scary— the boy swimming toward me— and my pulse calmed. Even though the shadows obscured his face, I always felt like I knew him. I drowned every time, but each night he got closer to saving me.

* * * *

In the morning, I woke still riddled with anxiety over my nightmare, but managed to get myself out of bed to shower. Once showered and dressed, I attempted to convince the worry lines on my forehead to relax, but was having no luck. With a heavy heart and an even heavier backpack I followed an enthusiastic Cherie to our first day of classes.

The morning was a humdrum blur of syllabi, textbooks, assignments, and teachers, except for Language Arts. Not only did the teacher, Mrs. Piper, assign an oral presentation that immediately made butterflies take flight in my stomach, but I had my first run-in with Brent since the library.

Brent, whose bangs were styled to hide his bruised temple, arrived at the classroom just as I did, starting an avalanche of emotions that crushed my lungs and made it hard to breathe. His lips were clenched in a straight line when he opened the door for me. "After you," he said in a tight voice, motioning me forward. I glared at him as I walked past, making my way toward Cherie.

At lunch, I found Cherie in the cafeteria saving me a seat, I was happy not to see Brent or Steve with her. I hadn't told her about my fight with Brent not only because I didn't want to make things awkward between her and Steve, but also because it might lead her to ask some questions about the content of the argument.

I plopped my blue tray on the table, dumping my back-pack with a loud thud, and slumped into the wooden chair next to her, mentally exhausted as we exchanged mutual "Why did we want to go to this fancy prep school?" looks. From the buzz of conversation in the room, it sounded like lots of students were complaining about the sadistic amount of work assigned on the first day of classes. If we had pitchforks and torches at our disposal, I would have led the uprising. My hostility level toward my teachers lowered after I polished off a brownie, stabilizing my crashing blood sugar.

"So how was Drama?" I asked as I bit into my turkey sandwich.

"Oh, it's going to be fabulous. There's a Drama Club and our first meeting is today. You're going to be there, right?" At first I thought Cherie had asked me that question, but realized she was talking to Audrey, a girl from our floor, who had just sat down beside me.

"Yep," Audrey said, pulling out the chair next to me. "It was a relief to know someone in class."

"Our first day of classes and you're already ditching me?" Travis, Audrey's boyfriend, joked as he sat down next to her.

"Oh, every chance I get," she quipped, giving him a wink and tossing her golden hair over her shoulder.

"What are you going to be doing tonight?" Cherie asked me as she stole a carrot stick from my plate.

"Um . . . were you in Language Arts? You heard we have to introduce ourselves in front of our whole class tomorrow, right? Where do you think I'll be?" I asked before popping a potato chip into my mouth.

Cherie put her hands to her head like she was trying to read the future. "I see you in the library . . ." she whispered eerily, "stressing out."

"It's uncanny, her psychic ability," I praised sarcastically, throwing a few of my chips at Cherie, who picked them out of her hair with a grin.

"I have to work on my speech, too," Travis said. "I can meet you there after school. That way we won't have to be alone while they ditch us for Drama."

"Sure. I'll want a second opinion about mine anyway." I gave Travis a grateful smile. The conversation then turned into a debate between Audrey and Cherie about which play the Drama Club should put on first. Cherie and Audrey were still debating between two plays I had never heard of when the bell rang.

After school, in the library, while browsing through some of the books on public speaking, I ran into Travis. We decided to work on the second floor, in the back corner, so we could practice reading our assignments out loud without disturbing anyone.

An hour later, I had my speech written out, and Travis was calmly making notes on colored index cards with his key points. I loved the fact that he was using bullet points about his own life. For me, prep work wasn't the problem; it was the actual delivery in front of my fellow classmates. I had found a book about public speaking, and was looking up ways to overcome the stage fright I knew would come. The book, however, was useless.

"Seriously— 'Be prepared'? Isn't that one obvious?" I grumbled under my breath. "Make notes? Picture people naked? So, do you think if I picture everyone naked, it will really help?" I asked Travis rhetorically.

"I'm afraid that might be a distraction, if I tried. I mean, Audrey's in that class." He chuckled.

I felt my face flush as I remembered Brent was too. No matter what had happened between us, he was still drool-worthy. "Okay, that one's out."

He looked at his watch and started gathering his stuff. "Speaking of Audrey, I'm supposed to meet her in about fifteen minutes. I better get going. You're going to do fine."

"Of course I am," I said sarcastically.

"You sounded fine when you were practicing it."

"Yeah, but it's different when you are doing it in front of a friend."

"Then just look at your friends while you talk."

"Okay, see, *that* is good advice. You should write a book."

"I'll keep it in mind," he said, standing up to go.

"Tell Audrey hi," I said. I watched him zip up his back-pack and sling it over his shoulder.

"Will do," he called as he left.

Dropping my head onto the table and sighing, I closed my eyes, mentally repeating the words of my speech. *Hello my name is Yara Silva. I...*

A book from a nearby shelf tumbled to the ground and

the pages rustled a moment before settling. I bit my lip, debating. If this was a horror movie, I would be yelling at the stupid girl to run— but I ignored my own advice and walked toward the book.

It was a copy of *Pendrell's Guide to Being a Top Student*. It didn't look threatening, so I picked it up. It was published in the fifties and seemed to be a collection of essays written by former students. I marked the page that had flipped open with my finger as I browsed the table of contents. There were suggestions on everything from acing a test to keeping one's dorm room clean. The page it had opened to had a small paragraph on public speaking by a T. J. Weld. I read the few sentences aloud.

"When I have to speak in public, I always find it helps to take a few really deep breaths until I am almost dizzy, then close my eyes for a second, and pretend I'm dreaming. It sort of disconnects me from reality and keeps me from over-thinking. I found this exercise to be very helpful and enlightening."

I frowned. I had hoped this book, brought to me by fairly spectacular means, would be more informative and have the real key to public speaking. I shelved the book with a sigh. I would just have to hope picturing people naked would do the trick.

* * * *

The sun hung low over the hills, striping the landscape with long shadows as I walked back to my dorm later that evening. The heat ebbed to the coming cool night air. It was a perfectly balanced evening that would make the rest of the world jealous. Once again I was envying my shadow's grace when a feeling of cold made me shiver.

I gulped and swallowed, tasting chlorine in the air. My heartbeat felt like it was tapping out danger in Morse code. I strained my ears to hear something, anything, but all I heard were my own steps. Then an arctic thread of air tickled the nape of my neck. I spun around expecting . . . I'm not sure what. But the whole campus was deserted and I was eerily alone.

Involuntarily, my step quickened and I started to glance around in search of a safe place or other people for that matter. I had the unnerving feeling that I was being followed. I paused for a moment, listening, but all I heard was a deafening silence. My lone companion was my shadow and even it seemed determined to abandon me as it stretched longer and slid further away.

I blinked at my other self. *How is my shadow moving if I'm standing still?* My possessed shadow raised itself from the ground like a zombie emerging from the grave until it hovered before me. The black mist that had attacked Brent. A geyser of terror erupted inside me, freeing my heart to leap to my throat and my knees to buckle in its wake. Landing painfully on my butt brought back some clarity of thought and my mind registered that the mist was thicker and more massive than I remembered. I scooted backward trying to escape, but its thick blackness snaked itself behind me, encircling me, blocking me in.

A hate-twisted face materialized in the mist while one of its slithering tendrils grew into an arm, with fingers stretching for me. A scream I didn't even know I was capable of left my throat, echoing off the buildings in a terrified refrain.

A scraping that made my skin crawl resonated in the air, as its nails hit some sort of invisible barrier mere inches from me. Screeching, it pulled back, then attacked again only to ram into the same unseen blockade. Refusing to give up, it battered against it, higher, lower, faster, slower, trying to find a weakness in its defenses. Despite being covered by my trembling hands, my eardrums pounded, threatening to burst at the mist's shrill cries of failure. Sensing its mounting frustration, I cowered, drawing my knees tightly to my chest, as the fear buzzing in my head grew louder. Then the whole entity attacked at once, circling me completely, its energy squeezing me momentarily in a breath-stealing vise before it was slammed back with a force that left me dizzy.

"Yara!" A familiar voice called. I spun toward Brent, who was waving his hands dramatically, trying to get my attention. His face tightened as he took in the horror in my eyes and the panic etched on my face, but his arms kept moving. "Over here, Yara."

My lips were mouthing the word my fear wouldn't allow me to voice. "Help."

My eyes slid past him, seeking the mist, when an assault of wind stung my eyes, forcing them closed as an explosion ricocheted around me. For a moment I feared I had died. But the hard concrete didn't transform into a billowy cloud; I didn't hear heavenly angel choirs, accompanied by harps. It took several blinks before my open eyes believed that not only had I survived, but that the mist was gone. I had no idea what had happened and chose not to question it as my body sagged in relief.

The air in my lungs that had felt thick and heavy instantly felt fresh, like pure oxygen. Black spots danced before my eyes and my head felt light as the rush of clean air overtook me. The encounter had drained me of the ability to sit upright and I felt my body give way under the exhaustion. More softly than I would have imagined, I collapsed onto the concrete.

My cheek lay against the warm walkway as my body shuddered with shock. Tears coursed down my face, my breathing shallow. I had never felt more weak or vulnerable in my life.

Brent crouched down beside me. "What are you doing on the ground? Are you sick?"

"Did you see it?" I whispered, my voice crackling with fear.

"See what?" Brent asked, looking around. The angry blue bruise on his temple convinced me that answering truthfully would just reignite our old argument.

"Never mind," I mumbled, suddenly wanting him to go away.

"Are you okay?" He asked.

Did he really want to know? I stared up at him. *No, he doesn't*, I decided. Still, he looked at me expectantly for some sort of answer, so I nodded. Not because I was okay, but because that is what people do in situations like this— they muscle through it, cowgirl up. When people ask how you are, they don't really want to know, they just want to hear, "I'm hanging in there." I was not as strong as other people, I decided, as I sniffed back tears. My hand covered my mouth to contain the sobs that were bubbling in my throat.

Brent accepted my answer and started to reposition himself. I thought he was leaving, and a tug of war between abandonment and relief fought inside me. Instead however, he lay down beside me, his ankles crossed, hands laced behind his head, face to the sky and began whistling.

"Please leave me alone," I muttered. He must not have heard me over the off key melody he was creating, because he didn't move. Even though I was angry at him, that didn't make me any less grateful. "Thanks for your concern but you can go." I pushed unsteadily off the ground to an upright position.

He didn't budge; the rhythm of his song swirled in the air, chasing away all of my fright and I found myself humming along to the old classic, "Can't Stop Dreaming of You." My teeth bit down hard on my bottom lip, trapping the melody in my throat as I stood.

When the world stopped swaying, I slowly began making my way back to my room. I took a few steps but stopped abruptly when I felt a presence behind me. I turned toward it, my heart racing, only to find Brent. He offered an apologetic smile and a shrug.

"You don't have to follow me," I told him, my voice weak.

"Well I'm all about chivalry," he said, with a formal bow and a flourish, "and you are so pale, I'm not quite sure you won't collapse again."

"I'm not going to collapse," I lied through gritted teeth. "I'm perfectly capable of making it home." In truth, my whole body threatened to keel over.

"Well in that case, I'll just be on my way."

With a nod I took a couple of steps only to find him still shadowing me. When I eyed him suspiciously he shrugged. "I happen to be heading toward your dorm to visit Samantha. Pure coincidence I assure you."

I stifled a laugh, which made his eyes twinkle.

"Thank you for helping," I mumbled under my breath.

The way he smiled into the edges of his mouth made me pretty sure he heard me but he asked, "I'm sorry— what was that? It was hard to hear you over my song."

Fighting to not grin, I continued on my path.

"Were you apologizing to me for hurling your book at my head?"

The smile on my lips died. My head spun toward him, my eyes throwing daggers and the tune died on his lips.

"Were you apologizing for calling Cherie crazy?"

"Touché." He grinned.

Taking a deep breath I said, "I really appreciate your help." I raised my hands to call a truce. "I don't want to fight anymore."

I started toward my room again, with him walking beside me whistling again.

"That is one of my favorite songs. Can you maybe whistle something else?" I asked, after listening to him whistle his asinine version of the song four complete times. The repetitiveness wound my nerves tighter than a bowstring and the only escape I could foresee was my dorm.

"Nope, it's the only one I know," he explained before continuing on with the song for the fifth time.

I slipped through the glass doors of my dorm house before he started whistling "Can't Stop Dreaming of You" for the sixth time. I made my way to my room only to be greeted with his loathsome song being carried in through the open window. I picked up my thickest textbook and made my way toward the window.

I leaned out, brandishing my book like a lethal weapon. The song stopped abruptly, replaced by a very amused laugh. He gave me a lopsided grin as he retreated out of range of my pitching arm, rubbing his temple. I slid the window shut, with a smile and dropped the book on my desk.

Complete exhaustion overcame me as I pulled my covers over my fully-clothed body. I lay there trying to convince myself that the dark mist wouldn't try to attack me again, though I knew I was lying.

"It's going to leave you alone," I repeated to myself, fingering Vovó's necklace as fatigue forced me to sleep.

*   *   *   *

I slept soundly the whole night, fully clothed, with

anxiety still humming inside me over the mist experience. Did Brent see the mist yesterday? No, I decided. If he had, he would have said something. So, that left me the only one who could see it. I didn't like that thought, so I tried to shove it to the back of my brain as I readied myself for school.

Language Arts came far too quickly for my taste. And somehow I had been given the honor of getting to speak first. Standing up, I walked to the front of the class and swallowed hard, resisting the urge to bite my lip. I carefully interlaced my hands behind my back and stood tall, lifting my eyes to face the audience. My mind raced, and my carefully prepared words suddenly eluded me.

Should I try to picture the people naked? I glanced at Brent, and flushed, glad he was too busy talking to the girl next to him to notice. Cherie, sitting behind him, stuck her tongue out and crossed her eyes, and trying not to laugh helped me refocus. I would have to let Travis know that his idea of looking into the faces of friends really worked. *Maybe I could write a testimonial for his book*, I thought, before realizing I had been standing in front of the class this whole time, and my mind was rambling. *How long have I been standing here?*

My face flushed deeper, my pulse reeled, the room started to spin— I was going to faint. Hoping to stop the swaying of the room, I closed my eyes, took several deep breaths— getting even dizzier— and tried to pretend I was dreaming. I hadn't meant to follow the book's advice, but somehow here I was, doing what it had suggested.

"Hello, my name is Yara Silva. People always ask what my name means." I took another deep breath.

As I talked, little drops of sweat began to trickle between my shoulder blades and my necklace felt uncomfortably warm around my neck. Still trying to calm myself,

I concentrated harder on pretending I was dreaming, distancing myself from reality, like I was outside myself, a mere observer. Suddenly the world around me seemed to slow, and I felt as if some part of me had detached from the rest. My head felt groggy, as if in a deep sleep and unable to awaken itself. I heard the words I was speaking, but at the same time, it was as if I wasn't the one saying them. It felt like I really was dreaming, but somehow I knew I wasn't. Had I hypnotized my own brain? Focusing as hard as I could, I tried to see if I could pull even further away.

It worked; I felt a cold rush of air as my spirit completely left my body. My dull, foggy brain was suddenly wide awake, alert, while the rest of the world seemed frozen in time. The words I had been saying stopped and I turned to see my body, still as a statue and ghostly white. What had I done? Could I get back? Raw panic overwhelmed me, constricting my chest, pulling my spirit back to my body.

I became whole again, except now I was freezing and shivering. Everything seemed back to its normal pace, but I felt sluggish, slightly out of sync. My shaking body had never felt colder and I crossed my arms and began rubbing them for warmth. A scattered chorus of giggles from my classmates brought me back to the reality that I had a speech to finish. My tongue was heavy like it had been coated with thick peanut butter. After rubbing it several times against the roof of my mouth it finally loosened. It took great effort to give my closing remarks.

"That was . . . interesting," Mrs. Piper said politely, looking surprised that I hadn't passed out. Still shivering and feeling dazed, I made my way back to my seat, nearly tripping twice. Brent's eyes were on me; I could feel him trying to get my attention but I refused to look at him. I sank gratefully into my chair, squinting against the glare of the lights in our class.

Cherie leaned over and practically shouted in an impressed voice, "That's the best you've ever done."

I shushed her with a worried glance toward our teacher. Cherie frowned at me, not liking being shushed. Still not quite feeling like myself, I started to explain, in a quiet whisper, the weird event that had just taken place, "It wasn't me; it was like . . ." I was interrupted by Mrs. Piper calling Cherie up for her turn.

She stood up in front of the class, and without any fear, launched into the story of her life. My head throbbed in pain and I dropped it to my desk, covering my ears with my arms to stop the pounding in them. My nostrils inhaled an overpowering and nauseating mixture of sweat, perfume, and deodorant. Worse still, my taste buds absorbed it and it settled down to my stomach, which turned over, threatening to be sick. Tears flooded my eyes, trying to ease the burning caused by the painful brightness of the room. The shrillness around me was like a live wire, scratching and tormenting my senses, zapping my nerves, in a series of painful jolts.

Soon Cherie sat down amid a round of loud applause that made my ears cringe. A thick sheen of sweat formed on my face as my body slowly warmed. With my head still down I raised my hand, begging Mrs. Piper to let me be excused. Cherie tried to ask me what was wrong, but I couldn't answer as I fled the room.

Outside the building, my head was still pounding, and I needed to be alone. I headed toward the trees that Cherie and I had cut through to get to the pool a few days before. After a short walk, I found a stone bench in the middle of a small clearing and dropped my belongings next to it. I gracelessly collapsed on the bench, stretching out on my back, and gulped in the fresh citrus air, ridding myself of the overpowering scents from my class. The sun heated my cold body, but was too powerful for my eyes and I let them slide closed. Slowly, the thudding in my ears faded, replaced by the soothing, lulling hum of the groves. The woods were peaceful and I let their tranquility wash over and heal me, lessening the severity of my surroundings. Refusing to even think about what had happened in class, I drifted off to sleep.

Some time later, I woke and slowly stretched, feeling refreshed. Noticing how high the sun now hung in the sky and where I was reminded me of what had brought me here.

My spirit left my body. Wow.

It was beyond freaky and I knew I should be scared but I found myself more annoyed than frightened. It's not like my grandma hadn't told me stories like these; I had just never thought they would happen to me. It was not uncommon among very strong Wakers, but this didn't bode well for me and my plans for complete normality. I laughed as the irony of the situation settled into my mind. Great. Not only was I a Waker, I was a *strong* Waker!

My grandmother would be thrilled. Vovó had plans for my future, and seemed to think it was me and my sister's destinies to take her place to help communicate and assist the ghosts someday, just as she had replaced her mother, and she had replaced hers. Since the gift for seeing ghosts was passed down through the female line, that hope jumped my dad's generation and now fell to us. With my dad marrying an American woman, Vovó was nervous that the gift might be too diluted and would not take root in me. I was nervous too— that it *would*. Now it had.

I wanted to go back to bed.

The hairs on the back of my neck prickled, interrupting my internal debate. I was being watched. Jerking to an upright position I spun toward my watcher, my heart beating hard against my rib cage.

Relief flared in me when I found it was Brent's brown eyes watching me, his arms folded across his chest, staring intently at me. He walked toward me and sat down at the far end of the bench.

"You missed lunch." He handed me an open bag of my favorite candy. "I took the liberty of eating all the greens."

"Thanks," I said, willing the sudden warmth in my heart to cool. I took the candy and poured a few into my hand, then tossed them into my mouth.

"You want to talk about what happened to you in class?"

My muscles all coiled, waiting to spring, my breath caught in my throat, and I choked on the candy. "What are you talking about?" I asked between coughs.

Brent made a tsking sound. "Do I really have to ease into the topic? Can't we just cut to the chase?"

I started to sweat. "What do you think happened?"

"Really? You won't show me yours until I show you mine?" Brent sighed reclining back on the bench.

"You wish," I spat, giving him my best "drop dead" look. I pulled a flower from the ground and twirled it in my fingers. "How's your head?"

"Fine, how's your crazy friend?" He multitasked by rubbing his bruised temple and glaring at me at the same time. "Of course, it might be safer to deal with her insanity than your temper."

"Temper?" I asked through a clenched jaw, my fingers compressing together so tight I bent the flower's stem in half.

"You chucked a book at me because I called her insane.

Yeah, I would say you have a temper."

"You deserved it, calling her crazy," I huffed, plucking the purple white petals from the flower and dropping them in my lap.

"I've been called a lot worse than crazy."

"Nothing is worse than being called crazy. You don't joke around with that word." My eyes bored into his intensely so he would understand exactly how much I meant what I said.

When he finally looked away he started chewing on his nails. "Yeah, okay. Your friend is playing with stuff she should leave alone but she isn't crazy. I never really meant she was nut-house bound."

My head dropped between my knees with a noncommital shrug.

Brent took my silence for agreement. "Good. So she might not be crazy but *you* . . . you have an awfully short temper," Brent teased with a smile in his voice.

Despite my current feud with Brent, I laughed. "I usually don't," I said honestly.

He chuckled. "So, what you're saying is I bring out your book-wielding, short-tempered side?" He hooked his foot through the straps on my backpack and brought it front of him. "Removing temptation." I gave him a look that communicated he should wither and die.

"So why did you follow me out here?" I snapped.

"I told you. I saw what happened in class and I wanted to make sure you were all right."

My hands immediately flew to my necklace and began twisting it nervously. "I got nervous," I said. "I felt sick, but I'm feeling better now." It was an edited version of the truth, but still not a lie.

"That's not what I meant," he said, shaking his head. "I

meant during your speech."

"I got nervous," I repeated slowly. "Stage fright."

He sighed. "Yara, are you trying to tell me you didn't astral project in the middle of talking?"

My jaw dropped.

He gave me a smug smile as he leaned forward and patted me on the knee. "I knew it. I think I knew it from the start. You're one of us."

I verbally stumbled. "One of who?"

"You're a *Clutch*."

"I . . . like in a car?"

Brent looked amused. "No, like in a Clutch, a person who can astral project."

My mind searched through all the fringe science stuff I had read through with Cherie and back toward everything my grandma had ever told me, but I came up empty. "I've never heard that term before."

"Well, you wouldn't have— it's what they called it here at school. It used to be Pendrell's secret society." Brent leaned in, his voice lowered. "No one is supposed to know any of this but I . . . know some things."

"A secret society?" I bit my lips together to keep from laughing.

"Yeah." Brent didn't notice my mocking of him; his mind was somewhere else. "It sort of disbanded a while ago, but I want to get it running again. If there are two of us, maybe we can." Brent whistled excitedly, his fingers drumming on his leg. "You didn't even need training, you did it yourself. I didn't even know a girl could."

The feminist in me bristled. "How very eighteen-hundreds of you. You're a regular misogynistic chauvinist pig, huh?"

"Now, now don't get yourself all riled up. They just

never had a girl member before, but we're going to have to let you in."

"Really? I can join your secret club? Do I get to learn the secret handshake and everything?" I clasped my hands together in mock glee. "Of course you've never had a female member here, idiot. You've never had girls enrolled here before. How did I dance with a guy who's never heard of feminism?"

"I've heard of it, but that doesn't mean a woman can do everything a man can do," he goaded. I went to smack him on the back of his head, but he ducked with a snicker. "I'm learning," he informed me. "How did I ever consider dating such a violent girl?"

"We're both lucky we got out early before we really knew each other."

"Oh yes, good thing neither one of is still interested in the other," Brent said with a playful grin. "You're not still mad at me, are you?"

"I may not be angry anymore, but it takes a while to forgive," I informed him honestly, wiping the flower petals from my black pencil skirt. They rained down over fallen leaves, adding a dash of color to the brown foliage.

"Makes sense." Brent nodded as he crossed his arms. "I only said that about girls because I honestly didn't know girls could do it. I was told it passed down through the male genes."

"Oh." He had me on that one; the Acordera gene only passed down through the maternal side, after all, as far as I knew.

"That's it?" He prompted, shocked. "No apology for smacking me?"

I yawned and studied my nails in reply.

"Okay then." Brent stood up and started pacing in front

of the bench, kicking leaves as he walked. "Obviously you're gifted, but you need help to hone your natural ability. There are some things that are essential to know."

"Look, Brent. I appreciate what you're trying to do but I'm not interested."

He looked startled and began, "I—"

I cut him off. "I don't want any part of this. The whole thing kinda freaked me out. I'm sure girls always do what you tell them because you're hot, Brent, but I'm just not that interested."

His head perked up with a wide smile. "You think I'm hot?"

I almost growled at him as my cheeks flushed. "I'm not interested in astral projection, so just leave me alone."

"Why?"

"I have some very personal reasons."

When I stood up to leave, he reached out to grasp my arm, but I pulled out of his reach.

"Yara, that isn't how it works. After the first time, you lose the ability to choose. You need my help."

My gut wrenched, like someone was tightening a loose screw. My chest tightened, my hands tingled, and I teetered backward. "I don't want to fight again, so please drop this." I picked up my backpack, and sprinted away from him, silencing the part of me that told me he was right.

CHAPTER 5

I had read, studied, written and typed until I could hardly see straight when I finally headed to dinner. I was starving because I had already missed lunch. Cherie hadn't been to our dorm yet but we ran into each other as I was entering the commons building. "Hey, what happened to you today? You just vanished after Language Arts."

I pulled her aside into one of the empty chair groupings on the bottom floor of the bustling building. "Yeah, I really have to talk to you about that." She gave me a quizzical look, as if questioning what she might have missed while sitting right next to me. I leaned in and motioned to the busy room around us as I told her, "But it's a long conversation I'd rather have in private. Nothing was really wrong, just strange."

"Strange as in my kind of strange?" I inclined my head to let her know it was. Cherie's eyes glistened with questions but she held them back. "We'll talk tonight. I'm very intrigued."

As we approached the cafeteria, Brent and Steve were waiting for us just outside the doors. Steve's face lit up when he saw Cherie, but Brent's face was calculating. A few girls walked by, yelling to Brent to call them later. I unclenched my fingers and followed Cherie to pick up my tray. We must have missed the dinner rush. The room was unusually empty and we had our pick of the tables after getting our food.

I squeezed lemon into my water as I told Brent, "I don't want to hear it."

His face was wooden. "I know, but I need to talk to you anyway. In private." He subtly motioned to our friends. "I was afraid you wouldn't talk to me if I approached you alone."

"You're right, but only because I know what you're going to say," I admitted.

Brent ran his hand across his eyes.

"Doesn't Steve think it's odd that you're willing to eat with me?" I asked, swirling my straw through my water.

Brent twirled his pasta around his fork. "I didn't tell him about your wicked throwing arm."

"Oh." I took a sip of water.

"Doesn't Cherie think it's weird that I'd want to eat with you? Why would she even want to hang out with me knowing what I said about her?" He asked before taking a bite.

I didn't tell her either," I confessed putting my napkin in my lap and smoothing it down.

A smile curled on his face. "I see."

"You see what?"

"More than you probably want me to."

"You two look cozy," Cherie said. I hadn't realized how close I had moved toward him while we were talking, and I scooted away from him. "What are you two whispering about over there?"

I've always thought fast on my feet and I smoothly lied. "I was asking Brent how Gifted and Talented P.E. went."

Brent smiled into his napkin. "Nice," he muttered

under his breath. He raised his voice so our friends could hear as his face drew into a painful grimace. "Torture! How was remedial P.E., Yara?"

"Um . . . better than torturous. So . . . good, I guess."

The conversation was soon filled from all three of them detailing the horror of how Mr. Molter, the cross-country coach, had pushed the runners beyond what they thought possible.

"So, why don't you join the team?" Brent asked, only half-joking.

"Besides the fact you three make it sound like so much fun?" I paused for comedic timing before answering honesty. "I never really thought of it as an option."

"Why?"

"I'm not a very fast runner," I said.

"Have you ever heard the expression 'slow and steady wins the race'?"

I laughed. "I have, but I've actually found that statement to be false. I've raced a hare." I motioned toward Cherie. "And the tortoise" I pointed to myself. "Always comes in last."

"So are you on *any* sports teams?" Brent asked, pushing around the vegetables on his plate with a fork.

"I have found that most teams appreciate my lack of membership. I do love sports, but I'm not a practicing participant of organized sports."

"Organized sports? Is that similar to organized religion?"

"Hey, I won't question your beliefs if you don't question mine, all right?"

"Okay," he laughed, raising his hands in defeat.

"And it may be totally lame, but I'm actually liking Social Dance."

Brent eyed me carefully. "Well, not totally *lame*, but—"

I threw my napkin at him. "Shut up!"

"Temper, temper," he chided, lifting his eyebrows with a smile.

I pointedly moved my chair closer to Cherie and talked to her through the rest of dinner.

*   *   *   *

On the way back to our dorm, Brent walked slowly beside me, while Steve and Cherie hurried ahead. The space between Brent and I was almost five feet wide; people probably wouldn't even guess we were technically together. A tense silence crackled between us and it was clawing angrily at my nerves.

Brent started to snicker and I turned to see what was so funny. "To think you couldn't even get through a single meal without throwing something at me."

I knew he was baiting me but this time I refused to get tangled in the hook. "So let's hear the speech I'm sure you've prepared."

Brent put his thumbs through his belt loops and rocked on his heels. "You need to learn to control your astral projection."

I brought my fingers to his lips, enjoying for a split second the feeling of his breath on my skin. "Shh. Not out here, someone might hear." Grabbing his arm, I dragged him into a dark alcove in the stone wall for some privacy.

"If you wanted to get me alone, you only had to ask," he said with a wink.

"I just couldn't control myself," I deadpanned, letting go of his arm. "I just don't want anyone to overhear this conversation."

Brent took a few steps back and rested his shoulder against the wall farthest from me. "I'm sure this is all a little bit startling to you, but you do need some help. It'll be better than you floundering around alone in this."

"Why?" I asked, fidgeting with the buttonhole on my sweater.

"There is so much to tell you . . ." His voice trailed off, his head cocked to the side, listening. "Someone's coming." In two large steps he was very close to me again. His citrusy musk cologne enveloped me, and my spine melted as I inhaled his scent deeper. It was a good thing I was against the wall; it was keeping me up.

"Are you okay?" He asked with a half smile. "You look , almost meek. Is my nearness affecting you?"

"Hardly," I scoffed, pushing him away. I turned my head, breathing in non-Brent scented air until my head cleared.

"Brent, is that you?"

Brent spun, his body rigid, his arm snaking around me. He made a show of wiping his mouth, trying to look sheepish, like we had just been making out while drawing me close.

"I didn't see you swimming laps at practice."

"Yeah, I missed tonight." Brent threw a sly smile my way. "I've been busy."

"I knew girls coming here would create problems," Coach Tait grumbled before bidding us good night. Brent kept his arm around me until the swim coach was out of sight, then stepped away from me.

"What was that about?"

"I didn't know it was him. I wanted us to have a good reason to be talking in such a secluded spot."

"I doubt people use that alcove to talk," I pointed out.

Brent gave me a wicked grin. "Exactly."

I rolled my eyes at him. "I admit I'd be embarrassed

if we got caught having that conversation, but you sort of overreacted back there."

Brent's shoulders slumped and he started chewing on his nails again. "Yeah. I'm just jumpy recently."

"Why?"

"Doesn't matter." Brent raked his fingers through his hair. "What matters is that I'm officially offering to train you." Brent shoved his hands into his pockets. "I'll be on your fire escape at one this morning."

I dropped onto a stone bench that rested under the branches of an oak tree, my jaw clenched in protest. "Is it really that dangerous?"

He sat beside me. "It can be. Unless you have training, your spirit can leave without you wanting it to any time you're scared or angry. There are some foods you have to avoid."

"You're joking, right?"

Brent shook his head. "No. You're lucky you have me. I had to learn this alone with some old notes. It wasn't fun." Brent started in on his nail again. All his fingers had ragged nails chewed down to the skin. "Black licorice, for example—avoid it. Some forms of it can push you out of your body with such force you end up far away from it and can't return for a while. It'll actually put up a barrier between your body and any spirit. Peppermint can—"

I cut him off. "No worries about licorice. I hate the stuff." I bit my lip trying to absorb the information Brent had spewed out. "It sounds like there is so much to know. Are you sure I have no choice in this anymore?"

"Once you do it the first time, it's part of you." Brent gave me a pitying look.

"How long have you been able to leave your body?"

He paused for a beat, loosening his tie. "I developed

that talent right before I started school here. How about you?"

"You saw my first time. Could the other guys in your family do it?"

He tilted his head. "Yeah."

I lifted my necklace out of my shirt and my fingers anxiously grasped the charm that dangled from the chain, rubbing it between my thumb and pinky. Brent stared hard at my necklace, taking a few steps toward me. He lifted his hands, stroking the beads almost lovingly— the amber in them burned a little brighter and warmed from his touch; its heat snuggled into my soul.

"Wow. It responded to your touch," I whispered, slightly awed. It was like something out of some fantasy novel, a magic talisman connecting with its master.

"Where did you get it?" Brent asked, ignoring my statement.

"My grandmother sent it to me from Brazil. Why?"

Shaking his head, he shoved his hands into his armpits while stepping back. "No reason. It's pretty."

I didn't believe him, but I examined my necklace with newfound interest. The amber beads were flecked with tiny preserved blossoms, and the intricately carved wooden flower pendant glowed beautifully in the moonlight. I lifted it, watching the way the material picked up the beams of light.

"It isn't all bad, you know. Once you can control it, it's downright sick."

It took a few moments for me to remember the conversation we had been having about astral projection. "What's so great about being able to separate your soul from your body?"

Bent looked around, making sure we were alone before

lifting his arm and running his hand back and forth in the air, creating a gentle breeze that lightly shook the leaves of the tree. I couldn't help but gape at him open-mouthed. Had he really just made the leaves move? He grinned at my wonder and raising his hand again, waved it around my face, lifting the hair off my shoulders so it floated gently in the air.

"That was incredible," I said as my hair fell back around my face and neck. I raised my hand, trying, but nothing happened. "How did you do it?"

"Meet me tonight and I'll tell you," he said, his low voice taking on a husky tone.

He was pouring on the charm, and it was working. I took a deep breath and refocused my brain. "Can everyone who can astral project do that?"

Brent paused, uncomfortable for a minute, before answering. "No, but I have this feeling you'll be able to."

"It's a date then." Brent gave me an odd look and I realized what I had said. My cheeks burned and I sputtered, "No, I mean . . . not a date, an appointment."

He puffed his chest out as he stood. "Gotta watch out for those Freudian slips." He grinned at me lazily. "See ya tonight."

* * * *

"So, explain to me one more time how you astral projected," Cherie demanded.

I lay across my bed, with my head hanging off the side looking toward Cherie's bed, my legs stretched up and my feet resting against the shiny white cinder block wall. "Well, when I first got up there, I was a wreck."

"Right, I noticed that. But that isn't out of the ordinary," Cherie interjected, as she dug through her makeup drawer and pulled out her nail care bag.

Although she spoke the truth, I gave her a nasty look as I sat up. "And then I remembered this advice I found in a book in the library. It said that when I was nervous I should take a deep breath and pretend I was dreaming, and it would help me get through it."

"So how did that make you leave your body?" She asked, her nail file pausing in her hands.

"I don't know how. I was panicking. It just happened. Anyway, and then when I did, I noticed that I sort of separated." I continued to tell her everything that had happened, hoping she wouldn't think I'd lost my mind.

To my relief, she set down her emery board and leaned closer to me, her eyes dancing with anticipation. "What was it like?"

"Everything around me slowed down, but my mind was so alert I felt like I was in fast forward. When I fully stepped out of myself, my body froze like an empty shell."

"So cool." I could almost hear the internal gears of Cherie's mind working. "Can you do it again?"

"I don't know," I answered, more than a little nervous of trying it again. I didn't feel it was my place to tell her about Brent being able to do it too, so I couldn't explain his warnings.

"What do you mean you don't know?"

"I haven't tried it yet. I did some research on it and found it could be dangerous," I lied, wringing my hands together in my lap. I wanted more answers from Brent before I told her more. "Some article said that if you do it once you won't be able to stop."

"Who says you'd want to? You need to embrace this, Yara. It's part of who you are."

"I'm not sure I want this, Cherie. It's too close to everything else I don't want to be part of. I need some time to process it."

Cherie pressed her lips together but her eyes spoke volumes. She wasn't done talking about it. Voices carried into our room from the hall outside and then grew faint as the girls walked by. A new song on the radio began, but still she said nothing. Finally she nodded. I'd bought myself a little time.

* * * *

I hadn't told Cherie about my training session with Brent, so I slid out the window and onto the fire escape as quietly as possible when my alarm went off. I shivered in the chill air, trying to find constellations in the stars as I waited for Brent.

I must have dozed off at some point because the next thing I knew the sun was peeking over the mountains behind the school. My body was stiff, sore, and freezing as I stood and stretched. A gentle gust of frigid air circled around me, tugging my hair away from my shoulders. Instead of moving on, the wind danced around me for almost a minute, like I was in the eye of a small storm. The breeze carried all the smells of Pendrell and a familiar scent that tugged at my memory. I tried to place it as I made my way back to my room. My bed was warm by comparison and I crawled into it drowsily. I drew up the blankets, wondering why Brent hadn't shown up and if I should be angry or worried.

By the time I got up, I had slept through first period, despite Cherie's attempts to drag me out of bed. In an effort to not be even later, I considered skipping a shower, but one sniff of myself and I ruled that option out. So I gathered my bathroom bucket, robe, and striped towel on my way to the bathroom.

After showering, I toweled off and wrapped myself in my robe. I emerged from the shower stall to find the whole bathroom deserted and full of steam. I hadn't realized my shower had been so hot. The row of shiny sink faucets dripped with condensation. The blue and white floor tiles were dangerously slippery and I slid along the moist floor toward the fog-covered mirrors. I wiped my hand across one of them and peered at my hazy reflection. I looked like I had been up half the night. The image of me vanished behind a new layer of steam.

The vapors of wet heat thickened, making it hard to breath and leaving me unable to see beyond my nose. I knew no one had come into the bathroom but I also knew someone was in there with me. Fear beaded into glistening sweat on my skin; my lungs seemed to wither, and I couldn't take a decent breath. Through the dank air, I smelled the same almost musky scent from the fire escape, sending a tiny wave of comfort through my frayed nerves. Not enough to make me less scared, but enough to give me the clarity of mind to get out of the room. My hands in front of my face, I started to scoot my way to the door, when a sound akin to a squeegee on glass echoed through the vacant room. I wheeled toward it and almost lost the contents of my bladder when I saw words on the mirror, written through the steam.

Do Not Trust Brent

I read the words aloud and once spoken they vanished along with the steam and I was alone in the perfectly ordinary bathroom.

CHAPTER 6

"Brent, wait up," I called, scrambling out of my chair after Language Arts. Somehow, I had been able to get myself to class after the bathroom experience. I kept trying to figure out why the ghost had written that, what it would gain by me not trusting Brent. I decided to ignore the warning, at least until Brent gave me reason to do otherwise.

He stopped with an impatient tapping of his foot. "How may I help you?"

"Thanks for standing me up last night," I complained. "I probably caught a cold waiting for you."

"Oh . . . right. I forgot about our date," he said slowly.

"It wasn't a date," I corrected with a shy grin. "It was a training session, remember?"

"Yeah, sorry. I got unexpectedly detained. Do you want to reschedule?"

"I figured you would. You're the one who thought it was so important I learn to control," I leaned in close, "my astral projection."

Brent staggered back, looking stricken. "I was wrong. You don't need training, you only need to avoid it."

My head cocked to the side, a feeling of unease sashaying through my stomach. "You said I couldn't stop."

"I just wanted an excuse to spend more time with

you," he whispered huskily. Blood rushed to my face. He licked his lips and got a faraway look in his eye. "I did some research last night and it turns out you can suppress it with herbs."

I frowned even as he gave me the solution I wanted. "Oh. I have to admit that watching what you did made me want to learn more."

"Trust me, you want to leave this alone. It's dangerous." He stepped toward me with a savage glint in his eyes. I studied them for a second, as his gaze dropped to my necklace, a slight frown pulling at his mouth. Brent's usually dark brown eyes were faintly edged in green, and with large flecks of jade I hadn't noticed before, they almost looked as hazel as mine. The words I had dismissed on the mirror flashed in my mind like a neon sign. Reflexively, my hand lifted to my necklace, my fingers toying with the wooden flower.

"Okay," I said, shivering. "So what do I need to take?"

He cracked his knuckles. "I'll bring it by your room when I can find some. You're in 222 right?'

"Yeah. How did you know?"

"I know all." He laughed, starting down the hall.

I stared after him, remembering the words on the mirror. Something about the conversation felt off and I wondered if I was starting to believe the ghost.

* * * *

That night as we were getting ready for bed, Cherie asked, "So, did you try to see if you could leave your body again?"

I was proud of her. She had lasted a full twenty-four hours before bringing up the subject.

"No, I haven't." Yesterday Brent had said that I had no choice anymore, that it was part of me now—but today he had said it was dangerous to try again. I wasn't sure which bit of conflicting knowledge to believe. But all day I had felt this intense urge to try it once more before I started taking the purple taro root powder he had given me after school. It looked like the pictures I had found online, but I still didn't know enough about it, and was hesitant to take it.

"Yara, you need to explore this for me. This is the sort of thing that validates all the stuff I want to believe in," Cherie explained desperately, perching on the edge of her bed. Tears had gathered in the corners of her eyes. "This is important to me. Try it again." Then she mopped her tears with her shirt sleeve. "Or better yet, teach me how to do it, too, and I'll come with you. Please, Yara."

I hesitated, considering. Cherie never understood why I didn't fully embrace my 'spiritual heritage' as she called it. The hours and hours she had spent with my grandma had created this insatiable desire in her to try and become, in her words, what I already was. Even knowing all of that, my answer was no, and I was going to tell her so. But then I saw her eyes. They were wide, innocent, and artfully teary, twinkling with hope and all kinds of unspoken things to guilt me into agreeing.

I sighed. I could never tell her no when she used that weapon on me. Would it really kill me to help her? Brent had said that it was bound to keep happening to me anyway, well before he had said it was dangerous and should be suppressed. If I tried it with someone else, maybe it wouldn't seem so much like surrendering to an unwanted destiny— it would be something we could do together.

"All right, fine. You win." I threw up my hands in defeat. "That was a lowdown, dirty maneuver," I couldn't help but add.

Cherie ignored me; she was grinning from ear to ear. "I

wonder how far we'll be able to go."

"I doubt we'll even be able to get out of the room. It's not like we can turn the doorknob."

"What if we had the door open?"

I thought for a minute. "That might work, but there are lots of other doors to go through." I bit my lip, contemplating alternatives. "Maybe if we had the window open, we could go down the fire escape."

Cherie's eyes lit up. "That's a great idea." She ran over to the window and slid it open, letting the cool evening air blow into our room. "So how do we start?"

"Beats me," I said.

Cherie had a few ideas. "How about if we sit in like some sort of meditative pose?" Cherie plopped down crosslegged and I sat down in like manner across from her, mimicking what I had done before, explaining it to her as I did. It was easier this time, as if my spirit knew what was coming and was anticipating the freedom it was about to experience. Energy exploded inside me as I separated.

Leaping up I turned to look at myself. A moment of doubt broke through when I noticed my pale, lifeless skin; it was obvious that my body was vacant of the spirit that normally dwelt there.

I look dead.

A warning swam through me but I refused to listen because no matter how I appeared, my spirit had never felt more free or alive.

Cherie would love this. Remembering my friend, I turned toward her.

Cherie's face was scrunched up in concentration. I wondered if I reached out and touched her, if maybe her spirit would join mine. My fingers gently touched her face. Her skin was hot and she didn't feel completely solid—more like she was made of gelatin, rubbery almost, rippling under my touch.

"Cherie," I called, my voice soft and melodious, heavenly almost. I hesitated for a moment, waiting to see if she'd join me, but she didn't. I wasn't sure what to do. *Am I brave enough to go further without her?*

After a brief moment, I knew my answer. I was.

I turned toward the window, leaned against the pane, and found it solid. Would the same go for the fire-escape? I imagined my spirit spilling through the metal grate like water through a sieve. I tested it first, sitting on the ledge and pressing down with one foot. It felt secure, so I stepped outside and climbed down to the sidewalk below.

The air itself was a complex tapestry of my surroundings and I could smell each thread. Fresh-cut roses, avocados, oranges, and from far away, blooming lilies. It was amazing, and I breathed in deeply, savoring it all.

When I reached the grass, I spun around in a circle with my arms stretched wide. Each star in the sky twinkled brightly as if warmly greeting my liberated spirit. A slight breeze brought in a new bouquet of smell as it gently caressed me.

The night felt like a blank canvas awaiting the first stroke, and I was the artist, picking the color from a near-infinite palate, able to go anywhere, see anyone, do anything. My personal tastes seemed to drift toward a pair of dreamy brown eyes, and my feet were soon heading toward Brent's room.

Since he could astral project, too, I thought spying on him might be fair, and I sprinted toward the boys' dorm only slowing when I neared the fire escape. The entire journey had taken seconds, but I didn't feel winded or tired.

My plan had one hitch: I didn't have any idea what

room Brent was in. I started on the second floor, and feeling every bit the voyeur that I was, I peeked through the window, hoping the boys would be dressed. Two boys I didn't know were both in the midst of studying at their desk, each frozen in time with a look of boredom on his face. I continued on to the next floor and peeked in through an open window. There sat Brent on his bed, his head thrown back and his mouth wide open. It appeared as if I had caught him mid-laugh. His head turned, his eyes glaring at me.

"I told you not to do it again!" His face contorted with rage and for the smallest fraction of a second, his image blurred, looking like someone else all together. His gaze was filled with such loathing and anger that my exhilaration turned to all-consuming, breath-stealing fear. My heart, clear back in my dorm room, lurched in terror. I recoiled as my spirit was sucked back to my body and I was grateful for my escape.

A crystal blue shimmer of light glittered at the foot of my bed for a second and a familiar smell perfumed the air. I squinted my eyes, trying to get a better look— when it vanished. I stared at the spot as if my sheer will alone would make it reappear.

My mind felt slow, weighed down by unseen sandbags. My body sagged to the ground and I shivered violently from the cold that suddenly encompassed me. Cherie pushed to her knees in front of me, her eyes wide.

"Are you okay?"

"I-I'm s-so c-c-cold." I stuttered. Cherie grabbed the green duvet off her bed and tucked the edges of it around me and then propped my pillow under my head. My teeth chattered and I hugged myself tightly for warmth.

When the shivers finally slowed, Cherie asked, "Did it

work?"

I flinched. "Too loud."

She dropped her voice to a whisper and repeated her question so low I didn't think I would have heard it normally. I managed a nod. The room seemed much brighter than it had before, and I squinted as I looked up at my friend. My eyes began to water and I snapped them closed.

"Too bright?"

I nodded again. Cherie hurried to turn the lights off and then returned. In the darkness I could see everything as if the light were still on. Four red dots stood out on her face, in the exact same spot that my fingers had touched her. "Did I hurt you?"

"What?" Her voice was still too loud.

"When I was out of my body, I touched your face, and it left a mark."

In a shot, Cherie was up examining her face in the mirror, leaning close to see in the dim light. She traced the marks my fingers had left behind. "You did this?"

My voice still felt feeble. "Yes. I'm sorry."

Cherie shook her head. "They don't hurt. How cool!" I heard myself try to laugh, but I didn't have the strength. Cherie's excitement gave way to frustration. "Why wasn't I able to do it?" She turned to me with questioning eyes.

"I have no idea." I could feel my warmth returning. The marks on Cherie's face were beginning to fade, too.

"Maybe I just need more practice."

"Maybe."

I sat up slowly, feeling more normal with every breath, although my room still had me on sensory overload.

"So, tell me all that happened," Cherie pleaded. I only got as far as where I touched her face before she interrupted me. "Why do you think my skin felt so flimsy to you?"

I bit the inside of my cheek thinking. "Maybe because we were on different spiritual planes or something. I mean, I'm still alive and yet I was without my body."

"So you think you still had substance because you weren't dead?"

I shrugged my shoulders. "Maybe. If I were dead I wouldn't be able to touch you, I guess."

"This is so amazing." She seemed to be digesting this new information. "How far did you get?" Her voice, seeping with curiosity, still hurt my ears.

"Boys dorm."

"Did you see the guys?" Cherie giggled in an operatic octave. She saw me wince and cut her laugh short. "So what did you see?"

In the safety of my room, hidden under a pile of blankets I felt stupid for having been so afraid. "I saw Brent, before I was pulled back to my body."

My feeling of stupidity didn't last long as I remembered the look in his eyes when he saw me. I had seen Brent angry before, I had seen him mad, but I had never seen him like I had tonight. When he glared at me, his eyes seemed evil and dangerous. Just the memory of them gave me a chill that made my toes grow numb. After managing to crawl into bed, my eyes grew heavy and were soon unable to remain open despite Cherie's continued talking. My thoughts were troubled as I drifted off to sleep. A pair of dangerous brown eyes haunted my dreams.

*   *   *   *

"Hey, Yara," Cherie said when she got back from her study date with Steve the following afternoon. I had woken up feeling lazy and had decided to stay in my room and study while Cherie had gone out. My homework was done, including my paper on "The Lady of Shallot," and as a reward I was indulging in some frivolous reading.

"Want to play hide and seek?"

"Are we five?" I asked, not looking up from the magazine I had stolen from her care package.

"Come on, it's going to be fun."

"Our room doesn't have too many hiding places."

"The cross-country team decided to play hide and seek in the avocado groves." I could tell from her tone that her patience was running thin.

I looked out the window at the dark, threatening clouds, and could see the tiny raindrops already falling. "Did you notice it's raining?"

"Exactly. It will be a blast!"

I deliberated for a moment. "Did you say the whole cross-country team?"

"Yes, Brent will be there." My heart thudded uneasily, as I remembered how angry he'd seemed the night before. I bit my lip, deliberating before finally bending to slip on my shoes.

By the time we made it to the groves, there was a large group assembled. From the size of the crowd it looked like the other team members had brought friends along as well. Brent was easy to spot among our numbers and I forced myself to meet his gaze. Instead of furious, his brown eyes were warm and friendly as was his smile.

"I'm glad you made it," he said as he strolled toward me. "I wanted to apologize if I scared you last night." He cracked his knuckles. People were milling around us and Brent lowered his voice, "I was really worried. You don't understand what you're playing with."

The game started before I could reply. It was raining heavily now and the dirt had become a thick mud. Bright flashes of lightning lit the sky, followed by loud rolls of angry thunder. Jody Lynn, captain of the girl's cross-country team, was the first person to be "it," and home base was the one avocado tree that looked like it had suffered some sort of fire damage. We all scattered. Scouting the area for a place to hide, I had the unsettling feeling I was being watched. I stopped in my tracks, looking around me, my shoes sinking in the wet earth, but didn't see anyone but my classmates scurrying for places to hide. I hoisted my feet out of the muck and shook them, splattering mud all over my pants.

It didn't take long to find a perfect hiding place in the leafy branches of a tree, allowing me to peek out without being seen, and I climbed up. Hugging the thin limb I was perched upon, I tried to ignore the prickly bark rubbing against my cheek. The pitter-patter of rain was oddly soothing, even if a few cold drops did manage to find a way inside my shirt, sliding down my back.

From my vantage point, I could see Jody Lynn coming and hear the giggles of people trying to get to home base. As Brent took off running, I watched Jody Lynn turn to follow him, giving me time to quietly slink down to the ground that was blanketed with brown leaves. I was poised, ready for the right moment to sprint when someone loudly screamed, "No!" Hand over heart, I jumped, twirling toward the shout, just as I was struck in the chest by something I couldn't see.

It hurled me backward, forcing the air out of my lungs. Breaking through branches that tore at and scratched my skin, I crashed down onto a muddy, foot-trampled trail several feet from where I had been standing. I pushed my fingers into the moist dirt, lifting onto my elbows, rocks embedding into my skin when a blinding flash of lightning struck down out of the sky on the very spot I had been standing mere seconds before. The air gleamed for an instant on impact, illuminating a figure that disappeared with the light. If any breath had remained in my lungs, I would have screamed. The world around me started to fade as darkness enveloped me.

* * * *

I woke up with a start. My body ached and my mind wanted to shy away from the fact that I had almost been struck and killed by lightning. My eyes tried to focus on an anxious Cherie, still soft around the edges, leaning over me. Steve and Brent flanked her shoulders.

"Are you okay?"

The world began to slide back into focus. I was on one of the couches in our dorm lobby.

"How did I get here?"

"Steve carried you while Brent ran to get help."

A small group of people stood on the other side of the room looking over at me anxiously.

"The nurse is on her way." Brent kneeled down beside me his hands behind his back. "What happened to you?"

"I tripped," I lied. "Good thing I did or I would have been struck by lightning." Every muscle in my body protested in pain and winced as I sat up; it felt like I had been the victim of a buffalo stampede. I closed my eyes and willed myself not to throw up.

"I think you should stay put until the nurse comes," Brent urged, backing up as I teetered to my feet.

"I'm fine! I want to go lay down in my bed," I argued, leaning heavily on Cherie. "If the nurse comes, she can come check me out in my room." It was a good thing that Cherie was strong, because she did most of the work as we made our way to the elevators. I stood confidently, waving goodbye to a worried Brent as the doors closed. As soon as they slid shut, I leaned my forehead against the metal doors, feeling soothed by their coolness, and took a steadying breath. By the time we reached our floor, I was able to walk with only minor assistance from Cherie, although my sore muscles caused me to limp slightly.

I was encrusted with mud that flaked off in a trail as I went, like Hansel and Gretel's breadcrumbs. Running my fingers through my hair, I found more mud and enough twigs to start a fire. My arms were not only caked in wet dirt, but were scratched and bruised, and the left side of my cheek felt tender. The reflection in my mirror was even worse than I had feared. I was a complete mess and in desperate need of a shower.

Cherie lingered in the doorway. "Did you really almost get hit by lightning?"

I slipped off my filthy shoes and sank into my desk chair, causing more flakes of dirt to rain around me. "Yeah." I hesitated. "Something saved my life."

That got Cherie's full attention. "Something?"

My wet socks stuck to my feet as I pried them off. "Yeah, someone screamed, 'no' and then I was hit here." I pointed toward my upper torso just below my collarbone, grimacing when my fingers brushed it. I swore in Portuguese, using phrases that would have made my grandfather proud, and unbuttoned my shirt, gasping as I discovered two red marks in the shapes of opened hands. They were bright crimson with welts along the edges and blisters forming in the middle.

Cherie didn't speak for a moment. "Wow. Well, someone was out there with you." I expected an admission like that to make her giddy, but instead she looked pale and terrified.

CHAPTER 7

The news of Phil Lawson's suicide the next morning shook the entire campus. It was only the beginning of his junior year, but according to the note left next to an empty bottle of pills, the pressure had been too much.

I had never talked to him, but I knew him as a basketball star and top student in our grade. Still, the loss of him impacted me strongly. Maybe because it reminded me how someone you loved could be there one minute and then gone the next. I wouldn't see him hanging out with his friends in the outdoor pavilion or dribbling a basketball in the gym. He was gone and his family and friends would never see him again. I wondered if he had a little sister who worshipped her older brother the way I had mine.

At lunch that afternoon, Cherie's worried eyes kept glancing to the spot where my red marks had been, even though they had faded already. She twirled a strand of her blonde hair, her blue eyes calculating. "It wasn't the curse," she told me, trying to sound reassuring. "If it were, it should have happened the first week of school . . . or at the end of last year. There is no curse."

Steve stormed toward our table. The salt and pepper shakers toppled over and my napkin drifted to the floor at the force of his orange tray banging down on the table.

"Bad mood?" I asked dryly.

His usually cheerful eyes were pure steel as he answered, "Something like that."

"What's wrong?" Cherie asked, her spoon pausing over her pudding.

"Just a big blow up with Brent—he is currently packing up his stuff and switching rooms, he got the RA's permission and everything." Steve combed his fingers through his dirty blonde hair.

"Must have been some fight."

"Yeah." He held his breath, cheeks puffed out before letting the air out. "I knew better than to try to talk to Brent about the suicide, but I pushed him until he snapped."

The table next to us was crowded with Phil's buddies, all of them grim-faced and red-eyed. "Were he and Phil close?" I asked, trying to keep my voice down.

"No, but considering the circumstances . . ." Steve trailed off with a shrug. Steve's eyes focused on me. "He didn't tell you about his brother, Neal, did he?"

"That his brother died?"

Steve looked down at his sandwich. "Not just died—he was the last suicide, the last victim of the curse."

Cherie dropped her spoon. "Neal was his brother?"

"I had no idea," I said. The apple in my mouth now tasted like sand. "He must be really hurting." My eyes were suddenly misty. The grief from my own brother's death washed over me. I imagined that being compounded by knowing he had killed himself. Phil's suicide had to have reinjured a poorly healed wound. "I've got to talk to him."

My hands and toes tingled as I jumped up fast and then I was caught up in a rush of cold air as my spirit separated from my body, without my wanting it to.

The entire cafeteria paused, the noises hushed, the

movement stilled. The world was like a photograph. Travis was throwing a handful of popcorn at Audrey who was studying from a book. Cherie and Steve were both looking toward me, mouths open as if about to speak.

Even though every human thing was frozen, birds still fluttered in the sky, clouds rolled by, smells of citrus and flowers were carried in the gentle wind moving through me from the open windows. The sun was beating down on me through the skylights, its warmth heated the chill my spirit felt without the protection of its human flesh.

Something blue flickered on the edge of vision and I spun around as it glided toward me with purpose.

A beautiful voice, vaguely familiar, came from the light. "Yara," it called. My heart in my body boomed, and my knees turned to oatmeal as my spirit reconnected. Shivering, I fell, knees smacking the stiff carpet with a thud as the voice asked, "Did you get my message?"

* * * *

It wasn't until later that night that I found Brent, swimming laps, his strokes a little less smooth than usual. The smell of the chlorinated room made my palms start to sweat. I wiped them on my skirt as I slipped off my flats, and sat on the edge of the water, dangling my feet in.

The day had been trying. The brief run in with the ghost was troubling but it was added to by other nuisances: I had spilled my soda at dinner, felt like I was being followed once, and found I couldn't find the taro root powder Brent had given me. I was kicking my legs in the water when Brent finally noticed me and swam over.

He gave me a hesitant smile. "If Steve sent you . . ."

"He didn't."

Brent lifted his elbows onto the concrete. "I don't want to talk about it."

"No problem."

"Really?" Brent hoisted himself out of the water, his wet hair splattering me with small droplets. My eyes followed the water trailing down his muscled chest.

I looked away. "Yeah."

"Thanks— I think you're the only person I've spoken to today who hasn't assumed Phil's suicide was overly traumatic for me." He seemed to be sincere but he had to be lying.

I decided not to tell him I was worried about that too. "I just wanted to make sure you're okay, but I'm not going to push, Brent."

"I'm fine." Brent got a strange look in his eyes. "Thank you for checking on me. You're pretty swell."

I swallowed a laugh. "Gee, thanks."

Brent leaned in close and I knew he was going to kiss me. His lips were so close they moistened mine with the excess pool water still clinging to his face, his breath warming my mouth. My eyes fluttered closed before he pulled back quickly and grimaced. I briefly regretted the onions on my hamburger at dinner— then a gust of wind brushed past us and something whacked me on the head, scratching my cheek as it fell.

"Ow," I complained lifting the potted palm tree that normally stood in the corner from off my head. The magic of the moment shattered, I stood and righted the plant while rubbing my head.

"Lousy timing," Brent said, his eyes surveying the room.

My lips twitched in a grin. "Yeah, stupid wind." I considered sitting down beside him again, but Brent had already slipped back into the water.

"I better finish these laps. Coach has been on me, saying

swimming should be my priority, not cross-country."

I nodded, letting him know I understood. I leaned against the glass walls of the pool house, letting my fingers stroke a leaf of the kiss-preventing plant when the temperature around me plunged drastically. Glancing at Brent, I checked to see if he had noticed the sudden chill, but his swimming rhythm hadn't changed.

I knew a ghost was near. My hands felt suddenly frostbitten, my teeth chattered, and the glass nearest me fogged. Sweat trickled down my neck and my lungs felt like they were caught in a trash compactor.

Taking a deep breath, I tried to stop the panic curdling my stomach. Except for scaring the crap out of me, the last time I had seen the ghost it had only tried to relay a message to me; before that it had saved me from the lightning. My pulse picked up when I also remembered it had attacked me and Brent. My ghost seemed to have conflicting agendas. One moment it was trying to kill me and the next it was saving me. It didn't make any sense to me. I bit my lip as I thought back to Vovó's teachings. She had always said there were several kinds of spirits: some meant to hurt us, others were trying to communicate with us, a few were confused and could become violent, and some just messed with people because they were bored.

I mulled over the idea of it being a confused ghost, but that didn't seem to fit. The encounter in my room was different from the one in the shower— well, except the scaring me part. There had even been a distinct smell in each case. What had attacked me had been the dark mist, smelling of chlorine, and what I had seen recently had seemed lighter, with an almost alluring scent. My nose immediately started sniffing for the chlorinated smell and it was faintly there, but no more than it had been when I first walked into the room. Warring with the chemical smell was another scent, one that felt like a hug from an old friend.

An idea formed in my mind, one so obvious that I deserved a smack to my head for not thinking it sooner. There were two ghosts. There had been more than a few tragic deaths here; it would stand to reason there could be more than one spirit haunting the place.

The first ghost seemed threatening, out to hurt me, but the second seemed more complex. I remembered the words I had heard this afternoon asking if I had received the messages. Maybe the second spirit was simply trying to communicate with me. It had told me not to trust Brent, but I wasn't going to follow that blindly. Vovó had mentioned that bored ghosts weren't above lying or toying with people's emotions to amuse themselves.

I gnawed on the inside of my cheek deciding what to do. Maybe if I opened a line of dialogue with the ghost and listened to what it had to say, it would leave me alone or move on.

"W-What do you want?" I stuttered, wrapping my arms around myself. I wasn't sure what I expected, but nothing happened. I stomped my feet, rubbing my hands together and blowing on them.

Something smacked the glass beside me, startling me. A large handprint shaped in the moisture on the window, and letters slowly formed beside it.

Warn you

All my joints felt rubbery, as I gasped out, "Warn me about what?"

Danger

"What's dangerous? Who's in danger?" I whispered, clasping my fingers together, my shoulder slick against the moist glass.

Not Me

What did that mean? Was the ghost telling me I was in danger? Or was the ghost letting me know he wasn't dangerous? I rubbed my head; maybe I needed to ask better questions. Before I could ask another one, the glass and the temperature instantly reverted to the way they had been. The pounding of feet on the floor behind me drew my eyes to a wet Brent who was hurrying over.

"I thought you left," he said stopping close to me, the dripping water creating a puddle at his feet.

"I was going to." I cast a nervous glance over my shoulder, still uneasy about having a conversation with a ghost. "I better get back. I'm behind on my Bio homework," I explained, spinning to leave.

He reached out but pulled short of touching me, retracting his hand quickly, a strange gleam in his eye. "Are you okay? You look like you've seen a ghost."

I gulped before answering. "I'm good."

I flashed him a big smile as I retreated from the pool house.

*   *   *   *

On the way back to my dorm my thoughts were befuddled. I wished my Vovó wasn't in another country; I could really use her guidance. I was starting to regret not having spent much time gleaning information from her the way Cherie had over the years. That's when I realized that even though I didn't have Vovó, I had Cherie and her surplus of knowledge, and not only would she believe me, she also knew Pendrell's paranormal history.

When I burst into my room I found Cherie laying on her bed, her feet in the air, studying. She took one look at me and rose to her knees knowing I had something big to tell her.

Suddenly nervous, I gulped, dropping onto my bed before revealing my two ghosts theory. I brought her up to speed on everything: the mist, the footprints, the steamy bathroom, being followed, not being able to control my astral projection, and finally my conversation with the ghost. The only thing I held back was Brent's ability to astral project; that was his secret, not mine. Cherie's eyes grew wide taking in every detail, the rosy color in her cheeks fading.

"Why didn't you tell me all this earlier?"

Hanging my head in shame, I admitted, "I was afraid you wouldn't believe me."

Cherie's voice was quiet. "Why would you think that?"

"My whole life people thought Vovó was crazy. I know you wanted to believe in all of this . . . but wanting to believe and actually believing it are two different things." I clutched my pillow to my chest as I asked the important question. "Do you believe me?"

"Every single word." Cherie reached out and ruffled my hair.

A breath I didn't even know I was holding escaped.

"You're not just able to see ghosts . . ."

I cut her off. "I haven't really seen ghosts, just fog like stuff. And it seems to come and go."

Cherie gave me the evil eye. "You can see ghosts," she reiterated. "And you can communicate with them, too." The light of understanding twinkled in her eye. "You're going to be a Waker, aren't you? Just like your grandma. Your abilities are developing!"

I smoothed down the wrinkles on my bedspread thinking the moment that I had dreaded had come and it wasn't nearly as bad as I had thought it would be. "Yeah. Apparently I am."

Cherie's eyes glistened with glee. "Frickin' awesome!"

She twisted a lock of her hair around her index finger. "So how are you handling this? It isn't every day your worst fear becomes a reality."

I sighed. "I know." I averted my eyes to the corner of the room, noting the need to vacuum, allowing myself to really think before I responded. "I'm actually doing better than I expected."

Cherie didn't say anything but I could see her almost shaking with excitement.

I shook my head with a wry grin. "So what's the plan? What do I do about the ghosts?"

"I'm not sure." She gave me a confident smile. "We'll think of something. I promise."

* * * *

The following afternoon I found Cherie in our room, unpacking red candles from the huge box she had been storing in the back of her closet. A thick book was open on the floor next to her and she was crossing off items from a list as she gathered them. As soon as she saw me she dropped her list and grinned, patting the spot on the ground beside her.

"I think we need to help you grow comfortable with your gift," she stated unceremoniously.

I groaned as I sat down next to her and leaned against her bed. "And how do we do that?"

Cherie flipped the page on her book. "We have to desensitize you so you're not freaked out by them anymore. Then when you see them you can just order them away or something."

I stared for a moment in surprise. "You think I can do that?"

"I hope so," she said, turning back to her book. "I think your grandma said the stronger you get, the more control you have over your interactions with ghosts. She said at first she was nervous, but she made herself be around them. It helped strengthen her."

"So how do I do that?"

"I'm throwing a formal dinner party for our closest friends tonight."

"That doesn't sound too bad." I wrapped my shoe lace around my finger. "How is that supposed to help?"

"It's not the party that's helping, it's the location. I'm having it in the old pool house."

Fear washed through me. "Why there?"

"It's the most haunted place on campus. So if a ghost is trying to communicate with you, it would be the best place for that to happen."

"Maybe I should ease into it a little more."

"No, you have to learn how to deal with this and fast. What better way than surrounded by your friends? The ghost won't try to hurt you if we're all with you. What's not to love— food, friends and a little training in your family business. It's a win-win."

"And it's formal because?"

Cherie pointed to a slinky black dress hanging in her closet. "It's formal so I have an excuse to wear that in front of Steve. You're going to come aren't you?"

I bit my lip and closed my eyes, trying to ignore the uneasy twisting in my insides before I nodded. Cherie clapped her hands and squealed.

I didn't know what to say, so I sat on my bed and watched as she began going through her mp3 player to create a playlist for the party.

"I'm throwing your bad musical taste a bone; I put 'Can't Stop Dreaming of You' on the list. Don't say I never did anything for you."

"Someday my music will grow on you."

She smiled as I helped her load up the black candelabras, whose dangling beads tinkled as I loaded them into several small boxes. The red candles followed and Cherie picked up the box, instructing me to come to the pool at exactly nine o'clock.

*   *   *   *

I was pretty much useless the rest of the evening while Cherie was gone, preparing for the party. I attempted to write my mom and dad an email, but had a hard time writing one that wasn't boring yet still didn't give details that might cause them to worry. After re-reading it, I knew I hadn't done a good job and my mom would know something was wrong. As I hit send, I knew a concerned and nosey phone call was in my future.

At eight-thirty I dangled my small silver purse around my wrist, debating about taking it. I hated carrying purses, but it matched my dress so nicely, I felt obligated as a woman to carry it.

I walked down to the lobby where Brent was reclining in one of the leather chairs, flipping through a magazine from the coffee table, wearing a black suit and a blue shirt.

"You look beautiful," he said, setting down the magazine.

"You clean up nice yourself."

I spun for him, letting my sequined violet gown swish around my ankles while teetering in my four-inch heels. Brent stood up and appraised me with a wide appreciative grin that did nothing to help my balance.

"Ready?" He asked walking toward the doors.

I followed mutely behind. Trying to control the nervous bounce house my stomach had become, my fingers reached to fidget with my grandmother's necklace, but met with only my naked throat. The necklace was still on my dresser since it hadn't matched my dress, and I felt oddly exposed without it dangling there. Brent noticed my fingers tapping my chest where the necklace should be and his eyebrows raised before he turned to open the glass doors.

He offered his arm, his shoulders stiff. When I took it, his posture relaxed and something flashed briefly in his eyes and was gone before I could interpret it. Together we walked into the chilly moonlit evening.

"Here we go," I whispered to Brent as we veered off into the restricted zones. He pulled out a flashlight and led me expertly toward the pool, a much wider and more direct route than Cherie and I had taken.

"Done this once or twice, have you?"

He laughed. "Yeah, sneaking out to the pool is like a rite of passage at Pendrell."

"Good to know I'm fitting in so well."

When we got to the tree that led to the window, Brent turned around and clasped his hands on my shoulders. "Do you really want to go to this party?"

"Don't you?" I asked, placing my hands over his.

He dropped his hands and ducked his head. "Truth be told, I'm not that eager to see Steve, and I hate this place. It makes me think of all that curse crap. Why did Cherie have to throw her party here?"

I hadn't told him the real reason for the location and lied with a smile. "She thought it'd be fun."

He cracked his knuckles and looked over his shoulder. "I'm not really sure why I came."

He gave me a wan smile before starting up the tree. I followed, and then crawled through the window, which wasn't easy in my formal dress. Brent took my hand and we walked together down the corridor that led to the pool.

When we entered the main room I stopped short,

utterly transfixed by the way Cherie had fixed it up. She had swept and dusted and picked up the litter, leaving the area amazingly clean. Sandalwood, frankincense, and cinnamon were wafting around the room, and as I inhaled I actually felt myself relax. The soothing music Cherie had picked out was playing from somewhere in the room, adding to the calming atmosphere. I had expected the setup to be chintzy, but it wasn't; it was beautiful.

The black candelabras with the red candlesticks were placed on tables in the four corners of the pool, giving the room more light than the moon did, and creating an almost romantic feel. She had placed a table with a white lace tablecloth in the middle of the pool. There were three white candles placed in ivory holders engraved with seashells in the center of the table, surrounded by plastic plates and cups, pitchers of water and several trays of food. Six chairs were arranged around the table, all but two of which were occupied. Cherie had found a ladder long enough to get us down and, more importantly, back up. As Brent and I climbed carefully down the ladder, I wished I had worn more practical shoes.

Cherie beamed as she watched me take in the room. "Do you like it?"

"It's amazing." I gave her arm a squeeze.

"Come and sit here, you two," she said, motioning toward the two empty seats.

I exchanged hellos with Steve, Travis, and Audrey, all dressed in their formal wear, too. I tucked my purse under my chair before Brent took my hand and we slid into our seats. Brent's cool fingers tickled my palm and I watched him trace circles along my wrist. His hand looked different and it only took a second to find the change.

"Hey, your nails have grown out. Did you finally stop

biting them?"

Brent held his hands out wiggling his fingers, before lacing them together and cracking his knuckles. "I think I broke the habit only to pick up a new one."

Cherie turned down the music and stood excitedly at the head of the table. "Thank you for coming. I'm sorry I don't have better food but it's all I could find from the cafeteria." She motioned toward the manicotti and the simple salad, before striking a match to light the candles.

As Cherie served herself and passed the dish along to Steve, something scurried across a corner of the room above our heads causing Audrey to jump. She swallowed hard as she craned her neck trying to peek over the edge of the pool.

"Why are we having your party here?" Travis asked grabbing onto Audrey's hand.

"It's the most haunted place around and I wanted to help Yara grow more comfortable being around the ghosts trying to communicate with her."

I kicked her under the table but her smile didn't dim.

Brent jerked slightly as he leaned over and whispered, "You've had a ghost trying to talk to you? For how long?"

"All year," I confessed spooning salad onto my plate. "Well there have been weird things happening all year but it's only been the last few days that one has actually been trying to talk to me."

Brent grabbed a bread roll and slammed it onto his plate. "I see."

"This place is haunted?" Audrey asked, the pupils in her eyes widening.

"Yes," Cherie said at the same time Brent answered, "No."

Their gazes locked in a sort of battle until Cherie turned toward Audrey. "You haven't heard the story about what happened here?" Audrey's face had gone white and she shook her head. Cherie leaned forward and her voice lowered. "About sixty years ago, a group of students snuck in here after hours. It was a night like this— the moon was full and the air chilly. They snuck into the pool house to have some harmless fun. They had no idea that what awaited them was death." Cherie had always been an excellent storyteller and her words were weaving an eerie magic, enthralling us all. Between breathing out and breathing in a now familiar musky scent became heavy in the air. The second ghost was here. The mp3 player skipped, cutting the current song off halfway through and a new one began, "Can't Stop Dreaming of You."

A cold wind rushed around the room and the candles on the table flickered in response. From the bottom of the floor, a blanket of icy dark fog began rising as it rippled out, reeking of chlorine. The mist was here, too. A loud sound like a footstep echoed through the pool, followed by a long banging noise that sounded like an old wooden rollercoaster going up the track. When it stopped my stomach felt like it was at the top of the ride about to plunge to my toes. Audrey screamed. Another loud thud came from the pool floor and my stomach plunged. My mouth went dry and I tried unsuccessfully to swallow. We waited for a second, no one breathing. When everything remained silent, we let out a collective sigh.

"What . . . what was that?" Travis asked as Audrey dove into his arms.

A deep chill settled inside me, crackling with a wintry intensity, raising every hair on my arms and neck in an electrified static. A cold sweat broke out across my forehead and I lifted my hand, still entwined with Brent's, to wipe it away, his fingers were like ice. A blinding white light exploded in the center of the table.

Its brightness was impossible to look at directly and I had to turn my head to peer into it, squinting my eyes. The intensity of the light dimmed slightly, leaving dancing spots in my vision as a figure appeared. Through the harsh glare, I could make out only a flash here, a flicker there— random details but never the whole picture. It seemed like a young man, about my age, almost completely translucent, standing on the table. His untucked white button-down shirt undulated in an unseen breeze, as did tendrils of his hair. I could make out his deep brown eyes— they seemed dazed and slightly unfocused as his gaze traveled rather aimlessly around our circle.

"It isn't safe. He will hurt you," the ghost whispered. My heart pricked with pity for him, sensing his loneliness, his innocence and I wanted to help him.

"Don't trust him," the ghost pleaded, recapturing my attention as he looked down on us, turning slowly on the spot. The way he moved, it seemed like he was lost, unsure where to go. As I glanced around the table no one seemed to be seeing him except Brent, whose thunderstruck expression I'm sure matched my own. "You must stay away from him!"

"From who?" I asked before I could think. My outburst caused everyone to look at me, including a startled Brent.

The ghost seemed to notice me for the first time. I blinked and jumped to see him squat to my eye level, his face directly in front of mine. He seemed familiar but before I could place him he screamed, "Stay away from him!" His voice was so loud and so shrill my ears throbbed in pain. The wind stirred up by his movement was no longer cold but hot, mirroring the anger in his words.

"He isn't me." Suddenly, without warning, he pointed

at me and my hair was sent flying behind me. The hot air that followed the motion of his finger seared my skin, burning me. I screamed as the wave of heat clung to me, like burning fabric and I clutched Brent's hand tighter as my head lolled back.

"Stay away from her!" His brown eyes turned scarlet, and I could feel the hate and anger that was boiling in him as the hot wind whirled around me. A heavy scraping echoed through the room, as the pool shuddered and trembled. I let out another scream. The intensity of the heat raged against my body threating to consume me, and my mind spiraled in chaos, breaking, losing reason, unable to stand the frenzied pain throbbing.

Then suddenly there was the sweetest release from the pain. I was blanketed in a comfortable chill, and the pool was eerily still. My soul had fled my body to protect itself, my body was frozen, my face contorted in pain, my lifeless eyes wide in terror. My friends, even Brent, were completely still.

Something chilly brushed my shoulder and I wheeled toward it screaming. It was the ghost, the intensity of light surrounding him had dimmed and we looked at each other. My ears pounded in confusion and my jaw went slack because it looked just like Brent, almost a mirror image, dressed in the Pendrell uniform. The ghost rubbed his eyes, his energy focusing on me, his brown eyes tender.

"Yara?" He asked before the candles in the room flickered out and I was pulled back into my body.

I looked toward him, shivering from the cold, but he had vanished. I freed my hands, pulled my knees to my chest, squeezed my eyes closed, and covered my ears.

"Are you okay?" Cherie pleaded, throwing her arms around me. There was a scraping of chairs as everyone gathered in around me.

"I'm okay," I said, not sure if I was lying.

Steve turned on an electric lantern that lit our surrounding area. I opened my eyes and saw Audrey clinging to Travis, white as chalk. Brent's eyes were trained on the ground as he shuffled his feet.

"Is he really gone?" My voice trembled as I forced my hands away from my ears.

"Who? Did you see something?" Cherie asked incredulously.

"The boy . . . the one who looked like Brent?"

"You saw a boy?" Cherie asked.

"Yes . . . didn't you?"

"No, I didn't see anything. But I felt the wind . . . cold at first and then burning hot. And I felt the ground shake and heard some loud noises. What happened?" Cherie pressed.

Steve let out a low whistle and nodded toward the edge of the pool above our head, "I think I see what that sound was."

Not sure my heart could take any more, I took a deep breath before glancing up. Something was covering half the pool— luckily not the portion where our ladder stood.

"What is it?" Brent asked, cracking his knuckles.

"Wow," Cherie said, mouth agape.

"The retractable floor," Steve answered, setting the lantern on the table.

"The one that closed and trapped all those kids . . . when they died," Travis concluded as his machine gun laugh nervously bounced off the pool walls.

"One and the same," Cherie said, her voice cracking.

"Yes, the floor thing is very eerie," I interrupted, "but what about the ghost? Did anyone else *see* him?" I questioned, looking from face to face and being bewildered as each person shook their head no. I turned to Brent. "I know you saw him." His eyes met mine and he hesitated for a moment before shaking his head and dropping his gaze back toward his feet. I knew he was lying but didn't feel like arguing.

"There was a boy . . . he looked exactly like Brent." I swallowed hard. "Was it your brother?" He shrugged. I looked around the group. "I think maybe it was. He seemed to be lost and wanting to warn us about someone." There was a collective gulp and Brent's head jerked up. "But then he noticed me and he became angry and I thought . . . I thought . . . I thought he was going to hurt me." Even though I had somewhat deadened myself to the experience, my breath was coming too quickly and I found myself gasping for air.

"She's hyperventilating," Travis said and was quickly digging through Cherie's box for something. He came back with an old brown lunch sack that he held out for me. I took it and tried to follow his deep breaths. But all I could manage were rapid, shallow ones. Cherie and Brent each put an arm around me and I mimicked Travis's deep breaths until my gasps had slowed to normal.

"Uh . . . can we go?" Audrey begged. "Personally, I don't want to be here. I'm not hungry anymore."

"I couldn't agree more," I said as I stood up and then swayed, grabbing the table.

"That's probably a good idea," Cherie said, steadying me. "You guys go ahead. Steve and I will clean up."

"Are you going to be okay?" I asked her, realizing the evening hadn't gone according to her well-laid plans.

"Of course!" Her entwined hands shook and her eyes glistened with unshed tears. "What else could I have asked for? We made contact." I reached out to her and gave her a hug before she shoved my purse in my hand and pushed me off toward the ladder with a sniff.

Travis and Audrey waved goodbye as soon as they reached the top and quickly disappeared down the hall toward the window, eyeing me curiously. I had a feeling they were anxious to talk privately about what I claimed to have seen and what had happened. Climbing down the ladder had been nervewracking; going up seemed twice as menacing because my body was still weak. I followed behind Brent, inching my way toward the top, gripping the rungs tightly.

When we made it to the window, I looked warily down to the ground as Brent climbed out the window and swiftly down the tree.

"Just get to the tree and then I'll catch you," Brent offered.

My shaking arms hugged the branch and I hoisted myself out the window. Brent smiled up at me, his outstretched arms ready to catch me. I landed in his strong embrace and clung tightly to him. I took a deep breath and let the crisp air cleanse out the anxiety I was feeling. He set me gently down but kept his arm around me as he started walking back toward our dorms. Involuntarily, I kept peeking at him out of the corner of my eye.

Brent stopped, leaning against one of the trees. "Do you want to ask me something?"

"I know you saw him," I said, picking at the sequins on my dress.

"Yeah. I was just overwhelmed. Still am." Brent sighed. "Aren't you?" I nodded wearily. "It's a lot to process. Could we talk about it?"

"I thought guys didn't talk about their feelings," I

teased.

His blank expression made me think he didn't catch my reference to his earlier statement.

"Sure, we could do that," I said, grinding the heel of my shoe into the walkway.

"Good. Let's go somewhere where we can be alone. I know the perfect place." He took my hand and tugged me forward.

The moon was full, immersing us in blue beams while a scattering of clouds inked the evening sky. Our lone steps echoed through the stone corridors and cobbled pathways as we wandered hand in hand around campus, ending finally at the new pool house.

"It's going to be locked," I warned, as Brent walked around the glass building, heading toward a side door.

"Oh, ye of little faith . . ." he smiled broadly, bringing a key out of his pocket and dangling it in front of me. "I might have borrowed this from Coach Tait."

"And is he aware that you have that?" I laughed, as he unlocked the door.

"He asked me to come back and clean up the bricks and towels after practice, and since it would be locked, he let me borrow his key. It's a shame I haven't seen him yet."

"That is a shame," I agreed, walking through the door he held open for me. It was a shade darker in here than it was outside and my eyes squinted slightly to make out the shapes in the room.

"I would turn on the lights, but then we might get caught," Brent explained as he followed me into the room.

Surprisingly enough, there was still enough light to walk around by. Sconces on the walls glowed dimly, providing enough light that it was possible to maneuver through the room without fear of falling into the pool. I was grateful. I didn't feel like trudging through campus in a sopping wet formal dress.

I made my way over to a plastic lounge chair, which squeaked in protest as I sat on it.

"So talk." I dropped my purse beside me on the chair and leaned back on my hands.

Brent held up a finger and walked toward the locker room. The sound of his footsteps echoed around the room, and I looked around absently while I waited for him. I noticed vaguely that a banner had been set up for tomorrow's pre-season swim meet against Sierra Academy, Pendrell's arch rival. Brent would be swimming in that and I planned to take advantage of the chance to admire him working in his natural habitat. He was fantastic eye candy, and I had earned the right to a few cavities.

The room felt cold and I rubbed my hands together for warmth. A sudden feeling of being watched crept over me. I wasn't alone in the room—I could smell the musky scent of the second ghost; he had followed us here. I tucked a strand of my hair behind my ear and glanced around the room, not seeing anything.

Brent came back with two cups filled with purple liquid and I attempted to look calm. "Grape juice," he said, handing me one of the cups. "I had a feeling we might be coming here tonight," he confessed with a grin. "I kept this in the coach's fridge. Cheers." He clanked his plastic glass against mine.

I lifted the cup to my lips prepared to drink when I lost my grip and it fell, spilling across my dress and crashing to the floor. I cursed at my clumsiness wiping the excess liquid from my lap and watched the juice stain the floor.

"More shaken than I thought," I said sheepishly.

"I think you need this more than I do," Brent said

extending his cup to me. My hands were unsteady as I reached for it. Brent smiled softly and shook his head. "You're a mess. Let me help." He brought his cup to my lips, the cup shaking, a sheen of sweat forming along his brow. The plastic cup pressed against my lips and I drank down the grape juice gratefully.

I coughed at the bitter aftertaste. "That might have fermented."

"Maybe," he laughed lowering the cup. "But you probably need more sugar in your system to keep from going into shock. One more drink." I frowned at him as he tilted the cup toward me, but I took another drink anyway, grimacing as I swallowed. "Feel better?" Brent asked, bringing his arm around my shoulder.

"Not from the drink," I choked with a smile. Then, being serious, I answered, "I think so. It's been a bad night. How are you?"

"There aren't really words to describe what that was like," Brent said setting down his cup and loosening his tie.

"Was it your brother?"

Brent shrugged in a noncommittal fashion.

I picked up one of the cups and rolled it between my fingers, swirling the last few drops of the juice over the thick clump of dregs stuck to the bottom. "The two of you look an awful lot alike."

Brent nodded. "I'm still thirsty. You drank all my juice," he said, nudging me with his shoulder. He looked me over. "You still look pale. Want some more?"

I shook my head. "Water, no more of that juice. It's awful."

"All right. I spotted some water bottles in the fridge. I'll go get those." Brent laughed as he stood and disappeared into the locker room.

I glanced at the clock and it read ten-thirty. I sighed, thinking of how much homework I still had left to do before I went to bed. I picked up my purse, checking to see if I had any breath mints. My tongue rubbed the inside of my mouth, trying to get rid of the bitter taste. A tickle in my throat spread to my toes as the world blurred and shifted. Something slammed into my body and hurled me across the room, through the glass walls and into the groves. Trees, people, and buildings sped past me faster than a striking snake. When I hadn't shattered the glass and sliced myself to ribbons, I realized I had astral projected. I landed prostrate on the ground with a thud; my stomach turned like it was seasick and my head felt fuzzy as I attempted to stand.

"What was that?" I asked myself, struggling to my feet.

"Yara!"

I spun around and my head felt like the inside of a blender as I found Brent standing beside me instead of back in the pool house. I noted with surprise that he had changed from his suit back into his school uniform.

"Get back to your body," he demanded, his brow furrowing.

"How did you get here so fast? Why did you change?" I asked, trying to catch my balance, my hands flailing in front of me. I stumbled over my own feet, feeling unusually heavy, as my hands caught the limb of a tree, the leaves scratchily poking me. Feeling sluggish, like I was moving through sand, I stretched out my hand toward Brent, my entire arm feeling like it was bound in heavy shackles. For a fragment of a second the corners of my vision seemed hazy and my vision blurred like I was looking through thick glass. I took a step back to find an odd squishing feeling between my toes, a heavy sogginess in my shoes.

Brent stretched his arms protectively to my shoulders,

his hand slipping on my slick skin now beaded with water. Lifting his hand he examined the moisture on his fingers rubbing it between his fingers, worry lines creasing his forehead.

"You have to get back to your body."

My hair clung to my face and shoulders, plastered there by the chemically-laced water that was suddenly dripping from it. I felt . . . wrong, and once again my vision grew fuzzy. I tried again to breathe but my lungs resisted like my chest was caught in an iron cage that refused to let it constrict. I coughed violently, chlorinated water gurgling from my lips.

"Go back," he begged, grabbing my shoulders, shaking them so hard my head rattled. Brent lifted my chin forcing me to look at him. His eyes were dark against his unnaturally pale coloring. "Listen to me, Yara, *you're dying*. You're drowning. You've got to reconnect with your body before it's too late." He rested his forehead against mine. "Please."

The words he was saying seemed important but my mind was slow and unable to make sense of them. He kept murmuring about my body, wanting me to go back. This seemed important to him so I quit arguing and tried to obey. I closed my eyes, concentrating, trying to find the tether that linked my soul and body so I could reunite them but couldn't find it, almost like the connection had been severed.

It's not there, I thought, unable to speak, my eyelids drooping.

He scooped me up in his arms, holding me tight, running faster than a shooting star toward the pool. The lights were off when we got there, and the door was closed but Brent paused only for a moment to readjust me and raise his hand before the door popped open. Once inside,

Brent ran to the edge and plunged us into the water.

Under the water, I could see my body sinking in the depths of the pool. Brent swam us toward it, but something invisible stopped us and flung us back with a flash of orange light. We tried again with the same result. Something was keeping us from getting any closer. It was like my body was wrapped in an invisible container that was keeping me from it.

Brent let go of me and swam alone toward the unseen barrier. He hesitated, his hands outstretched, feeling for the surface of it, until he smacked his palm against it, testing its strength. His face contorted with determination as he struggled, pushing, kicking and pounding with closed fists and flailing feet until the orange light blasted again, blindingly bright. Brent was right at the epicenter and I watched, horrified and helpless, as he was hurtled backward, like a rock skipping out from under a tire, and out from the pool.

I was alone.

CHAPTER 8

The shimmery orange wall lingered for an instant longer before it disintegrated into a glitter of glowing orange sparks that extinguished as they cascaded down, like fireworks fading in the sky.

"Brent!" I screamed, my heart booming recklessly from across the pool. I started to swim toward where he had just been but then, like a magnet, I was pulled toward my body, finally able to reconnect with it.

My first thought was for Brent; he was probably back in his body, too, and I had to make sure he was okay after receiving the full brunt of the blast. My body didn't want to cooperate, though; my mind was disoriented, and I blinked frantically to straighten my vision out. It didn't help much. The bottom of the pool was dark, the water was cold, and I was shivering.

I clawed toward the surface, determined to get out of the water, but I kept being dragged down by some unseen weight. My dress was caught on something, holding me captive under water.

I tugged and pulled, but no matter how hard I struggled I still couldn't wrench it free. I knew I didn't have much time, and I fought so hard that my bending, breaking, and bloodied nails tore at the fabric until it was ripped to shreds, but I was still stuck. My only chance of escape was to get out of the dress; it had to come off.

I tried to reach the buttons on the back of the gown but my hands were shaking too hard, and my frenzied fingers were unable to undo a single button. I was trapped.

The water was pushing me down further, crushing my lungs until they felt like they were going to burst. Stubbornly, I held tightly to the tiny bit of life-giving air hiding in them. Refusing to give up, my legs and arms kicked and pulled in vain. The stale air in my chest needed to be released but I knew water would replace it. My snarled hair and beautiful dress swirled around me like some eerie movie. This all felt familiar and then I understood why. It was my nightmare.

I'm dying, I thought as the hope inside me was brutally demolished by the terrible realization that my dream had not been a warning, but a foretelling; there would be no escape.

The hazy black edges of my vision started to spread into the center of my sight. I bit my lips together, fighting the inevitable, while hope still remained in my heart. I had seen this before, night after night. If I could hold out a little longer, help would come. He always came, and every night he got closer.

I closed my eyes trying to focus on the safety of that thought. That assurance slipped away as I felt the air inside me spoiling and knew it could do me no more good.

"Help me," I cried, my voice distorted by the deep water and heard by no one.

My eyes were closing in defeat when I saw him: Brent, swimming toward me, the white shirt from his uniform billowing slightly around him. He had come back.

"Please don't give up. Hang on," he pleaded. I nodded

clinging to life now that he was here to rescue me. He swam to my right side, trying to find where I was attached, until my eyes could no longer focus.

Just as everything went black, there was a blinding light, so bright I shielded my eyes from its overwhelming beauty, and all of the sudden my lungs didn't ache anymore, my sight returned, crisper than ever before. Some sort of miracle had happened and I knew I could hold on until Brent had freed me. I turned my head in sheer joy and amazement to look at Brent, just as I realized that something about this situation didn't make sense.

He had stopped fiddling with my dress in an attempt to untangle it, and he was now gaping at me, his eyes filled with horror. I was about to ask what was wrong when I saw it—the familiar darkness I had seen attack Brent on the first day and that attacked me only a week later as I walked back to my dorm.

We had to get out of here. Whipping my head to the right, I saw the light that had nearly blinded me seconds before. They were both there, and they both were coming for me on opposite sides, the warm inviting light contrasting starkly with the oppressive, heavy darkness that felt thick like tar.

The mist had changed; it was now more massive than before and infinitely more terrifying as its merciless edges moved toward me. I cowered back from the darkness, reaching for Brent, and threw my arms around his neck, clinging so tightly he winced.

"You'll be okay. Do you hear me?" Brent asked. I nodded weakly. "Hold tight," Brent commanded. "Swim."

"I'm stuck," I protested.

He frowned as he shook his head sadly. "No, not anymore. Swim!"

I was confused, but I decided to leave the details for later and just trust him. His arms were around me and with what little strength I had, I kicked, trying to help, wondering when I had become untangled.

Brent did most of the work as we swam for the surface, leaving both the light and darkness below. We emerged and Brent helped me out of the water, where I sat trembling on the ladder, staring straight ahead, rocking back and forth. The pool was now calm and the warring factions of dark and light had disappeared beneath the crystal surface.

"That was so close," I whispered, afraid to admit how near I had come to dying. Bile rose in my throat and I bent over, dry-heaving so violently that my spine cracked and neck popped. Finally, when I was no longer nauseated, I opened my eyes to find the world around me had changed.

Everything was exquisite: the colors were richer, the edges were crisper, and yet every object also had a soft glow emanating from it. I wondered for a second if the mixture of chlorine and oxygen deprivation had messed with my vision.

"Let's not sit so close to the water. Okay?" Brent suggested soothingly, interrupting my reverie. Silently he cradled me in his arms and led me away from the edge to a chair in the corner of the room.

That's when the shock kicked in. Brent kept his arms firmly around me while trails of tears started down my cheeks. Sobs I couldn't control escaped from my chest. I clung to him, squeezing my eyes shut, my pulse sprinted at world record speed. My heart seemed abnormally calm though; it should have been pounding from the adrenaline and exhaustion, but it was quiet.

"Are you okay?" Brent whispered into my hair.

I started to nod but then shook my head. "No. But give

me a minute to sit and I will be, thanks to you." I swallowed. "Brent, there's something that I need to tell you. Ever since before I came to Pendrell, I've been having this reoccurring nightmare. I'm drowning, and there's a man trying to save me. It was you," I explained, as Brent sat there looking at me with the wrong expression. I didn't understand why he looked so sad. Okay, so I was still in shock but after that wore off, I'd be fine. I gulped and a smile of appreciation spread across my face. "But tonight I didn't drown," I said. "You saved me."

The seconds ticked by as he sat on the ground next to my chair, fiddling with the untucked ends of his shirt.

"Uh . . . Yara," he started, lifting my chin so his eyes bored into mine. "There is something I have to tell you."

The scraping of the door and the lights flickering on drew my attention to Cherie and Steve walking into the pool house. I squinted at the sudden brightness, smiling at the sight of my friends, trying to figure out how I would explain to them why Brent and I were both sopping wet. Except . . . I took another look around and realized we weren't wet at all; in fact, we were perfectly dry. I stumbled mid-step and Brent deftly caught me.

"I swear I saw them come in here," Cherie mumbled. "He left, but she didn't."

"Nice to know you're able to pay such good attention to details and kiss me at the same time," Steve teased with a grin. He glanced around the room, looking right past us, ignoring me even though I was looking right at him. "Maybe they left," he suggested.

"What?" I gasped, coughing, my throat raw. "I didn't!"

"I guess," Cherie said, sounding unsure. "Wait, what's that?" Cherie asked, pointing to the water's edge where my purse lay haphazardly.

Cherie bent down and picked it up. "It isn't like Yara to leave things. You don't think . . ." she trailed off as she looked toward the water. She and Steve spread out each peering into the pool. Steve crouched low next to the water and pointed to something as the two of them gasped. Steve dove in while Cherie started screaming hysterically. They were jumping toward all the wrong conclusions.

"It's okay, guys. I'm over here." My voice, though, was still too weak to carry even across the room. I turned toward Brent who was watching the scene with a look I didn't understand. "Can you get their attention? Cherie's flipping out."

Brent shook his head. At that moment, I heard Steve resurface. He was pulling something heavy in his arms and Cherie ran to help him.

I turned again toward Brent. "What is that?"

"You really shouldn't watch this," he said, shielding my eyes.

"Watch what?" I demanded, pushing from his embrace. I took a few steps until my knees buckled at what I saw and a hysterical laugh escaped my throat. Steve was giving CPR to a girl. Had there been someone else down there with me? I looked at the broken body but didn't recognize her.

"One . . . two . . . three . . . four . . . five!" Steve shouted, pushing on her chest. He leaned toward her now blue lips.

Watching, I prayed for her to be okay; a moment of survivor guilt washed over me. I noticed how the poor girl's arms were sprawled out next to her limp torso with her legs twisted under the long ball gown. The once-elegant frock was now ripped into shreds, dripping with pool water as it clung to her still body, the shredded dress a chilling evidence of the fight she had put up to survive. The frayed material wrapped around her twisted ankle was so perfectly horrific that it almost seemed staged for a slasher movie. I couldn't bear to see her poor face, now a pale shade of baby blue, eyes closed and mascara running down her cheeks, lying on the lair of tangles and snarls that was her hair. My heart ached for her, still so beautiful in death.

"Breathe, Yara!" Cherie begged, tears running down her face.

Her words made me jump. "What?"

"Don't die, Yara," Cherie pleaded wiping at her damp face and clutching to the dead girl's hand.

"Is this some sort of sick joke?" I demanded spinning around toward Brent. I pointed toward the girl. "She isn't me!"

He shook his head, stepping toward me. "Let me explain."

"Stay back!" I warned. I looked down once more at the broken body. She did sort of look like me but . . . it was too much. The room around me spun. "But I'm alive. I'm here!" I shouted at the top of my lungs.

They ignored me. I turned toward Cherie, knowing somehow she would sense me. The slight grip on reality I held drifted away as she stared right through me and asked, "She'll be okay, won't she?"

Steve didn't answer.

"Of course I'm going to be okay. I'm here now."

She didn't respond.

"Don't you see me?" I tried to grab Cherie's shoulders so I could shake her and make her see me, but instead of making contact, I fell through her. I looked pleadingly toward Brent. "I'm going to be okay, right? I mean, I'm here and Steve's doing CPR on . . . me. Right?"

Steve's lips were against mine, giving my lungs the air they couldn't get for themselves.

"I think she's gone," Steve told Cherie.

"No! No, she's not," she cried, shaking her head, distancing herself from my body.

"Cherie," Steve said softly. "I'll keep trying. Go get help."

"I can't leave her," Cherie sobbed. She had her eyes squeezed shut, tears cascading down her cheeks. Her tears sliced my soul like a razor and I had to look away. Finally she left the pool screaming, "Help!"

"Don't give up! I'm still here!" I told Steve as he continued pumping on my chest.

"Yara," Brent said. He shook his head, a deep sadness in his eyes. "No, it's too late. You're not going to be okay. You're dead, just like me."

*   *   *   *

Brent's words echoed in my ears, 'You're dead just like me.' The refrain opened an emotional chasm at my feet and I was teetering on the edge about to tumble into it.

"There's still hope," I yelled, shoving Brent hard. I tried to block out Steve still attempting to revive my motionless body.

Brent rubbed his shoulder grimacing. "I forgot about your temper. I thought maybe dying would have cured you of that."

"Are you sure we aren't just projecting?" My eyes studied Brent's, waiting for a smile to crack his grave expression.

"Yara," Brent began warily. "You know you drowned."

"Maybe I did . . ." I gulped, forcing the word from my tongue, tears puddling in my eyelashes. "Maybe I did d-drown but you didn't. You're alive. Get back to your body and tell them not to give up because I'm still here."

"I can't." Brent said, his head swiveling to watch as Headmaster Farnsworth entered, a bathrobe pulled hastily over his pajamas, with two other faculty members in tow, each talking frantically on a cell phone.

"Brent, you're not dead. I would have noticed. I've been with you all night, at the party and then here."

"I was at the party, but I wasn't sitting beside you," Brent said, slowly rubbing the back of his neck.

"Of course you were sitting beside me. We both saw your brother when he appeared. He—"

Brent interrupted me. "That wasn't my brother, it was me."

"So you projected during it . . . as some sort of prank?"

"I wasn't projecting and I wasn't one of the guests."

"No," I said with a firm head shake. "You were sitting beside me."

"Let's try this again," Brent sighed and I heard his teeth grind together. "The guy sitting beside you wasn't me."

"Wait," I said, holding up my hand. "What?"

"The body next to you was mine but the soul inside of it wasn't. Think about it, if I had been projecting, I would have been wearing the same suit as the body sitting next to you. But I was wearing *this* thing, remember?" He asked in disgust, gesturing to his school uniform. "And you were wearing that." Across the room, now being encircled by faculty, my lifeless corpse was wearing a mangled version of the gown I was clothed in.

The truth started to sink in, but before I could mentally take it any further he interrupted and kept talking. "So yeah, I was at the party. I was the crasher, the entertainment, the rambling ghost who garbled out a cryptic message that made no sense."

"Yeah, what was up with that?" I demanded. "Why couldn't you just say 'Hey, Yara, the jerk next to you stole my body and he's trying to kill you'?"

Brent shot me an annoyed look. "It's not as easy as it looks! Ever since that jerk stole my body, I've been trying to tell people what's happened. I've had a hard time communicating with the living. Every time I did I've been rushed or interrupted by you freaking out and severing the connection we had. Tonight I was determined to get through to you. I turned on that song I used to whistle to let you know I was coming. But as soon as it began, this thick black barrier erected around me. Did you see it?"

"It was the mist. Or at least that's what I call it."

"Well, it took all my concentration and energy to break through. I made the whole room shake just trying to get through."

"That was you? Poor Audrey was so scared."

Brent tipped his head back and laughed. "That's right. The mouse even made her jump." He wiped away tears. "Anyway, after my little earthquake, there was this flash of bright light and you could see me. But I felt different. I was so tired and worn out, like I had short-circuited, like I was trying to wake up from general anesthesia. All I could muster were the simplest parts of my message and the basest raw emotions, like my anger at the guy who stole my body. I'm actually surprised I was able to get anything out at all."

My fingers pressed against my temples trying to stop the pounding behind my skull. "Were you the other ghost, the one who kept leaving me messages?"

Brent nodded as the sounds of approaching sirens ripped through the night, reminding me of what I had lost. I looked down at the floor for a few moments, trying to collect my thoughts. "How did you die?" I asked quietly.

"I'm . . . not sure. One minute I was studying with my lab partner, Phil, and the next thing I know I was pitched out of my body. And when my spirit left, someone else moved in, like a vacant hotel room. I bet there was something in those lousy snacks he brought." Brent punched the wall with a frustrated grunt.

My brain short-circuited, and steam probably escaped my ears as I tried to process everything I had just learned. It was too much.

Suddenly, I laughed hysterically, like a full blown, straight jacket-wearing lunatic, feeling my thin thread of sanity slip through my fingers. Brent stepped toward me and put his arms around me. I shook them off angrily.

"Leave me alone," I shrieked, gasping for shallow breaths. Uncontrollable tears flowed from my eyes and pure panic enveloped me; I was losing it.

Brent grabbed my arms, shaking me, knowing I was on the verge of a breakdown. He looked frantic as he took in my desperate panting and wild shuddering, my fingers digging into his arms. Brent lifted his hand and somehow I knew he was going to slap me.

"Don't . . . you . . . dare!" My teeth may have been helplessly chattering in my mouth but my eyes stabbed him with an angry glare that made his hand drop instantly.

Brent looked lost for a second, unsure how to help when I saw his eyes ignite with a plan. He gathered me in his arms and brought his lips to mine, engulfing me in a soothing warmth, and sending a little jolt of something into my dead heart that I chose not to acknowledge. Angrily, I shoved him away and slapped him hard across the cheek, snapping his head sideways.

"What was that?" I demanded, my hands resting uneasily on my hips.

Wincing louder than I thought my slap warranted, he held his cheek and worked his jaw. "Again with the anger. You could just say thank you."

"Thank you?" I shrieked.

He smirked. "You're welcome."

I shuddered with rage. "You want me to thank you for kissing me?"

Brent bit his nails with a flippant grin. "Well, you could thank me for that too, but I was referring to the fact that I stopped your volcanic meltdown."

It wasn't easy swallowing down my enraged retort but I managed when I realized my freakout had stopped.

I bit my lip hard, my cheeks burning. "So there was no romantic subtext there?"

"Don't flatter yourself," he scoffed, folding his arms. "My body's been hijacked; kissing you isn't high on my list of priorities right now."

"Oh . . . right . . . I didn't think . . ." I said, stumbling over my words while tucking a piece of my hair behind my ear.

Brent stepped toward me, slowly lifting his hands to my arms. "Everything is going to be okay, Yara. I'm not sure how, but it will be."

"Stop that! Stop trying to comfort me with empty promises." I glared at him for a second. "There has to be a way to fix this.

"There isn't a solution, only acceptance," he said, with a wisdom that seemed to go beyond his teenage years.

His words ruffled something deep in my soul and I stopped, my eyes finding his. "How? How do I simply accept my death? I have no idea how to make peace with this."

"You can start by saying goodbye to your friends."

Cherie now sat in a pool chair weeping quietly, her drama teacher, Mrs. Tolley, holding her hand. Steve stood behind her with his hands resting on her shoulders.

"I can't do that."

"It will make it easier."

"For who?" I asked angrily. "She needs me and I'm not leaving her. If you think I'm just going to accept this, then you don't know me very well. I'm not ready to die," I insisted through clenched teeth.

"It doesn't matter if you're ready or not, you already did," he reminded me evenly.

"There is always a solution."

"Not this time," he said, sitting on the edge of a glass table.

"Look . . . I'm willing to accept that I . . ." I couldn't bring myself to say the word drowned again, " . . . had an accident, but I just can't believe that it's over. If this is it, then why am I sitting here and not in the Great Beyond?"

He started to say something, but a look I couldn't read, maybe guilt, crept across his face and he kept quiet. With a deep breath, I began pacing around the room, still massaging my temples with my fingertips. I hoped rubbing them with enough force would somehow make sense of the last few minutes and help me see a way to make everything right.

I have no idea how long I went on like that, but when I finally sat down next to Brent, I realized the paramedics had arrived. Bright bursts of red and blue light swept around the room from the emergency vehicles parked outside. A paramedic was speaking quietly with Steve. A man in a police uniform was standing close by with a notebook out, jotting things down that Steve was telling him. Cherie, who was standing next to him, holding his hand, was staring blank-faced toward the pool. A photographer was taking pictures of the scene and several other officers were sealing off the room. I buried my head in Brent's chest, unable to watch as they zipped my body up in a long black bag before strapping it onto a gurney. He soothingly stroked my hair, murmuring comforting words into my ear.

I couldn't help but follow as I was wheeled out of the pool area and into the ambulance.

"They can't take me away," I cried to Brent.

"They have to," he said, tightening his arms around me.

"But if they do . . . how am I going to fix it?"

"Please believe me—you can't fix this, Yara." He moved my chin so I had to look into his eyes.

"*No!*" Cherie screamed, chasing after the ambulance.

Steve was right behind her, pulling her back. My unbeating heart wrenched painfully at Cherie's desperate pleading, at the way her body crumpled into Steve's arms as she sobbed. As I watched her mourn, the whole world began to spin dangerously fast and nausea swept through me. I couldn't take it anymore. Desperately, I fled the room and out into the trees to put distance between me and my grieving friend.

CHAPTER 9

I was thoroughly overwhelmed and I fled into the groves for refuge, sprinting at full tilt, branches and rocks all skimming past me, through me. Even though I couldn't hear him, I knew Brent was close behind me; I could feel him near. I stopped and clung to a tree, trying to get the last image of Cherie out of my head. Her expression had made everything far too real. I couldn't deny it anymore: I had died and there was no way to fix it. As I finally accepted this, everything fell into place, how everything had gone dark before Brent had been able to rescue me, my heart being so silent because it was no longer beating and the way everything was now bathed in a beautiful glowing light.

Brent's breath warmed my neck as he came close behind me.

"How did I die? I mean I know how . . . just, what happened? I was sitting by the pool talking to the imposter you, next thing I know my spirit was shot across campus, only to find my body had a restraining order out against me."

The corner of Brent's lips twitched as he ran his fingers through his chestnut hair. "I'm pretty sure your drink was spiked with some concoction, probably containing a special blend of black licorice. I knocked it out of your hands but his had stuff in it too. I did try to keep him from sharing his drink with you, but his grip on it was too strong." Brent sighed.

The groaning of brakes and tread of tires rumbled past us as the emergency vehicles left Pendrell. After they were gone the night became silent, even the insects hushing as if paying their last respects to me.

"That stuff he gave you can be pretty nasty for people who can project. It gives your spirit the old heave-ho and then won't let your spirit or anyone else's near the empty body."

"I died because I drank some stupid drink." My shoulders slumped. "So that orange thing you destroyed— was that created by the licorice stuff?"

"Yep."

"I was so dumb to not pay closer attention to your warnings. Thanks for trying to save me from my own stupidity." I lifted my head and looked at Brent, completely defeated. "At the risk of stating the obvious, I really wish you had saved me."

He sighed heavily. "Me, too. But I failed you again."

I startled at his unexpected word choice. "Again?"

"Well, besides drowning . . ." He stopped and somehow I knew he was trying to figure out how to explain the rest. "I saw the light coming and I wanted to watch you cross. I wanted to be there with you . . . so you wouldn't be alone. Then I saw the darkness trying to get to you as well . . . I wasn't sure which one would reach you first and I panicked. Instead of pushing you toward the light . . . I grabbed you rather . . . rashly. I took you away from them both."

"What does that mean?"

"Well . . ." he sighed again. "Honestly, I'm not sure, but I think it means that you are stuck here with me."

I blinked in sheer confusion. "I'm not sure what you're getting at."

Brent tucked his thumbs through his belt loops, not meeting my eyes. "I think you might actually have missed your chance at Heaven or whatever . . . because of me." My mouth dropped in complete surprise and I found I had no words. "I think my pulling you from the light might have . . ."

I found my voice and it wasn't happy. "So I'm dead, but I don't get to go to Heaven because of you!?"

Suddenly agitated, he started chewing on his fingernails as he spoke. "Basically, but I only did it because the darkness was coming."

For a moment the dual image of the light on one side of the pool and the sinister gloom on the other flashed before my eyes. Dread swirled through me at the memory of the heavy black that had felt like it desired to swallow me.

"What is the mist? Is it Hell? Have I been too bad to go to Heaven?" Every rule Cherie and I had broken replayed itself in my mind.

Brent chuckled quietly, which made me throw him an evil look. "Of course not."

I tapped my finger to my chin thinking. "It attacked me once on campus and it's what tried to choke you the day I saved your life."

"It was?" Brent asked astounded. "I always wondered about that."

"Yeah."

"So the mist is responsible for you and I meeting." He laughed. "It really is up to no good."

I eyed him suspiciously. "Did you ever see it?"

"No, but I think I felt it. That day it attacked you, I could almost sense it then, too. I could tell something was happening the way your hair was flying everywhere like you were inside a twister. I could almost feel something there, something trying to hurt you. I just knew you were in trouble and needed my help, so I blasted the area with a gust of wind. It was the only thing I could think to do, but it seemed to work." He fiddled with the knot of his tie. "And I didn't say anything because . . . because I couldn't see anything. Why didn't you?"

"I wanted to, but I was afraid you'd call me crazy."

He shrugged his shoulders, frowning. "Yeah, I guess I deserve that."

"But what is it?"

"Beats me. All I know is to avoid it when I see it. I thought I could protect you but that didn't turn out so well."

"What would happen if it caught me?" I asked.

"Again, I don't know but I'm guessing nothing good."

"If we're . . . dead—" It was still hard to say the word. "And we're not in Heaven or Hell, where are we?"

"Limbo, I guess. We're not alive, but we aren't with the other spirits either. I have no idea how long we'll be stuck here or what happens next."

"What kept you from the light? The black mist?"

Brent shook his head. "Nothing. The light didn't come for me." He dropped to the ground with a sigh. "It's almost like the Cosmos isn't aware that I died."

"When did you die?"

"I died a few weeks ago, or maybe it was a few days; I've lost track of time, but I've been dead for a while." Brent took a deep breath. "You'll probably remember it— the night I was supposed to start training you."

"That's why you didn't show up?" He nodded, and I chewed my lip. "So ever since then it hasn't been you?"

Brent shook his head.

"Then who has it been? Why did he kill you? And why kill me, too?" I asked in a rush of words.

A grim and determined smile carved itself into Brent's face. "That's the question, isn't it?"

My fingers drummed on my leg as I waited for Brent to continue but he didn't. "And the answer is?"

"Your guess is as good as mine."

"Really? That's it."

Brent nodded, resting his back against the trunk of a tree. He stretched his legs out and crossed his ankles.

"Any theories?"

"No. But I'm starting to wonder exactly how my brother died."

I slinked down to the bumpy ground as I asked. "Do you think his . . . death—"

Brent swallowed hard. "You can call it what it was."

I averted my gaze and licked my lips nervously. "Do you think his suicide is connected to this?"

"I have no proof, but my instincts say yes."

"What do you mean?"

"For some time after . . . my body was shanghaied, I had company." Brent scratched the back of his head.

"Okay . . ." I drawled out.

"Phil Lawson."

I leaned toward Brent stopping myself from taking his hand. "That isn't possible, Brent. He killed himself right after your body was snatched."

"That's just it— he didn't." Brent brought his knees to his chest. "Someone had stolen his body and had it for a long time before I joined him."

"Is he still around?"

Brent's voice sounded feeble when he answered, "No."

"What happened to him?"

"The mist got him, probably about the time of his so-called suicide. After his body died, the light and mist came for him, just like they did for you. I tried to help but . . . he didn't stand a chance. It wasn't pretty." Brent's voice was barely audible.

"But it never tried to get you?" My stomach lurched and it felt like my tonsils doubled in size.

Brent shook his head. "The mist knocked me on my butt a few times, but other than that, it never noticed me at all." Rubbing his eyes with the palms of his hands, he added, "The whole thing got me thinking— maybe that's what happened with the other suicides. Maybe their spirits got evicted and were stuck here like me. Maybe they didn't really kill themselves. Maybe Neal didn't choose to die."

He was quiet, his last words lingering. I lifted my hand and started rubbing his back, imagining Phil Lawson being captured by the mist. "Thank you for saving me. Maybe I'm stuck in Limbo but at least that . . . thing didn't get me."

"Oh, I wouldn't thank him so soon," Brent's voice said from behind, not beside me, as a chill crept into the air.

I spun in confusion, squinting against the now seemingly denser dark of the night. There stood Brent, his brown eyes edged and flecked with green, dressed in the same dark suit he had worn at the party. It took a moment for my mind to register that I wasn't looking at my Brent, but a fake Brent in a stolen body.

Fake Brent was watching me closely, and as soon as he saw a look of comprehension cross my face, he smiled in satisfaction. It gave me the creeps; I didn't like seeing Brent's face looking like that. I shoved the acid that was rising in my throat back down, but I couldn't keep it out of my tone as I questioned him.

"What do you mean? He saved me. Why wouldn't I

thank *him*?"

Fake Brent smiled even more greasily than before, if that were possible. "Isn't it obvious?" He taunted. "If it wasn't for him, you might still be alive. I might never have noticed you if you hadn't saved him from choking that day. And then, after he died, he tried to pass messages to you. I was left with no choice; I had to get rid of you. Well, and I have a few personal reasons, too."

After recovering from his shock, Real Brent hurled himself toward the imposter, his face full of fury. Fake Brent easily sidestepped Real Brent, his eyebrows slightly raised, with a look of light amusement on his face. "Feel better?"

Real Brent stood up and dusted himself off. "Who are you?'

"I've been many people over the years, but originally I was Thomas," he said with a formal bow.

"Well . . . Thomas, why are you here? What do you want? Do you want to gloat? I'll tell you what you can do with that gloating." Brent made a rude hand gesture.

Thomas laughed, completely ignoring Brent's graphic suggestions on what he could do with his free time, and interrupted him. "I'm here to collect Yara," he announced, meeting our shocked faces with an evil grin.

"Collect me?" I asked, my voice catching on my words.

Brent slid in front of me. "Like you did with Phil?"

"Yes— if I need to, I'll take her the same way."

Brent shuddered. "I can't let you do that."

"You wouldn't be able to stop me." Thomas held up his hands. "But I'm willing to make it easier on her. I need Yara. Why else would I have killed her?"

"Because you felt like it?"

"I don't enjoy it."

"Then why murder her?"

"I already told you why," Thomas said. "There were many reasons, but mainly because I need her."

"Why do you need me?" I couldn't help but ask, peeking around Brent, my hands resting on his waist.

Thomas turned toward and he held out his hand to me. "I'm giving you the chance to choose to come with me."

"Why would I go with you? Didn't you just admit to killing me?"

He held my gaze. "Yes, I did."

If Brent's arm hadn't circled around me, pressing my stomach to his back, I would have launched myself at Thomas.

"I can understand you being upset about that." He cracked his knuckles, then folded his arms behind his back. "You have to understand, I don't like killing people. I've grown accustomed to it, but it's never easy. Sometimes, though, it has to be done."

"So you have no choice in the matter, huh?"

Judging by the way his face brightened he had missed my sarcasm. "Exactly. It's a matter of survival. But I think your death, Yara, might be the last here." He took a few long strides so he was mere inches from me. His borrowed brown eyes pleaded for understanding. "I'm not a bad person."

"No, you're just a serial killer."

He looked past me and nodded before ducking his head. "I suppose I am. But I'm not a monster. I'm a prisoner just like you. You coming willingly will be of greater benefit to me. Please come with me, Yara— please join me."

The please caught me off guard and I almost missed Brent's arms releasing me. He circled slowly behind Thomas and I kept my eyes on Thomas so he wouldn't notice.

Thomas's gaze never left mine. "Will you come with me?" His voice was calm like what he suggested was perfectly acceptable.

"No!" I shouted, my whole body trembling.

"Fine— then I have a deal to make with Brent." He turned his back on me and spun toward Brent who had paused mid-crouch, having been preparing another attack. "I can see you're trying to play the hero here, but really you have no obligation to her. Do you realize that? I'm offering you a deal, Brent. I'm willing to give your body back and let you continue your square li— I mean *boring* life."

Brent lost his footing and struggled to right himself.

"That's right," Thomas crooned, with the lure of a cobra who's about to strike. "You'll get your body back, your life back, and you won't remember any of this. It will all be like it never happened. And to sweeten the deal, I'm even willing to let your brother's soul go free."

Brent pushed to his feet. "Neal? You have him?" Brent's eyes flickered with raw emotion and he stepped toward Thomas.

"Wait!" I yelled, throwing my arms out and jumping in front of Brent. "You're presuming that we believe that you have his brother. Well, we don't believe it. His brother died years ago."

"Oh really?" He asked lazily, and I felt the air start to chill around me. Brent raised his hand as if to attack, but Thomas lifted his hand in warning. "I wouldn't do that if I were you; you'll want to see this."

Thomas stretched out his fingers and pointed them toward the ground. Inky dark drops leaked from his fingertips, creating a vapory coverage around him that started to froth and convulse as it darkened into the mist. With a twirl of his finger the mist spun. Was Thomas the body snatcher also controlling the mist? Faces started to appear inside of it, rolling in and out of sight, until a face that looked strikingly like Brent rolled to the front and began to solidify in form. The charcoal gray began to colorize, like a black and white photo fading into life, and a man I could only presume to be Neal stepped forward.

Brent gasped. "Neal?"

Brent's brother wasn't in heaven either—he was caught in the very nightmare that had taken Brent's life, the thing that had nearly snatched me away when I died. Even worse, Neal didn't look right; his face was expressionless, like a mindless zombie from an old horror movie. Knowing Brent, I could fill in how Neal might have acted in life: animated and full of laughter. Even in death I would have expected him to struggle and fight against the force that held him captive. To see him standing there like some sort of robot, without any will of his own, just waiting to be controlled, was unbearable. I spun around to see Brent's reaction and instantly wished I hadn't. His eyes were awash in tears, hollowed and empty.

"A little family reunion." Thomas sneered. "I can see you recognize him, so there shouldn't be any more custodial questions. I'm offering to release both of the Springsteed brothers. Granted, your brother will be bodiless." He shrugged. "But he'll be free."

Brent's face was pale and strained. "W-what would I have to do?" He whispered casting me a sidelong glance. A nervous trail of sweat formed between my shoulder blades and I fumbled backward a step.

"Nothing," he announced, and Brent's brow wrinkled in confusion. "That's it," he continued, "do nothing. Just let me have her. That's all." The imposter flicked his wrist and a long black tentacle of darkness coiled around me. "Where are you trying to sneak off to?"

I gulped hard. "I-I—"

"What happens to her once you have her?" Brent started biting his nails.

Thomas waved off his question. "None of your concern."

The black arm around me tightened and reached up, one finger stroking my cheek. My stomach twisted and I started to panic as I leaned away from the inky finger.

"P-p-please, Brent. I know what it's like to lose a brother, but don't do this." The serpentine arm tugged me closer to Thomas and I struggled against the mist, my legs flailing and my fingers pushing into the mushy darkness imprisoning me. The mist started to absorb me and flashes of agonizing suffering that weren't mine forced themselves into my being. I screamed so shrilly my vocal chords strained to the point of breaking as the hopeless suffering of those trapped in the mist encroached on me. The fight left me, the defeated feeling of the others overwhelmed me, and I went limper than an overcooked noodle as I collapsed in the firm grasp of my enemy. A whimper escaped my throat, and tears traced down my cheeks.

Brent's hands were covering his ears but his eyes were locked on mine, swimming in indecision. It really wasn't a hard choice. There really wasn't a choice at all. Me, a girl he barely knew, or his brother's soul and his own life.

"Stop," Brent said weakly, dropping to his knees. "Stop," he repeated, louder and stronger.

The imposter froze for a second in apparent shock. "You must be goofing. You would give up your life, give up your brothers soul, for *her*? Think carefully about the choice you're making."

Brent nodded as he looked away from me. His troubled face was lined with creases as his sense of duty and his heart's desire battled. "I understand," he said quietly.

The body snatcher considered Brent for a moment. "I'll remind you I'm offering you what you want more than anything. In exchange I'm getting what I need. It's a fair trade."

"I know," Brent said, "and I'll consider it. But I need time to think. I can't decide right now." Brent stood up, his body stiff. "Until I decide, don't touch her. Let. Her. Go." His voice was firm and he took a few brisk steps toward me.

The imposter's green-rimmed irises glowed like a cat, the deep jade brightening. "You're going to want to accept my deal. I promise you, if you decline, it won't end well for either of you, and I'll still win. I don't make idle threats."

Brent nodded. "I believe you."

The tentacle around me unwound and the emotional weight of the trapped souls that had been crushing me lifted as it slithered back inside Thomas's body; at the same time, the mist seemed to lunge forward and swallow Neal back into it. Without a sound, it blew away, fading back into the darkness of the groves without disturbing any of the fallen leaves underneath it.

Thomas bowed toward me. "You have twenty-four hours. I'll be seeing you soon," he promised.

With that he turned and strolled away like he hadn't a care in the world. Meanwhile my own world had grown even darker.

* * * *

Brent turned slowly and walked a few steps, keeping his back to me. Then he dropped to the ground, his shoulders slumping in defeat. Awkwardly, I took a few steps back from him, not sure how he felt about me. Or how I felt about him. He had put off his horrible choice for a time, but it would have to be made soon. I was the one thing standing in the way of his brother's freedom. And his own life.

Brent took a long time to look at me again but when he did, his grim expression hadn't faded. He gave me a strained smile.

"Are you okay?" I asked.

He nodded.

Could I be brave enough and selfless enough to be willingly handed over to the mist? Tears gathered in the corners of my eyes as I dropped my head and studied my feet as they kicked the dirt. I decided to at least pretend I was. "How do you want to handle the exchange?"

"What exchange?" Brent asked, sounding lost.

My heard jerked up. "Me for Neal and your body."

Brent's eyes lightened to cinnamon. "Are you insane? You don't actually think I'd do that, do you?" I was too stunned to answer and Brent frowned at me. "What kind of person do you think I am?"

"I—I . . ."

"First, I would never be able to live with myself if I did that."

"But think about what you're giving up. Do you really understand that? You must . . . you seemed so tempted."

Brent let out a deep sigh. "Seeing Neal like that really threw me off balance." Brent rubbed the back of his neck with his hand and frowned. "I *was* tempted. Really tempted." He bowed his head and guiltily peeked at me from the corner of his eye. "I hate having to admit to that." He sighed and held up his hand to stop my obligatory words of comfort. "Don't. It sucked to really see myself for the first time and understand how weak I was. To know the things I would consider." He visibly shuddered.

Over the quiet chirping of crickets came the sound of

a dog howling from the city below. From where I stood, I could see Corona's lights twinkling in the evening air. In the homes, people slept, unworried about curses, ghosts and turning over a friend to save a beloved brother.

Brent came beside me, staring toward the town. "I *was* tempted, but it didn't take long to know I couldn't accept his offer. When he manhandled—spirit-handled you," he corrected with a humorless laugh, "I knew I couldn't let him hurt you. Neal himself would never forgive me. No matter what Thomas promised, I know I would never forget handing you over to him and I couldn't live with that. And I don't trust him. He'll never keep his word. Not to mention... I like you, Yara."

"Well, I thought . . ." I began, trailing off.

Brent grinned sarcastically. "Well, that might be the first problem."

I gave him a dirty look. "I thought you were considering his offer."

He shoved his hands in his pockets. "I said that to buy us time." I felt Brent's gaze heavy on me as he asked softly, "You really thought I was going to agree to his trade?"

Not wanting to answer, I changed the subject. "So what are we going to do?"

Brent's started nibbling on his nails. "I haven't figured that out yet. But we have to find a way to free Neal."

I had to ask, "How is any of this even possible?"

"Would you laugh if I said some sort of magic? Even worse— dark magic?" Brent grunted roughly. "Calling it magic cheapens it though; it makes it sounds trivial. Like some Vegas act."

"Maybe, but I can't think of a better term. You're right though; if it involves death, it's dark magic."

Brent gave me a knowing look, his eyebrows knit

together as he studied my face silently for a moment. "You sound like you know something on the subject."

My knee-jerk reactions tried to kick in, shielding me from embarrassment, but obviously things had changed. If any one person deserved the truth of what I knew, it was Brent. After all, he was a part of this, too; this wasn't just about me anymore.

"I'm not an expert," I said, "but I do know something about magic, or whatever you want to call it." I paused and looked at him, waiting to see if he was going to freak out or laugh or even worse, start the 'you're crazy' talk again. He didn't do any of that, though; he just kept looking at me in respectful, non-judgmental silence, so I pressed on. "I told you that I'm from Brazil." He nodded. "Vovó, my grandmother, she's like a wise woman in her town, making poultices to help the living with their grief, burning herbs to help ghosts cross over. She's able to see spirits and inter-act with them. She's almost like a . . . shaman . . . sort of. She's all about helping the spirits and those around her."

Brent pushed the sleeves up on his sweater. "Cool."

I started pacing around. "Something's wrong with this, though. I've heard lots of stories from her over the years, everything from possession to voodoo, but I've never heard of anyone being able to force someone out of their body and then steal it."

"Possession? Voodoo? Man, what must family dinner be like at your house?"

For a moment I was in my family's warm kitchen, eating *feijoada*, drinking *guaraná*, listening to Vovó's stories, laughing and joking. I longed for it so fiercely I could almost imagine myself there. The image faded into Brent, who was still watching me.

"Family dinners were never dull," I said. "I heard about

some weird stuff. Enough to know that whatever happened to you is dark magic, evil."

"Hmm," Brent murmured, thinking. "So what should we call it then? I can't call it magic."

"Trickery?"

Brent laughed bitterly. "Yes, trickery works. Him having my body is a trick that's fooling everyone."

I squeezed his arm.

The outlines of the tall campus buildings could be seen over the tops of the trees. Figures moved behind the windows and I wondered if they had heard about my death yet. My whole life, world, existence had altered only a few hours ago. It felt more like years than hours but it was still the same night that I had died. My life was over but maybe Brent's wasn't.

"Brent, it is a trick! You may not have your body, but you're not really dead. He said as much himself." I turned toward him. "We just have to get this other spirit out of your body and then you can move back in."

"It won't work," Brent said, sounding defeated.

"Why?" I demanded, tapping my lips with my fingers.

"It just won't." Brent drew his legs to him, sitting cross-legged, and rested his hands on his knees. "It might even make things worse."

My brow furrowed. "Were you always such a pessimist? I mean, we're already dead; how much worse could it get? I'm kind of thinking it can only improve."

"I'm being realistic."

"Okay, how can it get worse?"

Brent chewed on his nail again. "Other people might get hurt. Let's learn from my disastrous example. I died, I tried to fix it by reaching out to you, and that got you killed. The prosecution rests."

I pushed my bangs back off my forehead. "Okay, yeah. Well maybe we won't get anyone else involved. It can still work."

"There are other reasons it won't work. First, we aren't warriors in a fantasy novel."

"Says the man who can astral project and was kicked out of his own body by another spirit."

Brent rolled his eyes at me. "Second, we have no idea how to get him out."

I waved my hand, conceding he had a small point. "Let's say we figure it out. It should work, right?"

Brent nodded slowly. "If we managed to do that . . . maybe." He groaned at my eager expression. "Calm down. I didn't mean to get you all riled up; I was just thinking out loud." He gave me a playfully disgusted look. "Were you always so optimistic? Why, of all the people I could have as a companion here in limbo, would it be someone so... happy?" He made it sound like optimism was some sort of contagious disease. I gave him my brightest smile. He shook his head, trying not to return it.

The realness of what we were talking about settled around me, making me shiver. "If that guy is responsible for your brother's death, then you're right— he might be responsible for the rest of the curse."

Without touching it, Brent lifted a stone from the ground and tossed it between his hands. "That's sorta what I'm thinking."

"So the Pendrell Curse . . . is . . ."

Brent dropped his hands and the rock fell through his legs to the ground. "Real," he admitted, "and they should really be called the Pendrell Murders." He tried to loosen the tie on his uniform. "Couldn't I have died without this stupid thing? I can't get it off."

"So, we're going to uncover the truth behind the Pendrell Curse."

Brent held up his finger as he corrected with a rough voice, "No, we're going to break the curse."

"How?"

Brent's declaration was full of passion and promise; it showed on his face, but at my question it crumpled. "I don't know."

"Well, at least we have a goal."

"It does no good to have a goal if we don't have a plan." Brent smiled ruefully at my sudden frown. "But yes, at least we have a goal." He fought a moment not to return my re-established grin but finally gave in with a chuckle.

CHAPTER 10

A few minutes after discovering we had a goal but no plan, Brent was laughing heartily at a pathetic joke I had made. It reminded me of the first day on campus when I had thought his laughter sounded like a melody. It did now, even more so. It was music, beautiful, in a manly way, like a sensual, slow jazz. I loved jazz.

"Jazz, huh?" Brent asked, his voice suddenly husky.

"Uh . . . what?"

"My laugh reminds you of jazz? Is there anything about me you don't find attractive?" He rubbed his hand over his lips trying to cover his smirk. "So tell me, how much do you love jazz?"

I'm sure my face was pinker than the inside of a watermelon. "I didn't say any of that."

"You didn't have to say it, Yara, I could hear it." Brent tapped the side of his head. "I can hear your thoughts."

"You're not serious."

"Oh, but I am," he said, completely straight-faced.

My eyes opened wide in surprise. "So you can read my thoughts?"

"And you can read mine." He hadn't moved his lips; I had just known what he was thinking, his voice clearly in my head.

"How?"

Brent stood up and stretched slowly. "No, idea. It's like suddenly you were just there."

Whoa . . . how is this happening?

"I'm not sure. Maybe after you die there's no more need for secrets."

"Can all dead people read each others thoughts?"

"I'm not really an authority— I've only been dead a few weeks. But Phil and I could do it, too, although it's easier with you."

The whole limbo thing was going to take some time to process; there was too much to take in. Brent was handling everything in stride. Suddenly, I remembered I wasn't the only one who had recently lost their life. Brent had died, too, and yet while he was trying to help care for me, I had taken no thought at all for him. I was selfishly wrapped up in myself.

"Are you okay, Brent?"

"I'm doing all right," he answered, his voice cautious.

"You seem to be handling all this much better than I am," I said. He rolled his eyes at me. "Well, you are! How are you being so calm about it? Aren't you upset at all?"

He sighed in frustration. "Of course I was." He strode between the trees, walking with purpose. "It's just that I've had more time to deal with this than you. You're handling it much better than I did actually."

"Not that much more," I snapped, trailing behind. "You don't have to patronize me!"

"I wasn't," he said, turning toward me and walking backward. As he got further away I could feel an undeniable pull from him, like an unseen force tethering us together. The connection was stretched the further he got from me. It wasn't something visible, but a very real, stabbing pain pierced my gut, like someone had anchored a barbed hook in my stomach and was pulling me toward Brent. I bent over clutching my stomach. I fought the urge to follow Brent, though I knew intrinsically that the only way to ease the uncomfortable throbbing was to be close to him again. Finally, with a defeated grunt, I chased after Brent. He was waiting for me, resting against an unused smudge pot.

"That's new," he commented, holding his stomach and wincing. "Guess we'll be sticking close to each other, huh? Phil and I didn't have this." He gave me a wink. "Have to admit I'm glad it's you and not him; you're cuter." Brent studied me intently. "You get angry when you're scared."

"I'm not scared," I said, my eyes suddenly watery. I thought I had been doing a great job of ignoring the terror that had been gnawing at me all night.

"You don't have to pretend. I can *feel* how scared you are." He lowered his voice, "It's okay to be scared, Yara."

"You can feel it?" I asked, refusing to admit how frightened I was, even to myself.

"Yep. Wow, just knowing that's how you deal with being scared helps me understand you so much better," he said, walking again and disappearing behind the trees. The invisible hook in my gut was back. I closed my eyes, willing the tension and pain in my stomach to dim.

But I could still see Brent, his essence glowing behind my lids. To some internal compass, he was North, my guiding star. Following my Brent GPS led me to him in the Headmaster's garden where he had taken me the night after the dance. He was sitting on the edge of the gazebo with his eyes closed, his head following my movement. My tension unwound, the pain easing the closer to him I got. Opening his eyes, he watched me, sifting through my emotions until I cleared my throat loudly.

"Sorry." Brent laughed sheepishly. "It's just so . . . interesting. You're really sad and scared right now and you're trying to direct all of those emotions into making a plan."

"It doesn't do good to dwell on things you can't change. It's better to do something useful."

"But not being able to deal with them is just making you angry."

"Cut me some slack . . . I just died here, okay?" I said, gesturing wildly with my hands. I felt suddenly a little morbid at how casually I had addressed my death. "Am I supposed to curl into a ball and cry? How will that help?"

"Okay, slack given, but only because you just died."

I walked toward the edge of the garden, aware of how strongly he thought I needed to come to grips with everything. Just thinking of Cherie's haunted look the last time I saw her or imagining my family's faces caused acute emotional ache in my chest and I folded my arms around my middle, curling around them. I knew my feelings were simmering inside me like a beaker on a Bunsen burner and would eventually start to boil over, but I couldn't dwell on that now so I thrust them to the back of my mind. I promised myself that when I was ready I would reach out to my loved ones and somehow let them know that I still existed and was okay.

That idea comforted me slightly, but my heart was hit with a sudden tidal wave of pain as I thought of my poor parents and sister having to deal with another loss, burying another member of the family. They didn't deserve that. I buried my head in my hands and finally allowed myself ten minutes to cry and curse at the heavens. Anger, grief, and tears ruled me. And I let them.

After my allotted time I took a deep breath and found it odd that I still felt the need to breathe.

"I think it's habit," Brent explained. "Your mind says you need to breathe, so you do. We have a pulse, we cry—and, thanks to you, I can tell we still blush. It's almost like muscle memory and phantom limbs. But your all-important heart no longer beats."

A quiet thump-thump played in the silence. "But your heart is still beating. I can hear it."

His fingers went to the left side of his chest, checking. "It does, faintly, like it's miles away."

"Does that mean that I'm right that—"

"It doesn't mean anything," Brent said, cutting me off. He rubbed his chin. "You timed out how long you were going to wallow?" Brent's face was incredulous as he shook his head. He hadn't moved from the fountain, he was leaning forward, his arms resting on his legs. "Grief doesn't work that way. You know that, right?"

"It does for me," I replied defiantly, wiping the remaining tears from my face.

"If you say so."

"What's to grieve? We're going to fix this," I said, inhaling deeply the crisp night air.

I could almost taste the oranges, the avocados, even the flowers. I knew, without a doubt, somewhere on the other side of campus, chrysanthemums were still blooming. In amazement, I looked around, trying to gauge if I could pinpoint the directions of the smells. I could. It was similar to how aware I had been of everything when I projected, but much stronger.

Even though it was nighttime, I could see every detail and every color that surrounded me. Everything was so vivid and intense that I gasped at the beauty of my surroundings, as if seeing it for the first time. Nothing was one simple hue, but made up of subtle shades, highlights, and lowlights. I thought I had appreciated it before, but I realized my human senses had been too limited to recognize its true brilliance.

I sank onto a bench overhung by the branches of a maple tree. Its leaves blazed with color that could have inspired a sonnet; I wished I were a poet and could capture its beauty in words. Heartbeats of the young birds in a nest in the top of the tree made their way to my ears, bringing a smile to my lips.

"It is kind of amazing, isn't it?" Brent asked.

I nodded distractedly. "Okay, so let's work on our plan," I said, putting my problem-solving cap back on. "There's this really great bookstore down the street from my old school. It should have everything we need to know about astral projection."

"Well, that would be great if we could get there," Brent said grimly.

"Can't we just, like, appear there?"

Brent shook his head. "No, we aren't genies."

"Walk there?"

"No can do."

I let out a puff of frustrated air that lifted my bangs from my forehead. "Why not?"

"Well, we can't leave Pendrell."

"Why?" I questioned, feeling suddenly confined. I had never liked rules, and it irritated me that there were still rules even when I was dead.

"I wish I had the answers for you, but all I know is we can't leave."

"Is that a fact?" I raised my eyebrows in defiance. "Well, we'll see about that." I took off running as fast as I could toward the edge of campus. The wind and speed invigorating me with each step I took. Brent was next to me, jogging backward, easily keeping pace.

"You know, I really don't suggest trying this."

"I have to find out for myself. I just can't accept this on your word alone. You have to at least know that much about me."

"I do," he said ducking under a thick branch. "But it's extremely painful."

"Maybe for you, but it might not be for me. You can't be sure." I continued my sprint and tried to push aside the worry his warning had caused me.

"Maybe not," he said warily, "But I still advise against it. Don't be stupid."

"I have to know for myself," I explained, halting at the driveway that marked the edge of school.

He groaned. "Why?"

I bit my lip. "Here goes."

"Wait, Yara," he said, tugging on my arm. "Please, just listen to me."

I hesitated for a moment then cackled. "What, am I going to die again?"

"No . . ." he started, but before he could finish I flung myself with all the energy I had toward the other side of the driveway.

With a pain so severe it blinded me, I was hurled backward. I landed on the ground and skidded a few feet. It felt like every bone in my body had snapped, and that my internal organs were twisted and mutilated. If I had been alive, I was sure I would have died, leaving only a pile of gore on the driveway. I opened my eyes and the world around me undulated in harsh, blinding and over-sharp movements, making me dizzy. Sprawled on the ground, I was afraid to even try to move. Tears rained down my face, vanishing before they could wet the ground. Even their slow movement across my skin hurt. Fearing the rise and fall of my chest would be too much, I held my breath. When I finally took a breath, it felt like a jagged knife in my ribs. I sobbed in self-pity, longing for death before remembering it had already come.

My eyes darted toward Brent just as he winced. "Sympathy pains," he explained with a shrug.

Shame pulsed through me when I realized he was suffering right along with me. Despite the sting I knew I would feel, I opened my mouth to speak. "Can you block it out?"

"No, it won't let me." He grimaced. "You don't have to speak with your words, Yara."

I'm sorry, I thought.

"I know," he spoke into my mind. Brent stayed by my side whistling lullabies and talking about nothing at all, trying to distract me. The sun rose and was high in the sky by the time the pain eased enough for me to stand.

My knees buckled as I tried to get to my feet.

"Take it easy," Brent suggested, helping me up and slinging my arm around his shoulder.

"I have to get away from here. I don't think I can stand to dwell on my own stupidity any longer," I said, as he turned us and began walking us slowly up the driveway. "So, you were right."

"I was pretty sure I would be," he said without sounding arrogant. With each step toward the Headmaster's garden I felt my strength returning. The place was starting to feel like home.

"You've done that before."

"More than once," he said in a knowing voice.

"I would think once is enough," I shuddered at the thought of ever having to experience that again.

"The Phil thing really freaked me out."

"It must have been awful to be willing to endure that twice." I shivered. "So it looks like we're stuck here. Why?"

"I don't know, but it could be worse." He readjusted his grip on me.

"How? Maybe a bad case of food poisoning?"

"We could be alone."

My stomach tumbled like an Olympic gymnast. "Yeah, that would be a lot worse," I agreed, stealing a peek of him from the corner of my eye.

Somewhere between two steps my spirit recovered. I pushed from Brent's arms and twirled in a circle, giddy because there was no more pain, feeling free.

"I can see you're feeling better," Brent commented, leaning against a tree trunk with his arms folded.

"I do. I have all this pent-up energy; let's do something." I flashed him a smile to help convince him.

"We could play volleyball," he offered. "There shouldn't be students there now."

"The dead play volleyball?"

"Well *I* can, but I think I'll have to teach you how."

"I know how to play," I said icily.

"I wasn't trying to be demeaning," he said taking a step back in case I felt the need to elbow him. "It's just you haven't learned to move things yet." I thought back to my attempt to move the leaves on the tree and nodded in understanding.

"Can you teach me?" I asked.

For a moment he studied me hard looking for something, but I wasn't sure what. "Yes, I think I can. Besides," he said, taking me by the hand and leading me toward the P.E. building, "it might be vital for you to learn. You're going to have to defend yourself when the mist comes for us."

"What do you think he wants with me?" I asked, my palms suddenly sweaty.

"I'm not sure"

We walked in a heavy silence until we arrived at the volleyball sand pits. Several balls were still out, and without bending over, Brent stuck his hand out, palm down. A ball flew up to it.

"How did you do that? Are you actually holding it?"

He waggled his eyebrows as he smiled. "Well, I can feel it, but I can't quite make contact with it." He then made the ball bounce up and down in his hand. "Yet I can command it to do what I want it to, like a puppet with invisible strings. Catch!"

I ducked as the ball zoomed toward me. He laughed,

"Oh, come on. I know you aren't a practitioner of organized sports, but even if you catch like a girl, the ball wasn't going to hurt you. You're a ghost, remember?"

"Old habits die hard." The ball had rolled into a tangled, thorny bush, its white only barely visible.

"Now, you try it," Brent said as he moved the ball so it lay in front of my feet.

I stuck my hand out like Brent had, staring at the ball, concentrating and biting my bottom lip. Nothing. It didn't so much as vibrate. I tried it again and again and again. Still nothing.

"You have to visualize it doing what you want it to."

Focusing on the ball, I pictured it rising up to my open palm. The ball twitched slightly. I put even more mental energy into visualizing it. It flopped on the ground like a floundering trout.

"Yara, it's a little like faith. You can have no doubt that the object will obey you."

Biting harder on my lip, I pictured the ball again and tried to believe it would obey me. For an instant it lifted. A squeal of delight escaped my mouth and I did a dance of joy that may have included some really outdated moves. A proud smile spread across Brent's face as he commented, "You're picking it up pretty quickly."

He might have been stroking my ego, but I didn't care. In repeat attempts, I wasn't able to get the ball to move any higher, but I was able to recreate its small rise into the air.

"Let's try this," Brent said, throwing the ball at me. "Hit it back."

Instead of ducking, I moved my arm through the air, picturing the ball soaring back to Brent. While the ball didn't go that far, it did change course. After several tries, I was able to actually hit it all the way back to him and then he volleyed it back to me. I wasn't able to create the motion, but I could redirect something already moving. I hoped that would change with more practice.

Eventually, Brent sat down with a huge smile and ran his fingers through the sand. Following his example, I was surprised by the tickling sensation of its rough texture. The sun had begun to set and I leaned back on the sand to watch. I had been so absorbed in our game, I hadn't noticed that we had been here all day. The blazing palate of colors was breathtaking: red, pink, purple, and yellow. We sat in a silence disturbed only by a distant woodpecker as the most brilliant canopy of stars I had ever seen replaced the sunset.

The night was dark, but around us everything grew an even deeper black. Out of the corner of my right eye, I thought I saw something glide past. A familiar feeling of dread encompassed me as the temperature plummeted. The mist was creeping toward us, outlines of individual beings swirling inside it, their faces set in horrible grimaces.

Scuttling like an awkward crab I tried to back away. A heaviness settled over me, making it hard to move, impossible to speak.

From the mist, a spear-like tendril slithered toward us, aiming for me. I feigned to the right as it shot toward me but it wasn't fooled, and managed to stab me in the shoulder. Its point pierced me and an icy cold laced my shoulder, and warmed quickly to a burn that seeped deep into me. My hands wound around the inky tentacle and yanked it out. I screamed as blue liquid flowed from the ugly black wound.

The offshoot recoiled to strike again when something grabbed me from behind, like a strong firm hand had reached around my waist and was pulling me away, distancing me from my enemy. The wind was sucked from my lungs and my body folded in half, as if being pulled like taffy, and I was carried across campus. The air changed from fresh and flavorful to old and stale. Buildings, trees, and people zoomed by, and as they did I felt like I was being torn limb from limb. I cried out in agony.

My vision blurred as the pain grew. When it finally receded I looked around and found myself back in the glass pool house. I glanced at the clock; it read ten-thirty, just as it had the last time I was in here with Thomas, who had been masquerading as Brent. Had it really been only twenty-four hours since I had died?

The banner announcing a pre-season meet with our rival school still hung across the room, though the meet should have already happened. Even the moonlight shadows and the placement of the chairs replicated the night I died. The empty cups of tainted grape juice sat on the table beside me, and the concrete floor had a fresh stain from where I had spilled my drink. Every detail was the same, like someone had painstakingly recreated the night I died.

It was morbid.

I thought back to the ghost stories my grandma had told me about murdered spirits stuck in a homicidal loop, reliving their deaths every night. I gulped, hoping that wasn't about to happen to me. I didn't have time to worry over this because a loud crack thundered through the air and everything went black.

* * * *

Empty. I was nothing. No name, no sense of self, beyond and before this moment I was nothing. A heavy rhythm thudded around me as I was rocked, my limbs hanging uselessly from me.

In a rush my body and spirit were reunited. I was underwater in my heavy gown and impractical shoes. I was trapped and running out of air, drowning. I had heard when you're dying, images of your life flitter past your eyes, but for me pictures of my evening trudged through my mind: Cherie's dinner party at the old pool; sharing juice with Brent; being thrown from my body; trying to reconnect; Brent vanishing after the orange explosion underwater. My heart wilted with panic as I struggled to free myself from what held me captive, dragging me to the bottom of the pool. I peered into liquid darkness that seemed insistent on claiming me as it own, despite my frantic clawing and tugging at my dress. There was a clanging in my ears, a burning in my chest. I wasted my last few seconds of breath screaming futilely for help that I knew wouldn't come. Terror morphed into acceptance. My eyes started to close in defeat, my limbs stilled, and I knew it was the end.

Some time later my eyes opened slowly. The warped, disorienting feeling of déjà vu still clung to me. I was lying on cement, on my back, looking through the glass roof of the pool house, staring at the stars. My shoulder burned, throbbing from the mist's handiwork. I was back in the present, my memory intact, the instant replay of my death over.

I had been ripped from the present to experience again the final moments of my life. Reliving my death had been just as traumatic and painful as it had been when I had really died. In the reenactment, I had been powerless to remember anything beyond my final moments or do anything to change the outcome.

I turned to tell Brent but to my surprise he wasn't there. The last place I had seen him had been at the volleyball courts when the mist . . .

Did it get him? I started to get to my feet, but had to sit down as the room began to career. I thought of the mist attack.

My mind searched for him with an intensity that surprised me. He was near and just knowing that eased the pressure building behind my eyes. But beyond knowing he was close, I couldn't locate him, my Brent GPS on the fritz. The scraping of the door and the flickering on of the lights drew my attention to Cherie walking into the pool house, blocking the view of the person behind her. She wore the same formal black and white dress that she had worn at her party the night before.

"I swear I saw them come in here," Cherie mumbled. "He left, but she didn't."

Her words were familiar; I had heard them from her before, the night before. Her companion stepped out from behind her and my forehead crinkled in confusion to see it wasn't Steve with her, but Brent.

"Nice to know you're able to pay such good attention to details and kiss me at the same time," Brent teased with a grin. He glanced around the room, looking right past me, even though I was looking right at him. "Maybe they left," he suggested.

The words, his actions, even his expressions were identical to the ones Steve had used right before they found me dead. Brent was acting like Steve had, and was even wearing Steve's navy blue pin-striped suit.

"I guess," Cherie said, sounding unsure. "Wait, what's that?" Cherie asked, pointing to the water's edge where my purse lay haphazardly.

Cherie bent down and picked it up. "It isn't like Yara to leave things. You don't think . . ." She trailed off as she looked toward the water. She and Brent spread out, each peering into the pool.

"Brent!" I called, trying to get his attention. He gave no sign that he had heard me. "Brent!" I yelled again, stepping in his path so he would have no choice but to stop or run me over. To my surprise he did neither; he walked right through me, his eyes fixed on my dead body at the bottom of the pool, stopping only when he reached the edge, where he crouched low, gasping in horror and diving in. Cherie started screaming hysterically. Brent resurfaced, pulling my body along in his strong arms, and Cherie ran to help him.

Brent began giving me CPR. I kneeled across from him and called his name again, but he still didn't hear me.

I had heard of things like this, that other spirits could be drawn into the death loop. Like an actor given a role, Brent had apparently been assigned the part of Steve. In this moment, he, too, was given a script he couldn't vary from. His part as Steve had to play out to the end before he was himself again.

I didn't want to watch, so I walked toward the glass walls and stared out into the clear night, the searing pain in my shoulder helping to distract me from the scene re-unfolding behind me.

I was grateful when the CPR stopped, and the time twist ended. Cherie's distraught image disappeared like a wisp of smoke on the wind and Brent's consciousness reemerged as his own. The past faded into the present, leaving Brent standing there, looking dazed, rubbing the back of his neck.

"That was intense." He walked toward me shaking his head. "It's very awkward playing Steve and making out with Cherie. I'm not sure if I should feel guilty or grateful."

I shot him a nasty look but he didn't seem the least bit embarrassed. "What?" He continued. "It's not my fault that I now know way more about how our best friends kiss than I ever wanted to."

"Oh, shut up!" I said. I pushed down the feeling of jealousy I felt at the image of him kissing Cherie. "Thanks for the visual," I added, wondering for a second how far they had gone and then deciding I didn't want to know. "So you were Steve's stand-in?"

"No, I *was* Steve. I thought everything he was thinking, did everything he did. It was like I was him."

"Weird."

"I know. Why wasn't I me?"

"Maybe since you didn't have a body when it happened, you had to play someone who did." Dying again had drained me and I cradled my aching arm as I settled down wearily at the water's edge. "What was that anyway?"

"How you died," Brent said dryly.

"I guess I phrased that wrong," I conceded with a wry smile. "Why did I have to go through that again?"

"A hiccup in time, maybe?" Brent scuffed his feet on the cement. "Haven't you heard of murdered ghosts haunting the places where they died?"

"That was a rhetorical question meant purely for complaint." I bit my lip hard. "Is my murder going to echo here for all eternity? Am I going to have to relive my drowning every night?"

Brent's eyes wrinkled in concern. "I don't know."

Sadly, having listened to my grandma, I was afraid I did know. "Do you relive your death, too?"

"No, but we each died under totally different circumstances. I got invaded by the body snatchers and you went swimming with the fishes."

"Nice analogy. The real difference, though, is that you're not dead," I said softly. "Your heart's still beating."

"Well, I'm not exactly alive either, am I?" There was an electric frustration bubbling under Brent's surface. "You have to get past this belief that I'm still alive."

"I know, Brent. I'm sorry. Dying again was just really hard. It rattled me."

"Makes sense." I was surprised at his reply; I had been expecting another sarcastic remark. "So, how did dying go tonight?" He joked softly.

I snickered. "Oh, you know," I played along, "the usual. I drowned." Something that had perplexed me made its way out of my subconscious. "Something was different tonight, though. I mean, I wasn't in the groves with you before I drowned. I also skipped the whole not being able to reach my body part. Why is that?"

"I don't know. Was anything else different?"

I shivered as I replayed the horrific events. "Well, instead of being with you, everything was black and I felt like an empty shell. It was like I was . . . nothing."

Brent looked pensive as he ran his fingers above the pool, making small waves across the water. "Maybe your reenactment needed to keep you with your body the whole time."

"Why?" I placed my good hand over the water, willing it to move, smiling when it rippled slightly.

"I don't know. I'm just so glad that we were dragged here. I thought we were trapped." We shuddered simultaneously at the thought of the mist. "How's the stab wound?"

I winced, being reminded of the throbbing pain in my arm. *Burning. Agonizing.* I bit back my immediate responses and gritted my teeth. "Fine."

"Still trying to lie? Did you miss the 'We're connected' seminar held earlier?" Brent asked, rubbing his own shoulder. "Even if I wasn't having sympathy pain, I wouldn't have believed you." He rolled his shoulders again and cursed under his breath. "It sucks there can be this much pain in the afterlife." He turned toward me reaching for my arm. "Let me see it."

"It's fine." I angled away from him, suddenly tense. "No need to fuss."

He raised his eyebrows. "Good, then you won't care if I take a look."

"It's fine." I shoved his hand away.

"Yara." His voice was firm with a touch of warning. "Just let me look at it."

He gently took my elbow and eased me around. A long, low whistle pushed through his lips as his cool fingers touched the wound, examining it carefully. When I finally got the courage to peek at it, I felt nauseated. It was a gaping, jagged wound, black around the edges and crusted over by the blue liquid that had oozed from it.

Brent's hands were now covered in the sticky blue substance, but he didn't seem to care— he was concentrating on my injury, his eyes focused, his finger gently applying pressure. I could hear the words Brent repeated in his mind, like he was following a set of instructions, his soft fingers soothing the angry tear. Sweat formed on his face and his body trembled as my ragged skin fused back together, heating and molding like wax. Under Brent's fingertips, the wound then cooled, taking the pain away with the warmth, until the only sign of the injury was a jagged black scar. Brent collapsed onto his back next to me, totally spent.

"How did you do that?"

"I . . . I wasn't sure I could. I only read about it in Neal's journals." Brent breathed deeply. "I had to try. That injury was really serious. The mist wasn't playing around."

"What does it want?" I hugged my knees to my chest.

Brent rolled onto his back and draped his arms over his eyes. "Besides you?"

"That isn't funny."

"It wasn't meant to be." His voice sounded hoarse and weak.

"Do you mind if we get out of here? This really isn't my favorite place."

"Yeah, okay." Brent looked wistfully at the door, as if trying to make it move closer so he wouldn't have as far to go.

CHAPTER 11

The sun was rising and the air still chilly when we emerged outside. A few scattered clouds broke up the robin's egg blue sky. Rays of sunshine made diamonds of the dew glistening in the grass and clinging to the leaves. The campus was quiet, most students still asleep.

"Did you notice all the people in the mist?" I asked Brent as we neared my former dorm. I stopped at the fire escape, contemplating if I was ready to check in on Cherie.

"Yeah." Brent's eyes were on me, waiting for me to decide if I was going up or not.

"I noticed them when we first saw Neal, but I hadn't really thought of it before. They didn't seem happy there," I said, twisting away from the steps, moving onto the shrub-lined lawn.

Brent followed, his shoulders hunched. "Agreed."

"So why do you think they were part of it?"

"I doubt they had a choice." He let out a deep breath. "Probably they were captured souls, like Phil and Neal, forced to join. Soldiers being conscripted into an army. I mean we saw Neal was in it against his will."

"Who are they?"

"I assume they're the other victims of the curse." Brent's eyes glazed over with a faraway gleam as he started biting at his nails again. "I can't shake that image of Neal."

"But why would it capture souls?"

"Obviously for something bad. Power maybe?"

"To what end?"

"I don't know," Brent said tersely.

"It said it needed me. What's so special about me?"

"No idea. I'm sure it has nothing to do with your natural talent, your family lineage, and your ability to see evil ghostly fogs," he said sarcastically. "Then, to top it all off, your dead friend was trying to warn you and you were starting to listen. No matter why he needs you— I'm sure your attempt to contact me made him act sooner than he planned. You needed to be stopped before you figured it all out."

I gulped loudly and my mouth went dry as something new occurred to me. "I know Cherie. She's going to start poking around into my death. Will he go after her, too?"

"Don't worry Yara, she won't get far. I tried contacting her first. She has no paranormal radar." Brent was quite for a beat. "It surprised me. I thought after all the stuff you said she saw that she'd be easy to communicate with. Imagine my surprise when I got through to you instead."

I felt my cheeks burn in shame. "Cherie didn't see any of that stuff. It was all me."

Brent rubbed his temple where his bruise had been, a feeling of hurt in his eyes. "Why did you lie?"

"I was afraid you'd think I was unstable. And I was right."

"Fair enough," he said pulling on his gray sweater. "Well, it bothered me that people like her treat my brother's death like a game."

"I might be a tad touchy about the word crazy," I admitted, tucking a curl behind my ear.

"Why?"

"Vovó. Like I said, she can see ghosts. It's fine in Brazil—people accept it and admire her for it. But when she comes to the States and talks to ghosts in public or wherever, people start using the 'crazy' word."

"Why does she even talk to them when other people are around?" Brent asked rubbing his arm.

"She feels like it's her duty to help them."

"And you don't."

I chewed my lip in thought; this was getting to the painful parts that I didn't talk about much. Even Cherie had learned to sort of gloss over the finer points whenever our conversations got too close to this subject.

"I . . . I never felt that way," I admitted. "Ever since we moved here, my family was called crazy and lots of worse things because of her conversing with thin air. I was hoping I would be lucky and *not* get the gift. Then I came to Pendrell and started seeing the mist. And when I told you about it and you called me crazy—" The words spewed out of my mouth before I could stop them. "it hurt," I finished, staring him right in the eye so he would be sure to get the message.

Brent scowled at me for a second before he chuckled. "Yeah, well, so did that book." He lifted his head watching the clouds stroll across the blue sky. "If it makes you feel better, I believe you now."

I fought a grin as Brent leaned against a large tree crossing his arms deep in thought.

I was quiet for a moment, watching an elephant shaped cloud traipse across the sky. "Vovó felt I was the great hope for the legacy since my sister looked every bit the blue-eyed, blonde-haired American, and I every bit my Father's Brazilian daughter with hazel eyes, brown-tinged skin, and dark hair." I ran a finger through my dark locks. "I was relieved I was allowed to stay in California when my dad was transferred, missing out on years of unwanted lessons in the family legacy. But I ended up here . . . surrounded by ghosts."

"So you couldn't hide from who you really are, huh?"

"I guess not." I bit the inside of my cheek before confessing, "I'm a Waker."

"What's a Waker?"

"In Brazil they call it Acordera, but Waker is easier to say. It's a name for people who can see ghosts. I was just starting to be able to see them . . . the ability gets stronger with age. A Waker, though, does more than just look at spirits; she can communicate with them as well. If I had tried harder, you wouldn't have had to go to such dramatic lengths to talk to me." I let my shoulders relax. "If I hadn't been so afraid and trying to block everything, we could have been able to talk to each other just like this."

"That would've been nice," Brent said, still cloud-watching. I had been expecting some smart comment about how much work I could have saved him. Since I didn't get one, I knew his mind was mulling over something. When he reached his decision, he stood taller, tightening his jaw, his eyes cutting to mine.

"If I want Neal free and you want to make sure Cherie isn't in danger, we're going to have to fight the mist." Brent rolled around so his back was against the trunk. "Not just defend ourselves, but really attack it."

"I know that, but we barely escaped last time," I said, leaning against a tree opposite his.

"I wasn't expecting it to be so strong. Now I know; we'll be prepared. I swear I'll never let it get you."

"That's very sweet but I don't think you can make that

promise."

Brent shook his head in disagreement.

"I notice he didn't give you a chance to accept his offer," I commented in a small voice.

"I didn't expect him to." Brent shrugged. "Like I said, he isn't to be trusted. He was only hoping to get you without a struggle."

"That's not going to happen." I clenched my teeth, my eyes flashing. "You need to train me. I need to be able to fight, too."

Brent nodded in approval and his eyes twinkled. "I would expect no less from you." I caught his eye and a feeling of warmth heated my insides forcing me to drop my eyes. "Let's start training."

* * * *

"Concentrate," Brent said.

"I am," I snapped. My outstretched arm was shaking above a volleyball that rolled around but refused to leave the ground.

"Then concentrate harder." He was standing beside me, his feet spread apart in a solid stance, watching the stubbornly un-levitating volleyball.

"I can't." A storm of frustration was brewing inside me and my face grew red, sweat forming on my forehead.

"Then I won't let you fight."

"If you let me practice on you instead of this stupid ball, I could probably do it," I yelled over the tempest pounding behind my ears.

"Why should I let you? You can't even manage a stationary object." Brent moved his finger in a circle and the ball followed the motion. "You'd probably hurt me."

I dropped my exhausted arm, rubbing the base of neck to prevent the tension headache I felt building. "If I remember correctly, you *hurt* me when you knocked me out of the way of the lightning."

Brent's gaze dropped to his shoes, wringing his hands together. "That was different."

"How?"

"I had to act quickly." Brent dangled his fingers toward the ball and it lifted into the air and soared toward him.

"How did you know it was going to hit me?"

Brent twirled the ball, giving it the illusion of spinning on his fingers like a top. "Outside of my body, I'm always more aware of things. Heightened senses and stuff."

"That's true for me, too."

He waved the ball away and it bounced to the ground, rolling back toward the sand. "Yeah and I've always felt more connected to the elements, able to bend them to do what I wanted them to do." He studied his nails like he really wanted to chew on them, but shoved his hands into his pockets. "Since I died, though, my connection to them has grown stronger. I just knew you were going to be hit by that bolt. I'm sorry for hastily pushing that day. The lightning surprised me."

"Is that why it left huge welt marks on my chest?" I asked, cringing slightly at the memory.

"Yeah, I wasn't as careful as I should have been."

"Well, considering you saved my life, I'll let it slide. I never did say thank you. So . . . thank you."

"You're welcome." The muscle near his left eye twitched. "The thing is, Yara, the lightning wasn't near your game. That random bolt came out of nowhere."

I climbed to my feet, reading between the lines. "You mean that lightning was meant to kill me?"

A slant of uncertainty crossed Brent's face. "I think so."

"So he tried to kill me several times?" The baby hairs

on the nape of my neck stood on guard. I hadn't just been murdered; I'd been stalked like prey.

"Yeah. By then I knew he was trying to kill you. I wasn't sure what was in that vial he gave you, but I hid it."

"Oh, I thought I lost it. Not that it matters; I wasn't going to use it." Brent gave me a level stare. "Okay, I considered it the first time I projected accidentally." A group of students picked up the volleyball Brent had dropped and started a game. "If he did that, controlled the lightning, he's pretty powerful, huh?"

A patch of cloud covered the sun, making the day seem colder as Brent nodded.

"Alright— then I need to practice."

I stood the way Brent had shown me, my legs spread shoulder-width, pushing into my feet to keep me solidly on the ground. "Hmm . . . they took my ball."

"See if you can take it back," Brent said, a dare in his voice.

"Oh, I can do it." I pointed at the ball and concentrated.

While it did sail off course a few times during their game, it wouldn't obey me. From the corner of my eye, I watched Brent's shoulders slump in disappointment.

"It's okay," he said, giving up on me and rubbing his chin. "It can take a while to master. I've been pushing you too hard."

"I *can* do it," I yelled, my eyes focusing on the ball. All the pent up emotions unfurled from me and attacked it, for a brief, triumphant moment it glided toward us. I motioned for it to come closer, but felt myself losing hold of it. In annoyance I sent everything I had into the command, knowing I had done it, confident in my success until it exploded, leather and other odd pieces of material littering the sky before snowing down around us. The students watching shrieked; a few backed away, while the brave ones crept toward the ball.

Brent's face went pale and he licked his lips. "Glad we started with the ball."

"Told you I could do it," I said, stumbling to my butt as my strength deserted me. I expected to see Brent impressed or at least pleased, but his chestnut brown eyes darkened.

"You call that 'doing it'?"

My head dropped and I bit down on my quivering bottom lip.

"If we had been practicing together, you could have obliterated me."

"No. I wouldn't have hurt you." I panted for breath that I tried to remind myself I didn't need.

"You don't know that. You have no control." He cut me off as I opened my mouth to argue. "You let that childish temper of yours rule you. You wasted all your strength on that stupid explosion leaving you too weak to do anything else. If we were fighting, I would now be trying to defend not only me but you as well. Not to mention I'd probably be trying to correct whatever damage you created. You'd be nothing more than a distraction."

Like a human teapot, my blood boiled, my cheeks burned, and I could almost feel the pressure escaping like steam from my ears. "You said I was gifted and powerful."

"A battle is more than a flash of power, Yara. It's strategy and control," Brent said, trying and failing to keep his voice calm.

"I can learn to control my temper," I said, rising to my knees, each of my words clipped.

"I'm really starting to doubt that." His eyes were cold. "I'm starting to think your temper may be your defining characteristic."

His eyebrows lifted questioningly as my mouth opened to defend myself. My tongue rose to the roof of my mouth, becoming a dam to stop the rush of angry words that certainly weren't going to help me prove my point. I inhaled deeply, holding the air until it collected all the cutting words I longed to speak and then exhaled, letting them float away unspoken.

Brent applauded, nudging me with his shoulder, "I thought I had you there."

"It wasn't easy," I grumbled honestly, though part of me found his clapping condescending, treating me like a child who had learned the alphabet.

"Proud as a papa," he chided.

I gave him an evil eye before covering my face with my hands— I had forgotten he knew what I was thinking. "I can do it. It's just harder with you than with anyone else."

Brent's lips twisted up. "I wonder why that is?"

"Because you're so annoying?" I offered, watching the students abandon the court.

"I'm far too charming to be annoying." He tapped his index finger against his smooth lips. "If I remember correctly, you get angry when you're scared."

"You're right. I'm so afraid of you." I rolled my eyes. "I constantly worry that you're going to kidnap me or beat me up."

He stepped close to me, lifting his hand to my cheek. Brent's face moved close to mine, his intoxicating citrus and musk scent following him. Softly his fingers traced my cheek, turning my face toward him, his touch making my stomach pivot like a ballerina.

"There's more than one reason to be scared, Yara. More than one way a person can hurt you, too." The teasing tone was gone.

My useless dead heart floated up to my throat. "I . . . I . . ." I stuttered, staring into his silky brown eyes.

He chucked me gently under the chin before retreating back a few steps. "Of course, that's just a theory." Waving his fingers he lifted up some of the demolished ball. "I think we need to find you something new to work with." Brent grinned at me. "I bet I can open the ball closet and find your next victim."

"Isn't that an ironic turn of phrase?" Thomas asked, stepping out from the shadows, bringing with him an aura of gloom, a deepening to the night, and a dank iciness to the air. "My victim has a victim."

Brent instinctively pulled me behind him, trying to block me from Thomas's gaze. His muscles tensed, preparing to act.

"I'm not your victim anymore," I said in a trembling voice, peeking around the safety of Brent's shoulders.

Thomas didn't bother to stifle a yawn. "I guess this is your response to my kind offer, Brent?"

"I thought that was off the table, considering you sent your mist after us," Brent responded hotly. My shaking fingers rested on Brent's arm, trying to keep him calm.

Thomas cracked his stolen knuckles. "That was just a warning." Thomas scowled and his eyes looked disappointed. "I had hoped it would let you see you really don't have a choice but to cooperate."

A heavy fog from the mist started to leak from Thomas, its dark limbs stretched toward me. Brent pointed one finger toward it, swatting it away. Hoping to help, I stepped out from behind Brent and raised my hands, trying to channel power into my fingertips. A serpentine arm swiped Brent aside and then struck out at me, wrapping around me like the end of a whip, pulling me toward Thomas. I couldn't stop the gasp that exploded from me. The evil darkness formed into a hand and it jerked my chin up to look at Thomas. He breathed deeply as the tentacle tightened its grasp on me and then slowly started to sink into me. The impressions of suffering and pain started again. I screamed as his head fell back, his image shaking, blurring then sharpening before my eyes.

"Finally." His head shot up and there was a calculating gleam sparkling in his eyes and a smile plastered on his face. "You've grown stronger, Yara. I can feel it— you're what I've been waiting for. I can take you now and make you mine." He licked his lips in anticipation. His inky black fingers caressed my face in a possessive way. I tried to push him away but his grip didn't loosen. "Just think what you could bring with you if you came willingly." He shoved me from him; a ripping sound shredded the air as his tentacle released me. He wheeled around to face Brent who had been sneaking up behind him.

"No need for that. I'll be going," Thomas said, backing away from us. "I'll be watching and waiting." He winked before sauntering out of view.

"What did he mean?" I asked, chafing my arms with my hands.

"I think," Brent said, "that he's waiting for you to develop more of your power."

"But why?" I asked, balling my hands into fists.

Brent gave me a wry grin. "I think it's rather like fattening the lamb before the slaughter. He thinks you'll be more useful that way."

I shook my head. "Does that mean I should stop training?"

"No!" Brent said adamantly. "It's better to be prepared. The only way to win is to be strong."

"But I doubt we'll ever be stronger than he is," I whispered.

"He's not stronger, he just . . . caught me off guard before. Besides, I'm thinking of a strategy, Yara. I've got it covered."

"You really think so?"

Brent didn't answer. Instead, he left to retrieve another ball, and started whistling.

CHAPTER 12

My afterlife with Brent fell into a predictable pattern: every day we would train, and every evening we had the pleasure of reenacting my death. I did show improvement in not only moving objects and affecting the environment, but in controlling my temper, as well. It would have been almost boring if not for Thomas, who seemed to take a sick pleasure in watching me progress. I would often feel like I was being watched only to discover I was. He would mouth the word, "Soon," and then blow me a kiss before leaving.

As for my death reenactment, it was like watching a movie for the sixtieth time—I knew every line, I had seen it from every angle, and nothing ever changed. I had even stopped being emotional about it; it wasn't my death anymore, it was just an event that occurred and I was forced to watch.

I had just finished drowning again and was waiting for Brent to come in as Steve. He entered the room, really wanting to be outside kissing Cherie, but coming with her anyway. Cherie saw my purse and rushed toward it. Steve, following behind her, stumbled over a chair.

Wait, what? The tripping over a chair was new. Someone had left the chair by the pool earlier in the day and hadn't returned it back to its place before leaving, and for some reason it had been brought back into the past. I sat up watching carefully, waiting to see if anything else new happened.

Steve turned, looking at the chair in confusion, rubbing his knee. I felt Brent's consciousness shining through to the surface just then; Brent's familiar twinkle swam in his eye before it got smothered by the role he had to play. Steve turned back toward the water, squatting, looking in, circling the pool; when he finally dove into the water, the tipped chair caught on his foot and clattered into the water with him. I stood up with an idea so impossible I was afraid to let it fully form. I began tugging on my earlobes as my mind surged in hope and waited for Brent to become himself again.

"Did you notice anything different this time?" I asked Brent as he strolled near.

Brent stretched out his shoulders, feeling the importance of the question. "No, not really. Why? Why are you so worked up?"

"Well, when you came rushing in this time you stumbled over a chair that was in the way."

Brent scratched his head, nodding. "That's right. That was new."

"And for the briefest of seconds you were you, not Steve. Do you remember that?"

"Sort of," Brent said cautiously, turning his head toward the pool. The chair was still there, slowly sinking into the water.

"That chair was from the present and it altered things. It was only a little change—but what if something more than a chair, something bigger was added to the mix? Maybe it could change the outcome. What do you think?" My hands were rubbing together like I was praying as I waited for his answer.

"Yara, I know it must be hard for you but—" he started, his voice soothingly gentle.

"That isn't it," I argued— without anger. "Okay . . . it's part of it, but I just think there's a reason why we keep reliving it."

Brent dropped his head, not meeting my eyes. "I wish that were the case, but you die every night. Nothing changes."

"The chair . . ." I corrected.

He reached out and took my hand, completely engulfing mine in his. "Nothing significant changes. I wish we could fix this . . . it isn't just hard on you, you know? Every night I have to live through letting you die, knowing I was only a few minutes too late. Every night I fail," Brent said his voice breaking. "I wish we could change it. I really do."

In all the time times I had drowned I had never considered how hard it had to be on Brent, too.

"Brent, I'm sorry."

"Not your fault. I've got a hero complex," he said with a wink. "Let's get out of here?"

"Please."

As had become our nightly post-death habit, Brent steered me toward the fire escape that led to my old room. I still hadn't climbed those steps, afraid they might open up emotions I wasn't ready to deal with.

"Ready to see her tonight?" Brent asked as we paused before them.

I sat down on the bottom step and leaned against the metal handrail. After a few moments, I picked at one of the sequins on my dress and asked in a pleading voice, "Do you think she's okay?" I wiped away the tears forming in my eyes.

"I don't know," he said softly, "I've been here with you." He smiled as he offered, "Do you want me to go and find out for you?"

"I do want to know . . . I think I want to know . . . but I think I need to go with you."

"Are you ready then?" His tone was gentle, as if he had his own doubts about my readiness.

I took a ragged breath. "Uh, in just a few minutes."

He nodded as he stood and walked to the window. Ready or not, I decided I needed to do this, and followed him. I nodded to Brent, trying to exude a calm I didn't feel. With a glance of his eye, the window smoothly slid open. I paused for a second, awed by his strength.

"You really are powerful." I realized my words sounded strange, but I meant them. It was like Brent was some sort of warrior, but instead of leading people, he commanded the world around him with a wave of the hand, a flick of the wrist, or even a glance.

"It isn't a big deal," he said humbly.

I knew he was being modest; I had been practicing for over two months and didn't have even a sixteenth of his ability. *He's really pretty incredible. He—*

At that moment, I was aware of Brent trying to find out what I was thinking, and I quickly changed my line of thought.

With a warning grin I shook my finger at him. "I don't think so."

Rather brazenly, he said, "You were thinking something about me. I was curious."

I had several comebacks on the tip of my tongue. Instead, I smiled with a slight shrug. For a brief moment, I almost forgot what I was about to do, but as soon as I remembered, the tip of my thumb was in my mouth, being bitten on hard. It was a bad habit that I had broken when I was twelve.

I paced back and forth in front of the window, inspecting the empty, darkened campus. A few of the lights in the dorm houses were on, and I could occasionally make out shapes of students inside their rooms, most bent over books and laptops.

"You can do this," Brent offered encouragingly. He put a reassuring hand on my shoulder.

"I know," I said, trying to sound fearless. But I knew he wouldn't miss the spasms of doubt that flooded through me.

"What exactly are you afraid of?"

I turned to face him, leaning on the railing. "That she won't be okay." I bit my thumb again and then released it from my teeth as I added, "And I'm even more afraid that she will be." I sighed in self-reproach. "I'm the most selfish, horrible person I've ever met. How could I ever wish that on Cherie? She's been through so much."

I spun around and marched with determination down the stairs, toward the refuge of the groves. There was no way that I, being so self-centered, deserved to see Cherie. Brent caught up to me and blocked my way.

"Wait. Of course you feel that way. I don't think you could actually care for someone and not hope that some part of them misses you."

I shook my head, still angry with myself and unwilling to accept his words. "No." I covered my ears with my hands and squeezed my eyes shut, refusing to hear anymore.

"Yara, please listen."

"No, you are going to try to make me feel better and I refuse to let myself feel that way." I realized I was having a tantrum of sorts, but I couldn't bring myself to care.

"Oh, you refuse, do you?" He queried with slight amusement. Suddenly Brent was in my thoughts.

You can't shut me out. You'll hear what I have to say. It's normal to feel that way.

My eyes popped open and I dropped my hands to my side. "Do you really think so?"

"I'm very aware of your emotions. You love her. I know you don't want her to forget you—but even more than that, you want her to be okay."

"I do?" I looked at him with relief, knowing I couldn't hide things from him. I hoped he wasn't just telling me what I wanted to hear.

His eyes communicated with complete honesty the truth of what he said. "You do." He made sure I was walking beside him as he headed back toward Cherie. "If you don't go and see her while you can, it will haunt you for the rest of your . . . existence. I don't think I could bear that. Remember that your pain is mine now, too." We were at the fire escape again. "For both of us, please go see her."

I turned toward Brent. "Aren't you coming?"

"Nah. I'll give you some privacy. Besides I can always watch the repeat tonight in your thoughts."

He turned toward the groves with a quiet whistle. As he walked, I felt some sort of sadness in him that I hadn't noticed before. Part of me felt the need to go to him and comfort him the same way he had for me since I died. A small ache formed in my stomach as I stood watching him, hearing his tune carried toward me on the wind. I hadn't been this far from him since my death and I missed him. The string that connected us was stretching further than ever and it hurt me; I needed to be closer to him. I took a step down the stairs and at that moment he turned back toward me.

My hazel eyes found his brown ones. Suddenly, even though he was more than thirty feet away, I could feel Brent's hand lightly caress my cheek. I looked at him from across the distance separating us; he hadn't moved an inch. He was watching me with his thumbs still casually resting in the pockets of his pants. Only the intense look in his eyes betrayed that he was doing anything besides just standing there.

Could he really touch me from so far away? In awe, I raised my unsteady hand to my face where I could still feel his gentle, lingering touch. Our fingers intertwined for a second, and I smiled at Brent, enjoying the sheer impossibility of the moment. His touch was so tender, so caring that I felt my face flush.

Brent sensed my blush and I detangled our hands in confusion. I looked away, befuddled at the stirring of emotions arising in me. He was still watching me as I cleared my throat and looked up at him again.

He looked different, more content, wearing a calm smile as he whispered, "Go." Bewildered by the moment, I nodded. He turned away, whistling again, a song that sounded much happier than it had before.

The connection between Brent and me was stretched taut, causing me a twinge of bearable pain. I turned back toward her window and paused, preparing myself. Taking a deep breath I climbed through.

The room was stripped bare of both Cherie's belongings and mine. I took in the complete emptiness of my former room with an overwhelming feeling of having been blotted out. It was like I had never been there, my time at Pendrell totally erased like the click of a delete button. Without our personal items, the room was as stark and bleak as my mood.

I scooted myself onto my old desk, feeling completely insignificant. The faint scent of Cherie's perfume still lingered, but all other traces of our time here were gone. My hand brushed the bare wall beside me, and I smiled as I the felt tiny holes where I had tacked up pictures and the sticky remnants of hot glue that I had used to hang up posters, proof that I had once been here.

Brent slinked through the window, leaning on the its edge. "I was worried . . . you felt so sad. I can go," Brent said, half crawling back out.

"Please don't." I crossed my feet, the point of my heel scratching the top of the opposite foot. I patted the small space beside me on my desk. Brent backed in next to me and reached over taking my hand in his. His thumb tickled the inside of my palm and I laid my head on his shoulder. His other arm snaked around me, holding me tightly; I had never felt more protected.

He didn't make empty promises or cliché remarks like, "It'll be okay." He didn't say anything, and that was what I needed, just someone to be there. I snuggled in closer to him, my head so close that my eyelashes stroked the bare skin on his neck. Brent swallowed hard, dropping his arm from around me and stood up, striding across the room.

The inside of my cheek was feeling raw from my constant chewing. "Do you think she changed schools?"

"Maybe she changed rooms," Brent suggested, flicking the room lights off and on.

My thoughts spun out of control. *Is she okay? If she switched schools, will I ever see her again? And my family, had they come to the school and I missed them? Will I ever get to see them again? I'm alone. I'm going to be alone forever.*

All the grief, pain, and anger I had been repressing hit like a tidal wave. I felt knocked off my feet, awash in a current that pushed, pulled, and spun me around like a feather, drowning me in an emotional flood I couldn't swim through. The room tilted and veered like a carnival ride leaving me gasping for air as my chest constricted. I doubled over, clasping my knees. "I . . . I . . . can't breathe . . ."

Brent was beside me again, caressing my back, whispering in my ear, "You aren't alone, Yara. I'm with you. Breathe with me."

I tried, but small, desperate gulps were all I could manage. Brent pulled me close, holding my head to his chest. "Let's try that again. Breathe." He radiated calm, sharing it with me, battling the grief that attacked me with his touch like an antidote that soaked in through my skin. My ribcage shuddered as I forced my breathing to slow, Brent helping me gain control.

"Good," he said, pressing a kiss to my temple. "Good."

"I waited too long to say good-bye. Now it's too late." Tears welled up in my eyes again, then watered down my cheeks, down my nose and onto Brent's white shirt.

"Shh . . . shh," he soothed running his hands through my hair, massaging my scalp. "It's never too late. Did I tell you I said goodbye to Steve? It wasn't the ending I wanted either. Steve was ticked at me because the hijacker pretending to be me picked a fight with him. It's hard to say your goodbyes when your friend is cursing your name. He doesn't even know I'm gone. Still, it helped."

"I just wish I hadn't been such a coward and done it before." The purple fabric of my dress flowed around my feet as I tucked my legs beside me. "I knew the world would go on without me, but I didn't know it would be so soon."

"It has to," Brent informed me, winding one of my curls around his finger. "Look, there's something there."

My eyes followed the thrust of his chin toward the ceiling. There spelled out, in glow-in-the-dark stickers, the number 774.

I jumped to my feet so fast I felt a little dizzy, or maybe I was just giddy. "That's her room number. She's still here. She left it for me in case I came back as a ghost to tell me how to find her." I grabbed Brent's hand, pulling him up. "Let's go see her right now!"

* * * *

After climbing to the seventh floor, we quickly found the right room. Brent opened the door but let me stick my head in first to make sure she was decent.

"She isn't here," I said glumly, motioning for him to come in.

"Was she always this messy?" Brent asked, taking in the paper-littered floor and the wall adorned with pictures of students surrounded by hastily written Post-It notes.

"Not to this degree . . . not unless there's some project that she's urgently working on." I took the time to look at her wall and realized there was actually an order to the chaos. It looked like a timeline, the older-looking portraits to the left and Phil Lawson's to the right. My own face was below his with a sticky note question mark attached. I climbed up on her bed to examine the first two pictures on the left, stacked one on top of the other. The first, a pale, freckled, red-haired boy was labeled Dennis Parker. The other was olive-skinned with beautiful green eyes. The name "Weld" under his picture had me reaching out to grab Brent's hand. "That's T.J. Weld."

Brent had been examining the papers piled on Cherie's bed and shrugged, not looking up. "Who?"

"He was the writer of the article that led me to astral project." I looked closely at his name and gasped. "The T stands for Thomas. Could it be the same person?"

That got Brent's attention, and he stood up, coming beside me, examining all the little notes Cherie had scribbled under their names. "He's one of the two original victims of the curse." Brent clicked his tongue. "He is the curse."

"Does he look familiar?" I asked

"No." Brent started tracing the curse down its thirty victims. Brent's fingers gently stroked the image of his brother Neal. His eyes shot back to the picture of Thomas. "So that's what the guy looks like, huh?" Brent snorted. "No wonder he ditched his body."

I gave him a small grin as I thought through some of the new information. "Why would the ghost want me to be able to astral project?"

"Well, it already knew you could see it—or, at least, could stop it. Maybe it guessed you'd be able to project, too. You're a lot more vulnerable to it that way."

"Maybe."

"Then I kept trying to contact you. You're being a Waker must have made you that much more important to silence." Brent punched the wall. "You're welcome for that final nail in your coffin."

"It isn't your fault, Brent. I was a target from day one."

"Yeah, the day you saved my life," Brent growled, throwing up his hands and scattering the messy piles of paper into the air. They cascaded around us like snow.

"I'm not the only one with a temper, huh?" I asked. Brent scowled at me. "None of this was your fault, Brent."

"Sure," he mumbled, reading more of Cherie's notes about Thomas. "It says he had been diagnosed with cancer right before he died. And his best friend Dennis died in the fire with him. They were usually a trio but their other friend, Henry wasn't with them that night. He was the one who reported them missing."

"How did they die?"

"You don't know?" I shook my head and he continued. "They died in the fire . . . in the old pool house."

"The curse started there?" I shuddered, remembering how horrible I had felt in that room. Then another piece of information caught my eye. "Henry was the next person to die." I tapped my fingers against the wall knowing that piece of information was important but not understanding why. "Why every two years?" Brent shook his head. "Did your brother act any different before he died?"

"Well, he never came home. He always had projects and stuff; we had to come here to see him. The last time he came home, a couple years before his death, he seemed skittish and left some journals in his room that he didn't want to keep in his dorm room anymore. They're the ones that had all the information about the Clutch."

"So he didn't come home for two years. Isn't that strange?"

Brent smirked at me. "You're new to prep school, but no, that isn't unusual. Not until that college acceptance letter comes in the mail."

"Oh. Why wouldn't the guy posing as your brother come home or take off to a different country or something?"

"Maybe he was afraid he wouldn't be able to control the body? Maybe he knew he couldn't really fool us?"

"Or," I proposed as a thought popped into my head. "What if he can't leave campus either? Thomas said he was a prisoner like us."

Brent nodded. "Yeah, that makes sense." He started snapping his fingers as his mental gears started to grind. "Yeah, and people eventually have to leave school. He'd need a new body if . . ." Brent didn't finish his sentence, trying to piece things together.

I inhaled slowly and smiled, Cherie's perfume heady in the room. I had been so excited about finding her and then so caught up in her notes, I hadn't noticed her signature scent at first. The significance of her perfume faded as the sound of feet in the hallway had my fingers clasping tightly together in anticipation until they continued past her door. The corners of my mouth drooped.

I turned my attention back to Brent to quiet my disappointment. "Did your parents worry about sending you here after your brother . . . died?"

Brent laughed without humor, staring out the window. "No, they wanted me gone. I got in the way." Brent held up a hand against my forthcoming denial and apology. "They love me, but they're busy with their own lives. A good college was just an excuse to send me here. To ease their conscience, they have me meet with a therapist every few months though."

"Did it bother you to come here?"

Brent rubbed one of his shoes against the back of his leg. "Yeah. Didn't seem to matter though, did it?"

I really had no idea how to respond to that, so I didn't say anything. Instead, I watched Brent crouch down to read the last of Cherie's notes about me. Beside my picture was a big red question mark. Next to it another scrap of paper listed everything I had told her in detail. He swore, pointing to an arrow that led from my picture to a small snapshot of Brent we hadn't noticed before.

"She suspects him." My knees gave out on me and I plopped onto Cherie's bed. "She won't let it go, either."

The curtains at the window fluttered in a chilly breeze and the room seemed darker. Brent tugged me to my feet, across the hallway, down the stairs, and outside, while my mind swirled with the danger Cherie was in. I had to warn her—I wasn't sure how, but I had to. My arm ached where Brent's fingers dug into me as he cursed. The air around us had grown frosty, pressing in on us.

Brent stopped and spun me so I was looking at him. "Yara, run. Get as far from here as you can," he pleaded, his fingers loosening their grip on my arms.

"What are we waiting for? Let's go," I said reaching for his hand, but he pulled it back.

"I'm not coming."

"What? Why? Come with me," I begged, not understanding.

"I can't. We can't both get away from it and I'm not about to let him get you." I looked at him, dumbfounded. "You go hide, I'll hold it back. Go," he commanded, trying to push me back with his wind, but I planted my feet in rebellion.

"Not without you." I tried to breathe deeply but the air lodged in my throat refusing to go further. "It's me he wants." Tears trudged down my cheeks. Another gust of wind pushed against me, away from him, soft but insistent. For an instant the wind stopped pushing, instead circling me in a gentle hug, like Brent was holding me in his arms. When I closed my eyes, it felt like he was physically next to me and I was in his warm embrace.

"We can get away together," I stammered. The wind forming the shape of his fingers wiped away my tears then gently stroked my cheek. Something I didn't know existed stirred within me. Despite the upcoming fight, he was much more content than I had ever seen him before.

"Go," he said softly and I was again being pushed back against my will. My arms reached out toward him and I screamed his name as I strained to touch him. Frantically I tried to cling to trees, to branches as they whipped past me.

Tears blinded me and I sobbed, "Please, let me stay." My feet dragged on the ground through leaves and gravel despite my hysterical kicking. My limbs continued searching for anything to get leverage, to help fight against the wind Brent was commanding, until he was no longer in view.

My determined fight was interrupted by Brent's urgent voice in my mind, *Please . . . stop resisting, please. I don't think I can fight you both. I need to be able to concentrate.*

With that I stopped and dropped helplessly to the ground, bawling, rocking back and forth. As it drew close to him, I could feel his terror grow. That fear made my tears stop and in some twisted way gave me courage. I couldn't hide like a coward; he might need me. Brent thought he knew me better than anyone else. If he truly did, then he knew he couldn't keep me away. I would help, not complicate things. I hoped.

I crept from tree to tree until I was able to see Brent and the huge blanket of vapor approaching him. He seemed so small against such an enormous foe that my heart careened in my chest. Thomas had left Brent's body behind for the fight; there was nothing human in the villain moving toward Brent, only the mist.

I watched as Brent, standing firm, raised his hands to the heavens as if summoning something. And it came. The cloudless blue sky grew dim; dark rain clouds moved in, quickly blocking out the sun altogether. The ominous clouds were drawn to him, thunder rolled, a crash of lighting brightened the suddenly dark sky. Rain poured down, drenching the world around us. Birds flew from their nests and far-away dogs howled in fear. Brent's hands were spread wide and I noticed that as he brought them close together a small ball of the elements he had summoned swirled there. As forms began to take shape in the gloom, he dropped his hand pointing it toward the shadows. The ball he had created attacked the mist, scattering the forms back to vapor. Before they could re-form, his hands were raised again. I had thought him a powerful warrior and he was. I would gladly follow him into battle.

I clung to the tree as the wind whipped my hair and dress in its fierceness. The separated mist was gathering to go against Brent one more time but a small part of it broke off, gliding toward me.

Trying to control the wind as I had the volleyball, I tried to push back the slithering darkness, but my frantic attempts had no affect.

Thomas's voice seeped out from the mist. "So glad you've come to play, Yara. It's time."

Brent cursed loudly as his head snapped toward me. He pointed a clenched fist in my direction, cursing again, and a strong gust pushed me back with such force that I lost my grip on the tree and was hurled backward, landing heavily on my right side. The small vein of haze that had been moving toward me scattered and slid back to join the whole. I turned my attention back to Brent and gasped.

The mist had encircled him entirely. He held both hands out wide as he slowly looped around, sizing up the strength of his foe. He was strong enough to keep his enemy from advancing any closer, but couldn't repel it entirely. He looked toward the skies and a small cyclone formed directly above him. The twister descended and engulfed him, safely keeping him in its eye as it twisted and whipped away the darkness.

Run, Brent commanded me in his thoughts. *You need to get away. I'm not sure I can hold this off any more.* The cyclone lifted just high enough for him to duck underneath and run toward me. Things seemed to be moving in slow motion and I watched as the remaining mist swirled around Brent's legs and pulled him to the ground with a thud. His fingers grabbed futilely into the dirt as he was being dragged away from me.

I opened my mouth to scream but no sound came.

"Go!" He yelled.

Suddenly I felt faint, unable to move. The mist grew denser and again several distinct beings became evident. I could feel it growing stronger as it rejoiced at capturing Brent. I stood, unsure what to do. I couldn't run. I couldn't leave Brent. He needed me. I was scared, I was angry, and it was the mist's fault. I wanted to throw all of my erupting emotions out toward the enemy in all-out assault. My eyes locked on my foe, concentrating, channeling my fury into my fingertips. A movement out of the corner of my eye caught my attention. Brent was shaking his head adamantly.

In an instant, his lessons came back to me. I needed to be smarter than that—I couldn't be ruled by anger or fear. I had to keep control or risk being left completely power-less— or, even worse, hurt Brent. Not sure what else to do I mimicked what I had seen Brent do; I lifted my hands up toward the sky.

I felt a surge of power around me, awaiting my command. My eyes focused on the fog holding Brent. I dropped my hand and I pointed at it with all my might, all my heart, all my determination. The power I had summoned obeyed, scattering the dark substance. To my astonishment, the wind felt like an extension of my hand. It bent to my will as if attached. I reached out with my elemental hands and grabbed Brent's.

I pulled with all my strength, but he didn't budge.

Our eyes met and I felt his strength combine with mine. His power surged through me, burning my insides with its intensity. I felt invincible as I leaned back to give myself more leverage, wrenching him free. The mist's tendrils reached for his ankles, trying to reclaim its grip. The air rang with its anguished cries as Brent stumbled into my arms. A sense of completion filled me, like some long forgotten half of me had suddenly returned. I set that thought aside, promising myself to ponder it at a better time. Like when I wasn't fighting for my soul.

We were both panting heavily as we wheeled together toward our enemy. I faltered for a second when I saw a face that had emerged from the mist. It was Thomas Weld. He looked just like his picture in Cherie's room; he hadn't aged in the sixty years since he was thought to have died.

"Focus," Brent hissed as he grabbed my hand, and together we raised them to gather whatever force we could. We sent a wave of hail, rain, and wind so strong it knocked the leaves off all the trees in our area and ripped at branches that creaked in protest. The mist, instead of spreading, huddled together in a tight ball, the independent shadows joining the whole. With one last glare in my direction, Thomas drew the mass into himself.

I had been so surprised to see Thomas that I hadn't realized Brent was still working. With a final push of air, Thomas was knocked back a step before retreating out of sight. The storm quickly cleared and the sun shone as brightly as it had before the battle. Brent lowered our hands and collapsed on the ground, cradling one of his ankles. We had won the skirmish, but the war was still not over.

CHAPTER 13

"Is it gone?" I asked hopefully, wiping away the sweat on my face.

"For now," he said, his chest rattling with exhaustion. "It'll be back."

A knot formed in my stomach. "How do we get rid of it for good?" He shook his head. "How did it know to find us in Cherie's room?"

"I'm pretty sure it was looking for Cherie and found us by mistake," Brent said, resting his hands across his body.

"How come he wasn't in your body this time?" I asked, arranging the length of my dress around me.

Brent let out a tired sigh. "He was done toying with us and was moving in for the kill. I know I'm stronger when I'm without my body. I'm guessing it's the same for him."

"Do you—"

Brent held up a hand to stop my flow of questions. "Can we do this later, after I've had a chance to rest?"

I bit my tongue, but my mind began theorizing and trying to make sense of what had happened.

"That includes thinking too loud," Brent said wearily, his eyelids fluttering closed.

"Sorry," I apologized sheepishly. He had risked everything to save me and I moved closer to him, taking one of his hands in mine. A lump of gratitude formed in my throat, so strong it was almost painful. Without thinking I threw my arms around his neck and went to kiss him on the cheek.

Or, at least, I meant to— but at the same moment Brent turned to me and started to say, "I was thinking—"

I'll never know what he was thinking because his lips met mine. My eyes popped open in surprise. His eyes were wide in astonishment as well. For a long second, we sat there staring into each others eyes, our lips touching, totally frozen. My mind was a blank except for wondering if I could will the mist back to take me now and save me from this uncomfortable situation.

Finally, my wits returned to me and I pulled back hastily, my cheeks flushing with color. My fingers rushed to cover my offending lips. Brent tried to sit up but was still too weak and finally settled on scooting further away from me. Wanting more distance, I retreated back a few feet. I looked up at the sky, at the ground covered with fallen leaves, at the bare branches of the trees, anywhere but at Brent. Silence can be deafening.

Finally Brent cleared his throat. "Can't say I'm that surprised that you succumbed to my charms."

"I didn't mean to kiss you," I said, embarrassed beyond belief.

"Really? So your lips just ended up close enough to touch mine by mere coincidence?" While his words almost seemed to be teasing, his tone wasn't.

I dared to glance at him and saw that he too was avoiding looking at me. He was studying the palm of his hand like it was the most fascinating thing in the world.

"I went to kiss *your cheek* as a gesture of thanks but then you turned to talk to me and . . ." it was far too humiliating to finish the sentence so I didn't. The fact that I had to explain my actions bothered me. "Don't you already know this? Can't you tell through means other than having to speak?"

He seemed as flustered as I did, his cheeks tinged pink. "I could, but you're all muddled right now. And I really do try to respect your privacy." Finally Brent seemed to have composed himself and he laughed. "I told you I'm irresistible. You've got it bad for me."

"Aren't you glad I came back?" I asked, deciding to ignore his loaded comment and change the subject.

He tilted his face toward me and frowned. "Having you close was a distraction, as I thought it might be," he said. "But in the end, I think it was good you were there."

Warmth rippled through me. "Were you afraid?"

Brent closed his eyes. "Yes," he answered honestly. "At first I thought I had things under control, but then you changed that confidence. I had a moment where I knew I was going to fail. When it got a hold of me, I was sure it was over. It's a miracle we weren't taken."

"I know you didn't want me here, but I had to—"

"I'm glad you were. Turns out you came in useful," he half-teased.

"I'm still amazed at how you did that. I had no idea how much strength you had. You were right about him just having caught you off guard before. It was like watching a sorcerer."

His chest puffed up in pride. "Really?" He paused thoughtfully. "I might have been showing off a little. I didn't really *need* the lightning. I just thought it gave a dramatic flair."

"That sounds like something you would do." I laughed, breaking a small twig off one of the leafless branches that had fallen to the ground during our skirmish. "I have never seen anyone else do what you did today."

"Have you looked in a mirror recently? I have never seen anyone, besides myself, able to do what you did, especially after such a short amount of time. You are . . . gifted."

I gave him a withering glare. "Right. Please don't tease me."

Brent laughed heartily, ruffling my hair. "I was being serious. According to Neal's journals, hardly anyone can do the sort of stuff I've been teaching you."

I waved off his compliment. "I think we need to go. I feel like we're too easy to find here." Brent was still lying on the ground, completely exhausted, surrounded by what looked like the aftermath of a hurricane. The skirmish hadn't taken that much out of me, so I stood and hoisted Brent up, placing his arm around my shoulder and my arm around his waist. As we slowly made our way out of the clearing, Brent was practically limp at my side, unable to walk by himself, his left leg dragging behind him. I kept checking on him out of the corner of my eye.

"Will you please stop peeking at me like that? This is degrading enough as it is."

"Did it ever occur to you," I said, with a sly smile and a wink, "that you're so irresistibly handsome, I can't keep my eyes off of you?"

He threw his head back in a laugh. "Of course. I should have realized."

I stopped for a second repositioning my grasp on Brent. We had only gone a few yards and it felt like we had walked miles. As he tightened his arm on my shoulder I realized how tired I truly was.

When we finally arrived in the Headmaster's garden, I helped Brent down beside the gazebo and gracelessly plopped down beside him. He reclined heavily against the wood panel. The dark circles under his eyes contrasted against his gray skin.

A dull ache in my ankle I had been feeling since the fight became a painful throbbing. I lifted my dress to check out the damage, only to find it perfectly fine, but still pounding. My eyes narrowed at Brent. I was pretty sure I was experiencing sympathy pain from Brent's injury. I reached out for his leg and his closed eyes flew open.

"What are you doing?" He asked, snaking his leg away from me.

"What does it look like?" I snapped, grabbing his leg firmly. He relented with a grunt. Sometimes I could be persuasive, especially when he was too weak to protest.

"Just don't make it worse," he retorted, crossing his arms grumpily.

I scowled at him as I rolled up his pant leg and gasped. "Ouch."

A piece of the mist was stabbed into his ankle wriggling like a worm burrowing into the flesh. The whole area surrounding it was black, the same blue liquid that had been on my wound leaked around the edges. "When did this happen?"

"When you pulled me free."

The black on his ankle was slowly spreading like a spider web, climbing up his leg. It reminded me of blood poisoning, climbing up his veins toward his heart. I moved to grab it when Brent stopped my hand. "Don't touch it."

"Right." I bit my lip and raised my fingers over it trying to pluck it out using my mind. It clung to him, refusing to let go. I could feel its resistance and I tugged harder. It wobbled a little until it finally pulled free with a loud sucking sound that was lost in Brent's stream of profanity.

It landed a few feet away from us and shimmered and wiggled gelatinously before vanishing. The wound was blistered and oozing, but the black continued to spread higher. I lifted my fingers and tried to pull the infectious liquid out but it wouldn't come. Without even thinking about how dangerous it was, I lowered my mouth to the wound and my lips pressed against Brent's leg, closing over the cut. Brent's leg jerked and I looked at him, mentally asking if it was hurting him.

He strangled a laugh. "Not exactly."

Not really feeling reassured, but knowing I needed to hurry, I began sucking on his leg, pulling the poison out, much like my grandpa had done for my sister after a rattlesnake bit her when we were young. The poison had my gag reflex working as it touched my tongue. It tasted horrible, like a mix of moldy grapes, rotten eggs, and open septic tank—chilled, fermented, and topped off with rotten milk. Slowly, the black in his leg began retreating.

It took several times of sucking the poison and spitting it out before I got it all. As soon as the black substance touched the earth, it vanished, absorbed into the dirt, killing the grass. I bent over and heaved, black and blue saliva trickling down my chin. I drew the back of my hand across my mouth, clearing it away, then wiped it on the browning and brittle grass. If evil had a taste, that was it.

Brent looked at me strangely, rotating his ankle a few inches off the ground.

"What?" I asked, leaning my back against the gazebo's white-painted boards.

He didn't respond right away and I checked to see if he had fallen asleep, but he was watching me. "I can't believe you just did that."

"Did it help?" I asked, trying to determine whether

he sounded impressed. He nodded mutely, holding up his leg, his pant leg fell enough to see the small, newly formed black scar on his ankle. It looked like a tattoo of a black rain cloud. "Good, because that was totally gross, and if it didn't help I think I would cry."

"Weep not, m'lady; it helped," he said, with a slight bend of his waist. "You can't keep your lips off me, huh?"

I rolled my eyes at him. "Yes, I'm sorry my motives are so transparent." I mentally threatened to dig up whatever poison I could find and reinsert it into him, causing him to sputter a laugh.

"In all seriousness, thanks," Brent mumbled, dropping his leg with a hard thud. "That was brave. Stupid, but brave. What if you got some of it in you?'

"I didn't . . . besides, you would have done the same for me," I said simply, stretching my sore body.

"Yes, I would have," he answered without any hesitation at all.

I felt the nightly pull of my death and I slumped.

"Oh, man." Brent groaned. "I'm too exhausted to watch you drown again."

"I'm even less up to it than normal," I complained as we were lifted from the ground and carried toward the pool.

After I had drowned and Brent had failed to revive me, we again walked toward the garden.

"I'm so tired." Brent yawned, dropping to the ground and pulling me down beside him. "I think I need to sleep."

"Sleep then." I started humming softly, a melody I made up as I went along.

"I shouldn't, though. I need to be ready in case it comes back." He sat up straight, slapping his face lightly, trying to wake himself up.

"I'm perfectly capable of keeping watch."

"Maybe for a few minutes," he said. He smiled weakly as his eyelids drooped, his face toward the sky and his arms folded across his waist. I could feel the tension still coiled inside of him, leaving him too anxious to sleep.

"It's okay, Brent. Go to sleep. You kept us safe," I whispered, leaning close to his ear, resting my hand lightly on top his. I continued humming until he finally drifted off.

When I was sure he was asleep, I pulled my hand away. Alone with my thoughts, I was able to really concentrate on what I had learned in Cherie's room. Eventually a dull pain pulsed behind my eyes, and my head lulled back as I massaged my forehead. My eyes slid closed as my murky thoughts merged with my unconsciousness to form equally horrible dreams.

* * * *

I was in the center of the groves, running hard, trying to make it to the edge of campus. Brent was beside me, holding my hand, urging me to move faster. My lungs burned, trying desperately to breathe. I could feel the mist growing stronger as it chased me, nipping at my heels. Cherie stood at the edge of campus, frozen. Brent was on the ground beside her, and yet still beside me. I was there, too, lying next to him, wearing my necklace.

"Brent," an eerie voice called from behind us. "Please don't run from me."

Without warning, he stopped and spun around, dropping my hand. "Neal?"

"Brent," I begged, "we have to keep going."

I frantically grabbed his hand but he shook me off, stepping away from me and closer to the dark.

"Brent," I began, but he ignored me and took another step further away.

Tears ran down my face, and my burning lungs were no

longer getting air as I started hyperventilating.

"He needs me," Brent explained. I reached for his hand again, but missed. I looked up and saw that the shadow had grown stronger. Two figures stood out from the rest: Neal, who was calling out to Brent, and Thomas, partially hidden in the shadows.

"That's right, Brent." Neal smiled with his mouth, but it didn't reach his brown eyes. "Come to me."

"I can't leave her," Brent explained to his brother.

His smile became more sinister. "Then bring her with you."

Brent smiled at me like this was a good solution. He started toward me, and I fell to the ground, devastated, as the rain started pouring down. My heart broke in betrayal as I watched him draw closer, a vacant look in his eyes.

The mist hovered, closing in on Brent as he slunk toward me.

"We've been waiting for you, Yara," it hissed as it glided ever closer. "You've avoided us for too long."

I began crawling backward on the ground, trying to get away, slipping in my haste and whimpering in fear. I knew it was over. I heard myself scream as it overpowered me.

*   *   *   *

I sat up screaming, my eyes wide with panic. I gulped hard, urging my breathing to slow. It took some coaxing to convince myself it was only a nightmare. Brent still lay sleeping beside me somehow undisturbed by my scream. I rolled onto my side and watched the rise and fall of his chest, appearing untroubled in his sleep. Even though my nightmare had the same vivid texture of my prophetic dreams, I refused to be scared by this one. I knew Brent wouldn't betray me. He had his chance and he didn't take it. He hadn't abandoned me. He had already made that choice. Right? Brent stirred beside me and I scooted closer to him, feeling safer as I did. My fingers rested next to his, a whisper away from touching. I closed my eyes, listening to his rhythmic breathing.

The terrible sentry that I was, I must have dozed off again because when my eyes slowly blinked open from a heavy sleep, the sun had risen over the mountains surrounding Corona. I wasn't sure if I had dreamed, but at least I hadn't had another horrible nightmare and I awoke feeling peaceful. My mind started dissecting the earlier nightmare, but found it was still too terrifying and shoved it aside until I was ready to deal with it.

The sun's rays warmed my face, languidly rousing me even further from sleep. Birds were singing and the fountain was on. It was a beautiful day and I couldn't help but smile. I felt happy, connected to this gorgeous garden, to Brent, and to my limbo existence. I lifted my arms and stretched, realizing that my connection to Brent at the moment was literal. His arm was wrapped around me and he was snuggled in close. My body involuntarily jerked in surprise, rousing Brent from his sleep.

I managed to free myself from his embrace and turned to look back at him, trying to appear normal, but feeling awkward. With me kissing him and then sleeping in his arms he was going to start getting the wrong idea.

Brent, now fully awake, rolled onto his back and put his hands behind his head. I heard the smile in his voice as he sang softly, "As I was drifting off to sleep, a dream washed through my mind and carried me to our embrace, so warm and soft and kind, and then you promised me your heart and told me you would stay, but when the morning broke at last I found you'd gone away. It breaks my—"

"Shut up, Brent," I growled, my good mood souring

like rotten milk. I recognized the verse from "Can't Stop Dreaming of You" and cut him off before he got to the chorus. I let out a frustrated breath of air and glared at him. "If you keep singing and whistling that song, it won't take long until I don't like it anymore."

"I'm surprised you even know it."

"Kevin was really into older music, mainly jazz and folk, but this was his favorite song. I'm not sure why. But after hearing it so often, I started to like it, too."

Brent nodded. "Still, the lyrics fit our situation perfectly—you waited until I was asleep and crept into my embrace—" I put my hand over his mouth to stop his words.

"I had a bad dream last night and . . ." I trailed off letting my mind explain the nightmare and my fear.

He was silent for a minute. "I'm sorry for teasing you. I—"

"I know."

"Interesting dream."

"Yeah, but it's just a dream, right?"

Brent sat up straight, looking at me strangely. "What do you mean by that?"

I shook my head. "Nothing."

"I don't believe you."

I bit my lip, thinking about the dream and how it had frightened me. "I've had dreams like that before, ones that were scarily vivid. I think it scared me so much because it felt similar, like the dreams I had of me drowning. You know, before I drowned."

I suddenly had Brent's undivided attention and he leaned toward me. His brown eyes narrowed as he grabbed my hand. "You dreamed about drowning?" I nodded. "Was it similar to how you actually died?" I nodded again, not exactly sure where he was going with this. "Was your dress caught on the brick bag they use for the swim team?"

"I couldn't tell; is that what happened?"

Brent thought for a moment. "Yeah, Steve had to rip it free to pull you out."

"I didn't know that."

"Tell me, Yara, the first time you had that dream, were you wearing your necklace?" I told him I was. "How about when you left your body?" I nodded again. "But not when you died?"

"No, it didn't go with my dress. Does that matter?"

Brent scratched his chin as he thought. "It might. Tell me about this new dream again." With as much detail as I could, I explained everything to him.

"But this dream is different, right? I mean I was with Cherie and I felt . . . alive."

"I'm not sure." Brent pursed his lips, still mulling over this new information. "Is that the only time you've had dreams like that?"

I took a calming breath before I answered. "No. The week before my brother Kevin died, I . . . I saw it in a dream." I plucked a blade of grass and watched it hover in the air before me. "I didn't tell him about it; I had no idea it would come true. If I had, maybe he wouldn't have gone to that stupid party with his loser friend. Maybe he wouldn't have let his friend drive."

It was impossible to miss the loud sound of Brent sucking in a lung full of air. "Oh, man."

I let the blade of grass that I had shredded to pieces fall to the ground. "I never told anyone. I was afraid they'd blame me."

Footsteps padded on the stone walkway as a man in a groundskeeper uniform crossed to the fountain and began cleaning out the leaves that had fallen into the water.

Brent slid himself closer to me and wrapped his arm around my shoulders. "Why didn't you pay attention to your drowning dreams then?"

"I thought it was a fluke. I hoped it was. I . . . I don't know," I admitted slowly. "I did try and be careful around water though."

Brent chuckled. "Yes, that seemed to work well for you. Let's pay attention to this one, then."

"You're going to give me to your brother and let the mist have me?" I asked, shaking his arm off of me.

"That's not going to happen. Haven't I already proved I wouldn't do that?" He rolled his eyes at my stare. "The situation might be the same, but the difference will be in the details."

A lawnmower rumbled to life and the grounds employee began guiding it across the grass. We climbed onto the ledges of the gazebo as stray pieces of grass floated through the air.

"We fight, we lose?"

"What happened to your undying optimism?" Brent asked, raising one eyebrow.

"I traded it for your sense of reality." I traced around the black scar on my shoulder with my fingertips. "How's your ankle feeling?"

"Changing the subject? Sure, I'll stop talking about the important topic if you feel uncomfortable." Brent stretched his legs out in front of him. "I'm much better. I dreamed too."

"What did you dream?" With amusement I noticed he blushed and protected his thoughts. "Aren't you going to tell me?" He shook his head as he stood up and rolled his shoulders.

"But you made me discuss mine in detail."

"I'll tell you what, if I have a dream that might be that important, I promise to tell you all about it." He flexed his muscles in several body builder poses. "My strength is back. Let's start training again." I groaned as he yanked me to my feet.

* * * *

Later that night we walked toward the center of the school, wandering around while waiting to reenact my death. The moon shone brightly on the campus and even without my heightened senses I would have easily been able to see by its beams. It was chilly, cold enough that if I were still alive, my breath would have hung around my face in the air.

"It's a beautiful winter evening. All that's missing is snow. I'm never going to see snow again." I frowned at this realization.

Brent smiled at me mischievously and lifted his hands above his head, mouthing words I couldn't hear and my mind didn't understand. The temperature plummeted, and clouds formed, covering the bright moon. Within moments, tiny fluffs of white flitted to the ground around us.

I laughed in amazement, tilting my head back. I stretched out my arms and twirled in the falling snow. The small flakes gradually gave way to larger ones as the pace of them picked up, coming down in a flurry, until several inches of billowy white blanketed the ground.

"How did you do that?" I asked, sticking my tongue out to catch the snowy flakes. They didn't stop, but fell through me unimpeded.

"It wasn't hard. It's the same basic technique I use to control the wind. It just took more time, energy, and concentration. I didn't do it everywhere, just around the school."

"How are the weathermen going to explain that?"

Brent chuckled, reaching out his hand and letting a few flecks of snow fall through him. I took a deep breath and inhaled the chilly air. I was surprised to find I felt different. Something in me had changed. After a minute I realized, for the first time since I died, I felt content. Yes, there were things I longed to change, and people I wished to hold, but I could feel myself slowly moving past my life. It's not that I was losing the memory of my loved ones, but I was coming to accept things as they were. There was a word to describe how I felt. Happy.

Brent turned to me in shock. "You're happy."

I stopped walking and bit my lip, turning to face him with a surprised grin. "I am. Or at least I really think I can be." At that moment I noticed that the room that had once been mine was still dark, but only a little sadness squeezed my heart.

"You can't already be losing your happiness," Brent said as he formed a perfectly round snowball. He took aim at me. "This is a happiness-rejuvenating snow ball," he explained in a very serious tone. He threw it at me, but with a wave of my hand, I forced it to miss its mark.

"Really?" My eyebrow arched in defiance as I created a snowball of my own. I tossed the snowball from hand to hand.

"Now you're going to want to be careful with that," Brent warned with a wag of his finger. I ignored the warning and tossed it at him. It didn't even come close to hitting him thanks to a deflection on his part. Soon the world was nothing but cold wet snow being flung between us. He managed to "hit" me twice but I returned the favor three times. Having snow go through you is an interesting experience; it made me feel briefly like a rain cloud. When I was tired I collapsed on the wet ground, breathing heavily.

"I haven't laughed that much since I died," I wheezed.

Brent plopped himself down beside me. "Me either." He rested his head on his arms that were crossed above his head.

"Thank you for making this possible. Imagine how surprised everyone will be in the morning."

"It was nothing." Brent waved his hand across the sky and the snow began to slow.

I rolled toward Brent, resting my head on my hand. "Why do you always do that?"

"What?"

"Try to make it seem like this ability you have is no big deal?"

Brent stared up at the sky, watching the bright stars and moon. "I don't know."

I watched as with a flip of his fingers he began to roll a snowball. "Doesn't matter. My ability wasn't able to save us from dying."

"It saved us when the mist attacked."

Brent smiled warmly as he sat up. "It did do that," he admitted—but amended his statement, "but only with your help."

Brent continued to make his snowball until it got so big that I would no longer be able to get my arms around it. "It's so cool you had this ability with the elements while you were alive. I never got the chance to try."

Brent nodded. "Yeah, and unlike everyone else, I could do all of it off campus as well."

"You mean all the body leaving and moving stuff was limited to campus?" I chewed on the inside of my cheek, thinking. "Are my abilities limited to here, too?"

Brent stretched his neck again rolling his head in a

circle. "Maybe . . . probably."

I looked around Pendrell with its sturdy trees, seasonal flowers, and brick buildings. It all seemed so normal, so unthreatening, but there must be something not right about it. I turned to Brent, curious. "What is it about Pendrell exactly that lets its students project?"

Brent laughed. "I was wondering if we were ever going to have this conversation." I could hear him shuffling his thoughts, trying to organize them and decide where to start. "Well, Pendrell was founded by Christopher Pendrell," he said. He seemed satisfied with his snowball and began to roll a new one. "He thought his sons needed to get into an east coast prep school to be able to get into the right college. He was devastated when they weren't accepted. He set out to make Pendrell better than the schools that had snubbed them. He wanted the kids from his school to be smarter and more successful than any of his competitors. About this time his brother returned from a trip from South America with a plant called pankurem."

"That's the same plant my necklace is made of," I interjected. I could picture the plant perfectly, its tiny leaves growing in little clusters, their edges jagged. I had seen those leaves many times and I knew them well; each one of the amber beads on my necklace had been hand crafted to include a leaf within it. "Vovó uses that plant all of the time in her work."

"I know about it being in your necklace," Brent said, still working on his second snowball.

"You knew?" I thought back to when he had seen my necklace and how it had reacted to him.

Brent listened to my thoughts. "Yeah, that stuff responds to people like us. It's supposed to keep spirits safe, and can protect us while we project. I never found any but when I saw your necklace I knew what it was. Like some part of me recognized it." The corners of his mouth sagged. "I thought it would keep you safe."

"Maybe it would have if I hadn't been a slave to fashion."

Brent tilted his head to the side considering before continuing. "Anyway, back to our story. His brother told him about the plant's ability to help people reach their highest mental potential, helping them see connections they might have otherwise missed. Christopher was eager to learn more about the plant and invited a few people who knew about it to teach at the school. He planted it all around campus and started growing it in his sons' rooms. He even put a small amount in their tea and food."

"Well, I am sorry to discredit that theory, but that is the same plant I had in my necklace and it didn't seem to do me any good at all."

"Yara, please, I'm trying to tell you a story here." Brent sighed. He examined the beach ball sized snowball, nodded, and began to make a third. I pretended to zip my lips and continued to listen. "So, not only did it help their grades, but it also had a side effect: they were able to leave their bodies. And they shared that secret with a select group of their friends. And thus began Pendrell's secret society, the Clutch. Each class passed it on to the next group of students, until two boys died in a tragic fire. After that, some members tried to keep it going, but too many weird things started happening— guys getting hurt on their way to meetings, strange accidents when they met, just. . . weird things. Eventually things got too hard and they gave up. The society sort of petered out."

"So you're telling me that we had a secret society at our school? Really? You weren't kidding about that? One that never made it into any of Cherie's stories?"

"It was a secret," Brent pointed out, exasperated.

"It must have been hard not to be able to project after they left the school."

Brent confirmed this with a nod. "Every New Year they would all gather in the pool house and celebrate together. You see, once you could do it, you could always do it when you were here. The only problem was that you couldn't do it when you anywhere else. Well, most of them couldn't," he added with a sheepish grin.

I tapped my lips with my finger, thinking. "Even if you had enough of the plant?"

"Yes— believe me, they tried everything," Brent said. His third snowball was now also complete, around the size of a basketball.

"How does Thomas fit into all this?"

"I'm pretty sure he was Clutch and probably behind all the weird stuff after the fire. I don't have any details on what scared them so badly though."

"So how do you know all this?"

Brent shrugged. "I read it Neal's journals."

"How did he know?"

"Well, my grandpa was a member, but it had disbanded before my dad came along. And he couldn't find anyone else interested and could only barely project himself."

"So, genetics plays a role?"

"Seems that way. All the bushes on campus died years before dad started school here. He thought maybe that was why he had a hard time doing it . . . and he was afraid any of the plant left in the soil would have faded even more by the time Neal came along. I think my dad had hopes of Neal starting the Clutch again. He was worried not having the plant would make it impossible."

"But how did we leave our bodies without the plant?"

"Well, my grandpa had a different theory: that the plant wasn't really necessary to project, it just made it easier. He was convinced the plant's most important purpose was to protect the body from harm while the spirit was gone. Once I read that in Neal's journals, I started practicing it at home."

"Wow." I was once again impressed at his power.

He shook his head in annoyance. "It's dangerous to leave your body. I was stupid. Not to mention, you did it with one lousy paragraph from a book. Believe me, I'm much more impressed by that. You didn't spend hours sweating for nothing in your bedroom and accomplishing nothing but body odor."

I laughed at the mental image. "It wasn't me. It was my necklace and the step by step instructions from Thomas."

"Maybe." Brent piled his three snowballs on top of each other. "A snowman," he said.

"I figured that out all by myself." I spotted two thin branches I thought would work for the snowman's arms and I commanded them over toward the piles of snow.

"How come your grandpa and dad didn't tell you about this? How come you had to read it in Neal's journals?"

Brent shrugged. "Not sure."

I watched as five stones floated through the air and then became a pair of eyes and the buttons on the snowman's chest. Brent stood and examined our little snowman. "It needs a good nose."

I stood up, looking for something that would work while Brent made a mouth with two leaves.

"It was supposed to protect me," I said, positioning an orange flower above his green lips. Sitting back down in the snow I examined our masterpiece. I didn't really see it, though; my mind was still on my necklace. I wished I had it on now so I could examine it more carefully. I found it odd that, from another country, my grandmother had sent me a present that was tied not only to my death, but to the mystery of Pendrell itself. "Maybe the necklace did work."

Brent turned to me, stunned. "How exactly do you explain that?"

"Well, it allowed me to the see the mist and save you, and it protected me that time it tried to attack me. Well I guess you helped that time, too. That *is* what all that frantic hand waving was about, right?"

"That frantic hand waving is a highly polished form of defense that saved your butt."

"Anyway, as I was saying, it allowed me to save you, protected me and probably even made my Waker genes finally develop. The plant is supposed to protect pure spirits—" I blushed at the compliment I had just implied about myself. "—from being hurt by evil ones. I never really thought about the plant inside the necklace actually working, but it does seem that the necklace really helped me." I scratched my collarbone where my necklace should have been and bit my lip. "Now that I think about it, Thomas couldn't even touch me when he was pretending to be you... until I took it off. And if I hadn't been so heedless of my grandmother's request to wear it all the time, I might still be alive."

"Or," he countered, "it led you to your death by letting you leave your body and attracting the mist's attention in the first place."

"Or maybe it's just helping me see connections that I haven't figured out yet. My grandmother is a smart lady."

Brent didn't reply. He didn't have to. I could feel how strongly he disagreed with me. He was silent for a while and I could hear him thinking. "Yara, do you believe in fate?"

"I suppose it depends on the context."

"This plant. It can't be coincidence that your great-great-grandfather worked here and that this plant your family uses in their spiritual work also ends up here. I'm willing to bet he's the one who brought it to the school. You said he was a science teacher, right?"

I nodded, starting to see where his line of thinking was going.

Brent continued, "Your family knows so much about herbs, it must have been him Christopher chose to teach him about the plant. Even though the plant eventually died, it still managed to somehow imbue its magical powers into the soil. Then you arrive here decades later, a girl who's been raised with this stuff, who's special even among those who are already considered special. It's no wonder you astral projected so soon and so powerfully. I don't think you could have stopped it even if you wanted to." I blushed. He either didn't notice or had the grace to pretend not to. "And you bring your unique gifts and a necklace infused with this plant to school," he continued, pacing around. "Maybe you're tied to all of this somehow."

"My grandma didn't want me to come to Pendrell. Grandpa always swore there were evil things happening here. My parents didn't listen. I didn't listen." I bit my lip considering. "But if he was so sure, why didn't he do anything about it? I mean couldn't he have fought it?"

Brent looked at me like I had missed an important piece of information. "Didn't you say only the girls in the family could see ghosts?" I nodded. "Maybe he knew there was something going on, but didn't know where to look."

I stared at him, shocked and open-mouthed. It all made sense; everything fit. How did I feel, though, about the idea that I was tied to every paranormal happening at Pendrell over the last sixty years? I didn't have time to think too long on it though, because the pull of my reenactment was tugging at me. Once again, it was time for me to die.

CHAPTER 14

The next day, students were slushing through the melting snow, trying to make the most of it. Brent was watching the crowd carefully. I followed his gaze and found my eyes resting on Thomas, in Brent's body, playing ball with Brent's friends.

"So how does he go from piloting your body to controlling the mist? He was in the mist fighting when it attacked."

"I'm guessing he has to leave his . . . my body to do it."

I bounced on the tips of my toes. "That means the next time it attacks, you should search for your body while I—"

"Not going to happen," Brent said through gritted teeth. "I'm not risking you to help myself."

"But I . . ." I let my sentence trail off when I caught the fury in Brent's eyes. "Okay. Okay. It was just an idea."

"I don't ever want you to take a chance like that." Brent seethed, still watching Thomas, who winked in our direction tossing a football to Travis. For the briefest of moments, Thomas's green eyes flashed inside Brent's brown ones.

"Was that wink meant for us?" I asked Brent, who was eyeing Thomas carefully.

"Yes," Brent said as he folded his arms. Finally he turned and looked back at me. "How can everyone think he's me?"

"Maybe because he is literally inside your body?"

Brent looked at me, exasperated. "Obviously there is that. But that's not what I mean."

"What is it?"

Brent dismissed the conversation with a wave of his hand. "It doesn't matter." Brent studied Thomas with disgust. "All of those girls are around, some of my buddies are with him. Can't they tell it isn't me?"

"They probably know something's up. The girls just think you're cute," I said, ignoring the pleasure in his eyes. "And they're still getting to know you; most of them didn't really know you before you died."

"I thought *you* knew me," he admitted. "Turns out you didn't. You thought he was me."

"I didn't," I lied, examining my nails.

Brent gave me a knowing look. "You almost kissed him."

"Yeah, sorry about that." My cheeks burned.

"I just thought . . ." Brent trailed off, his eyes looking hurt. "He isn't anything like me. I guess that's why he picked the fight with Steve; Steve would know. I mean, I would never act so cocky."

I struggled to hold back a laugh. "Yes . . . you are so different that way." The floodgates of my laughter burst open and I giggled uncontrollably for a full minute.

Brent cleared his throat and glared at me. "Are you quite done?" My laughter dried up immediately. "I can be a bit cocky, but mine is good-natured." Brent peeked at me from the corner of his eyes, making sure I agreed with him.

"Okay, I'm actually willing to admit that. You aren't mean-spirited."

Brent flashed me a sincere smile. "My cockiness is charming, endearing . . ."

I nodded piously. "As is your humility."

The snow was all melted now, leaving only muddy ground behind. Classes were about to start and my one-time peers were migrating to where they needed to be. I sat down on a stone bench, leaned back on my hands, and tilted my head toward the sun.

Brent sat next to me and I felt his eyes on me. "What?"

"You said that you were ashamed of your Waker abilities because you wanted to be normal, but what's so great about being normal?"

I closed my eyes seeing the red of the sun through my eyelids. "You, being normal, wouldn't understand."

"Oh, so I'm normal? I can astral project and move things with my mind. Does that sound normal?" It was impossible to miss the sarcasm in Brent's voice.

"Well . . . no, but your stuff is cool."

"Your stuff is awesome. I think it would be great to talk to ghosts."

"Well, you're currently talking to a ghost and I'm here with you for all eternity, so feel free to talk away."

Brent laughed, the melodious sound of it brought a smile to my lips as big as I used to get when I heard the ice cream truck.

"Seeing dead people isn't cool. Even if it were, I suck at being a Waker . . . I fought against contacting you . . . I got scared every flipping time I saw a spirit. Vovó never got scared."

"Has she ever dealt with a murderous ghost?" Brent asked pointedly.

"No, but if she had, it would have gone down a lot differently. I should have paid more attention to what she did. If I had, maybe I could have handled this better."

"Why *didn't* you pay attention to her?"

The glass door under the schools arched entrance slammed open and Mrs. Piper thudded out. She wobbled on her thin heels as she hurried past us checking her watch. I pretended to be engrossed with her to stall answering.

Finally I admitted, "It was shame. I totally believed in everything she taught me but it embarrassed me when people laughed at her and me by proxy. When I was a kid I defended her and started more fights than I can count." My fingers found their way to the scar on my eyebrow. "After a while I stopped because the arguments never changed anything. As I got older, I just wished she would cut it out and pretend to be normal. She knew I felt that way and I think it hurt her." I let my head loll forward so my chin was resting on my chest. I had barely spoken the words, needing to say them, but not wanting to own them.

"But if you believed her, why would you want her to pretend she couldn't see ghosts?"

"I wanted people to think we were normal," I confessed in a small voice, feeling like my insides had been carved out with a melon baller.

"Who cares what people thought?" Brent asked, sounding genuinely confused.

"At the time, the gossip, stories and stares were horrible. But now it seems so stupid that I cared."

I brought my fingers to my lips about to start chewing on them. Brent caught my hand, lowering it. "Nasty habit you don't want to start." There was a kindness in his eyes I didn't deserve.

"If I hadn't been so stubbornly stupid, I might have been able to listen when you were trying to reach out. I could have figured out it was you. I mean, some part of me knew it was different. When it was Thomas haunting me, there was a chemical, chlorinated smell, but with you, it was a comforting, alluring scent that—" I bit my tongue, realizing what I had admitted.

"What?"

I pulled my hand away, the blood draining from my face. "Nothing. It smelled like you, is all."

"And my smell makes you feel comfortable and is, at the same time, alluring? Even when I was alive?" Brent smiled wide. "I knew that new cologne was working for me."

I focused on the orange flower that had once belonged to our melted snowman to give my eyes something to do other than look at Brent. "Anyway, as I was saying, I knew it was different. When I was in the shower—" I stopped for a moment and gave Brent a sharp look. "You were in there when I showered?"

It was Brent's turn to blush as he pulled on the hem of his sweater. "Yeah."

"So you saw me naked?" I asked, my voice cracking.

Brent shook his head aggressively. "Of course not."

"Really?" I arched one eyebrow at him.

A flush crept up his neck, his face crimson. "Alright, I'll admit to being tempted—severely tempted, but I waited outside the stall. I'm not a perv." Brent quickly changed the subject. "I realized something the other day. If I get my body back as you keep insisting I can do . . . you'll be stuck here all alone. I probably won't even be able to see you. You missed your shot at heaven and—"

"It doesn't matter. We're getting your body back," I said, standing up and putting my hands on my hips. "One of us is getting out of here."

"What makes you think I'll be okay leaving you here alone?" Brent stood up and glowered at me.

"I," I started but stopped when I noticed a familiar

blonde head walking across campus.

"Cherie!" I laughed and cried at the same moment. I was laughing because it was Cherie, but crying because she was so different from the friend I remembered.

I was surprised at how emaciated she had become. Her usually creamy skin now seemed chalky. The dark circles under her eyes complimented the hollowness inside them. It looked like some part of Cherie had died with me. She stood at the edge of the sidewalk, hovering, as if making a choice. Her hands were stuffed into the pockets of her black hoodie and twitched nervously. Gathering her courage, she nodded her head as if more determined. She pulled her hood over her messy ponytail like a coat of armor and took a tentative step onto the sidewalk. She began walking slowly, a sharp contrast against her usually quick pace.

I stepped in front of her, hoping she could see or sense me. She stopped short and for a moment I thought it was because she knew I was there. I smiled hopefully, but her head turned away from me and searched for the window of our old room. With new determination, she began walking again.

Brent was still where I had left him, watching the whole scene. "Why can't she see me? Or at least sense me?" I asked.

"I think she's in a place emotionally where no one can reach her. It's like there's a black cloud surrounding her. She isn't doing well."

"How can I help her?"

Brent sadly shook his head. "I . . . don't know."

Turning quickly, I followed after my friend until she entered the pool house where I had died. "What's she doing here?"

"Confronting her ghosts?" Brent guessed, catching up

to me.

Cherie sat down on a pool chair and leaned her elbows on her knees. I sat down next to her, wishing I could hold her or offer her comfort of some sort.

She began speaking aloud. "My whole life, Yara, I've dreamed about ghosts and adventure. I've believed we could make contact with those who have died. And now that I really need to believe it, I can't." Cherie looked all around the room and bit her trembling bottom lip. Tears slipped down her cheeks and she didn't bother wiping them away. "What good does all this belief in ghosts do for me if I'm unable to have enough faith to try to make contact with you? But what if—" She choked back a chest-rattling sob. "—if I try, and I find out you aren't here. What if you're gone forever?" Cherie pressed the palms of her hands into her eyes. "It will take away my last hope. I can't live without hope, but I can't live like this either."

She sat up straight and took a deep cleansing breath, as if ridding herself of doubt. She stood suddenly, trying to keep her newfound composure, and walked to where they had pulled out my body, her face drawn. Minutes passed as she stared at it before bending down and placing three candles on the spot. After lighting them, she stayed crouched down. The candles were scented: lavender, chamomile, and another I didn't recognize. As I inhaled their fragrance, I felt myself relaxing, these were the same candles Vovó used when speaking with ghosts.

Cherie pulled something from her pocket, a small bottle of liquid. She poured it around her in a large circle. Then swiftly she smashed the vial onto the concrete, shattering it with a loud crash. Tiny pieces of glass flew everywhere. One shard cut her hand and blood oozed from it, but she didn't seem to notice.

In a loud commanding voice she called. "Yara Silva, if you're there, will you come and speak with me. Please."

She knelt down and blew across the wet circles she had made. Her breath combined with the smoke from the candles, creating a shimmering, sparkly mist that slowly wound itself together into hair-fine threads of light, which twisted into a glistening rope. It glowed a faint blue as it lengthened itself, swaying from side to side. It was beautifully hypnotic as it slithered, searching for something: Me.

I could feel it calling for me. I wanted to answer it, but found I had no words. I had little sense of who I was or where I was going. All I cared about was that the rope was coming for me. I tried to move toward it, but was frozen in place with no control of my limbs. I was eager for it to reach me, to possess me, because I knew it was meant for me, at the other end of the rope, someone who loved me was waiting.

From somewhere far away I could hear a man calling my name. He pulled on my arm and tried to turn my head toward him, but unsuccessfully. All I could do was watch in anticipation as the rope stretched longer and longer, mere inches from me. Finally it reached me, slowly winding itself tightly around my leg and continuing to creep up, binding me in its twine. As it reached my throat I could smell it, breathing it in deeply as my eyes closed. The fragrance was comforting and familiar. I opened my mouth and it slid gingerly down my throat. It was healing the places of hurt and sadness in me. I felt whole. I was aware of it taking root in me, becoming one with me.

As it lifted me in the air I felt cradled. I continued to inhale the length of the rope until I had swallowed all of it and was gently being set on the ground. One scent stood out from among the others. As my sense of self returned, I recognized it as Cherie's perfume, *Feu et Glace*, permeating the air. It was the scent the rope carried and the liquid with which she had made the circle. I opened my eyes and found myself in a blue translucent bubble, and I was not alone. I was with Cherie. She smiled and all the pain on her face vanished.

She cleared her throat and wrung her hands together.

"Is . . . is that really you, Yara?"

"Who else would it be?"

My question erased her fear. She threw her arms tightly around me and I wrapped mine around her. She didn't fall through me. It was as if I were made of flesh and bone once again.

"Cherie," I cried, "I was afraid I would never see you again."

A loud thud made us both jump. We wheeled toward it, grasping hands tightly only to find Brent's concerned face peering in as he banged on the outside of the bubble with closed fists. I could see his lips moving and calling my name, but he seemed unable to see us. The tension in my shoulders relaxed as Cherie bristled.

"Br— Brent?" Cherie asked, stepping back, tugging me along with her. "Can he see us?"

I shook my head. "He is Brent, but not . . ." Cherie looked at me questioningly. I had so many things I wanted to say and I had no idea how long this moment would last. I knew the most important thing I needed to do was to make sure she was okay. "You *need* to stop looking into the curse, Cherie. You need to let my death go."

"Why?"

I wanted to tell her the truth but I knew if I did, it'd only make her more determined to solve the case. In that moment I knew I was sacrificing others' lives, other people who might be victims of the curse, to save Cherie's life, but I didn't care. "There is no curse. What you call the curse is really just a string of overworked desperate students. As for my death, it was nothing more than an accident. There is no one to blame but me, Cherie."

Cherie shook her head. "I don't believe you."

"It was. You need to let it go and move on with your life."

Cherie eyed me skeptically. "So, is there a Heaven? Are you an angel?" An image formed in my mind of her balancing on the edge of some great cliff and my words having the power to push her off or pull her to safety. *Do I tell her the truth? That I'm stuck between worlds, forced to relive my death every night? No*, I decided instantly, *I offer her comfort.*

"Yes, I'm an angel. It's beautiful here."

I saw some of the weight lift from her shoulders, and could almost see her take a step away from my imagined cliff. "I'm so glad. I was worried. If you weren't okay. . . I don't know . . ." She swallowed hard, and I knew my lie had been the right answer. "So, are you a guardian angel or something? Can I put in an official request to have you be mine?" Before I could answer she continued, "I was so mad at you, Yara. For dying and leaving me alone. But the truth is, I was really mad at myself for that stupid party." I noticed she was eyeing Brent cautiously as he continued to walk the circumference of our bubble. "I still don't trust Brent."

"Stop it. Stop it right now. I won't let anyone else take credit for my death. It was a stupid accident. It wasn't your fault." I forced her to look at me. I saw her hard blue eyes soften under my scrutiny.

"Really?"

"Really." I let go of her face and she carefully studied

the back of her hand trying not to cry. "As for Brent. The guy you see there isn't him, they just look alike. As your guardian angel, I'm telling you to stay away from Brent. He's bad news."

Cherie sighed with a small grin. "Noted."

"Stop pestering him, Cherie. I mean it."

She nodded. "Alright." Her hand went to her pocket and she pulled out my necklace. "Maybe this would have helped, or changed things. Your family was really mad that you took it off. I think you should take it now."

I was stunned. "I don't know if I can."

She smiled broadly. "Your grandmother has a few theories about that."

"Vovó?" Tears welled in my eyes.

Cherie nodded. I lifted my hair and bowed my head as Cherie clasped the chain around my neck. I felt a jolt go through me, my balance faltering for a second.

"Did it help?"

"I felt something. What did she think it would do?"

"She didn't say. Your mom wanted to bury you in it, but your grandma thought this would be better. She said your grandfather wore something like it when he went to school here and that it should be a mandatory part of the Pendrell uniform. He appeared to her in a dream before you started school and said you would need it."

My hand flew to my chest. "Really?"

Cherie looked like she was trying to remember something else. "She mentioned something to your mom that I thought sounded interesting. She scolded your mom for letting you come here. I guess she told them it would be dangerous for anyone in your family, even though your grandpa had used up all the plants to put a barrier around the school. I have no idea what that means. Does that mean anything to you?"

"My grandpa was the one who put up the barrier?"

Cherie nodded and raised her eyebrow. "Yeah, that's what she said."

I nodded as my mind absorbed this new information. Had my Grandpa used the last of the pankurem plant to create a barrier meant to trap the evil he knew existed but couldn't see, making sure no plants remained so that others wouldn't try leaving their bodies unprotected as their secret society had done? Everything in me screamed yes.

Cherie dropped her eyes sadly and her little sniffle interrupted my thoughts. "See, it *is* my fault you died then... because I begged you to come to school here."

I gave her a forbidding look. "It was not! **Do. Not. *Ever*. Say. That. Again**."

Cherie looked sheepishly happy as she nodded.

I shook my head and brought myself back to the present. "I don't know how long we have, but I have to tell you, Cherie, you're going to be okay. You have to try harder to be all right," I scolded her without meaning to.

"I'm trying. I promise I am."

"You were always the leader. You were always the strong one."

"I was?" Cherie sounded so unsure, so unlike herself.

I nodded. "Yes. I've been following you my whole life."

"Maybe I'm only strong when I have you watching my back."

I pulled her in for a tight hug, "You are always strong. I love you, Cherie. You're my best friend—always."

"You, too." She reached for my hand, but instead of connecting, it went through me. She shook her head desperately. "No! It wasn't long enough. I need more time!" I could hear the hysteria creeping into her voice.

"Just remember, you need to cause enough trouble now for both of us. I love you." There was an ear shattering pop as our bubble burst. The force of it threw me back and I collapsed on the floor. I shook my head, dazed.

Brent was instantly by my side, his face still strained with worry. I sat up, feeling dizzy.

"You vanished. I was afraid I had lost you," Brent said, his voice ragged. "I had no idea what had happened and I was afraid I'd never see you again." Brent leaned toward me and rested his forehead against mine, breathing deeply, his eyes glistening with more moisture than normal. "I've never felt so alone. It was like I had lost . . . Yara, I . . ." he stopped, closing his eyes.

I could feel the blackness and emptiness the incident had caused in him, surprised by its intensity. He lifted his hands to my cheeks, opening his eyes and staring into mine. Something unspoken passed between us, creating an intimacy that hadn't been there before. A gush of warmth spread through me. My dead heart did a little flip in my chest as I gazed into Brent's eyes; they were liquid, like melted chocolate, full of unspoken promises I could almost hear. His minty breath was warm on my face, his thumb traced my bottom lip as he leaned in closer.

"Yara," he whispered at the same time Cherie called "Yara," from across the room.

My eyes slid past Brent toward her, slamming the door on the moment we had just shared. There wasn't much I could do for Cherie anymore, aside from stopping Thomas. She was beyond my ability to comfort. I was past the point of being much use to anyone . . . anyone but Brent. My eyes cut to Brent, then darted back and forth between the two, my past and my present, settling finally on Brent's cocoa brown eyes.

My world lurched, a spasm of dizziness spun through me, and I brought my fingers to my head to steady myself. When the emotional earthquake stopped, I climbed to my feet, stumbling slightly. Brent held out his hand and made sure I was stable before releasing me, my skin hot from his touch. I peeked at him, shyly, from the corner of my eye hoping to see some proof that something had altered in him as well, but he seemed unchanged. He still had the same teasing smile, the same mischievous eyes and casual stance. By all appearances, he was the same old Brent, not one who had been so shaken when he thought he'd lost me. I had to wonder, inside the part of my mind where I could hide such thoughts from him, if I was imagining these significant moments.

Cherie reached out to where I had been standing in our bubble then wrapped her arms around herself. Her grief was still strong, but I could also sense that a kernel of hope had been planted inside her. Her eyes swept around the room as if she knew I was still there, smiling as her hope took root and blossomed.

"Bye, Yara." She waved goodbye, walking a little taller than she had when she came in. I trailed behind her, following her outside, then watched her leave, knowing she'd be alright. Another hurt that had haunted me was now starting to heal itself, right now it might be like putting a Band-Aid over a wound that needed stitches and was gushing blood, but eventually it would get better.

"Is it always harder for the ones we leave behind?" I asked.

"When you disappeared into that bubble, I thought I was the one left behind. And yes, I think it is."

My eyes followed Cherie until I lost her shape in the night's gathering shadows. The moment seemed symbolic— me staying behind with Brent, while wistfully watching as Cherie moved forward in a yet undetermined future. For a few minutes more, I stared at the place where Cherie had disappeared from my sight, trying to imagine myself still beside her. The image wouldn't form in my imagination; all it could conjure was me walking the path in the opposite direction, next to Brent.

A serene smile plastered itself on my face as I angled toward him, resting against one of the glass walls. "I had no idea that death could be so complicated. One death influences so many people."

Brent stared past me, thinking. "Yeah."

I pushed off the wall and walked back into the building feeling Brent behind me. He almost gagged before he covered his mouth and nose. "What is that awful smell?"

I breathed in deeply with a smile. "It isn't awful. It's beautiful. It's Cherie."

"Well, 'Cherie' is so potent, we're going to be smelling her everywhere on campus for days."

"I love it." My fingers played with the necklace Cherie had given me. "She brought me a gift."

"She was able to put that on you?" Brent's eyes opened wide and he rocked back on his heels, as he studied the necklace curiously.

"Yep— it was Vovó's idea." I then told him all the new information I had received from Cherie.

Brent bit his nails, thinking. "Your grandma seems to know a lot."

"Yeah, she does. All that time I wanted her to be normal; turns out she was smarter than the whole bunch."

"It seems to be that way with life."

I felt the familiar pull, taking me to reenact my death.

*   *   *   *

Everything was black. I felt empty, like some part of me was missing. I had no idea where I was or who I was. I was being rocked gently and I could hear the sounds of heavy footsteps, the crunching of broken glass and labored breathing. I felt a vibration around my neck, lulling me out of my hypnotic slumber, forcing me to pay attention. Still everything was dark, but something was familiar in the air, a smell that I recognized. It reminded me of something, but I didn't know what. Still, it pulled and tugged at my memory, urging me to remember. I inhaled deeply and for the briefest of seconds a girl with blue eyes and golden blonde hair flashed in my mind. She had a name. I knew it... *Cherie*. I dredged the name from somewhere deep inside my foggy brain.

Where am I?

I was being rocked . . .no, I was being carried to. . . someplace horrible. The person holding me against him wanted to hurt me. I was in danger. My muscles twitched as I feebly tried to break free. Fingers sunk into my skin, and the pace picked up. I tried to lift my heavy eyelids, only managing to open them a crack, enough to see everything was draped in darkness. My tired arms lifted and I scratched at the face I couldn't see. The figure held me tighter, squeezing even harder, crushing my ribs. I gasped as the air was forced from my chest. Flailing, my foot made contact with my assailant. His grip slackened and I fell into the pool with a huge splash, sending water up my nose.

Wiping the water from my eyes I swam away from him toward the other side of the pool.

"Help," I screamed between frantic strokes. Another huge splash rippled the water. My heart shuddered in my chest as I glanced over my shoulder, breathing raggedly, afraid he was coming after me. I couldn't see what had caused the splash, but something was sinking behind me. I reached the far edge of the pool, my trembling fingers curling around the cement as I started to pull myself up. But something strong pushed down on the top of my head, shoving me cruelly underwater.

Water flooded into my open mouth, tunneling down my throat. My mind cried out, trying desperately to communicate with my friends, *Help me. He's trying to drown me.* He dove in beside me and the warm blood in my veins crystallized in fear. Struggling to the surface I gasped for life-giving air. I panted for a few glorious seconds before a painful tug of my ankles pulled me down. I clamped my mouth closed just in time, before being forced back under. He crooked his arm around my throat and pulled me like a rag doll across the pool and further under the water. He held me firm while I elbowed, kicked and swung my arms at him, trying to break free. He responded by tightening his hold on my neck and yanking me down further, while white spots of light burst behind my retinas. His free hand grabbed the hem of my dress and looped it through something.

My arms flailed again, frantically trying in some way to stop him or at least to injure him as he bent his legs and pushed off from the bottom of the pool. His foot struck my face as he kicked his way toward the surface. I reached in vain to grab onto his legs.

I watched his distorted image climb out of the pool without a backward glance. I was alone in the pool. Alone in my fate. The water was crushing me, pushing me down. My lungs burned with the pressure and swam in lethal levels of carbon dioxide. I groped desperately at my dress trying to pry it free from where it was caught. It was no use. Reaching behind my back, I tried to undo the slippery buttons. But there were too many and my numbed fingers were too clumsy to undo them. I kicked and pulled at the water with all I had but my body hovered at the bottom of the pool.

I'm dying.

My hair and beautiful dress swirled around me like an eerie scene from a movie. And it seemed familiar, that I had watched before. It didn't scare me anymore. I already knew the ending. I remembered in a brief instant of clarity that I had died before, that I was already dead. Everything came back to me in a rush. In my mind I directed my thoughts toward Brent, but pictured Steve's face. *Help me! Brent, hurry! I'm drowning. It's my dress; it's caught. You'll have to cut it free.*

I was tempted to waste what little air was left in my lungs on a scream, but I didn't. Even as it felt like my insides would burst, I held on. I knew help was coming this time. Through the water I saw the lights flip on, followed by Steve and Cherie's images flickering down to me. I smiled as the world around me went black.

* * * *

There was light behind my eyelids and they fluttered open for a second. I was on the ground with Cherie and Steve around me. My lips lifted in a wan smile before my eyes slid closed.

When I reopened them I was standing beside Brent, watching my friends work on my body. I stretched and felt quite giddy about having put up a fight before I died.

"I feel different. Did I fix it?"

Gruffly Brent answered, "No." He slammed his fist against one of the plastic tables making it quiver. "You still died. I was so close." He swore angrily, then sighed deeply. "I got your messages loud and clear, though. That was smart."

"Messages?"

"Well, your first one for general help made Steve stop for a second and wonder what was going on. That got him coming toward the pool, worried about you. But the second time, when you called directly to me, I woke up and took charge. I knew exactly what to do. It was weird because I had all of Steve's knowledge, but I was in control. It was genius."

"It almost worked. Maybe another night?" I offered with an encouraging grin. I examined myself lying on the ground and saw my dress had been torn to shreds.

"I had to cut you free. It was caught on the drain this time," Brent explained, watching the CPR. "Steve carried a pocket knife and I made sure he had it ready before we even came into the room."

"I figured you would have to cut it. Too bad I was wearing this impractical dress."

Brent eyed me up and down. "Still, it does look nice on you."

I pretended to ignore the compliment, while secretly relishing it. Fighting the urge to preen, I changed the subject abruptly. "When I was my empty shell, the necklace woke me up a tiny bit and then I was able to smell Cherie's perfume. It almost saved me."

A smile formed at my lips as I sent Cherie a silent thank you.

Brent sat on a pool chair and dropped his head. "If only we had been a minute earlier. If only Steve could have run faster. I . . . he could have saved you."

"I don't think you were supposed to. I think . . . I was meant to die." I was grappling to find the words to explain to Brent the peace I had already made with death.

"You didn't *die*; you were murdered."

"True." That fact still chilled me to my very soul. I found myself still trembling slightly at the thought that someone had killed me. "I think I changed it enough to set it right. Maybe I created some sort of physical evidence so they can catch the jerk. And bring him to justice. Perhaps it was meant to be this way."

I sat down next to Brent as understanding flooded through me, understanding I had refused to see before. "I do think I was meant to die. I think . . ." I blushed as I struggled to find the words. "I was meant to save you. This proves things can change. It's too late for me, but we can still get your body back." Brent looked uncertain but I knew I was right. "That's what all of this is about— stopping the curse and returning you to your body."

Did I want to die? No, but if my death saved Brent, then it meant something. Brent was such a good guy and still had so much to offer the world.

"So, you're proposing that it was the universe's design that you die so I can live?"

"Yes, and break the curse," I said, wrapping my finger around one of the shredded ends of my dress.

"Well, screw the universe." Brent started out of his chair and leaned against the round table he had punched earlier, his back toward me.

Gathering my courage, I went to Brent and placed my hand on his arm. "It's okay, Brent. I'm not sad. I never really understood how people could be willing to die to save someone they love, but I get that now."

"Love?" He asked the question guardedly, clamping down on the emotions I could read from him.

My heart rose to my throat. I tried to speak but found myself stuttering instead, "I . . . that . . . isn't what I meant

. . ." I gulped, dropping my hand from his arm.

Brent spun around. "What did you mean then?"

Words, thoughts, feelings all abandoned me as I stared into Brent's eyes. A wide chasm seemed to separate us now and I wasn't sure if a bridge could be built. A drop of water landed on my arm and was followed by more plinks of moisture. It took me a moment to realize that it was my tears that were wetting my arm. I was crying and I wasn't sure why.

Brent rocked back on his heels and rubbed the back of his neck, not knowing how to respond. My slip of words had totally freaked him out. My chest constricted as I stared at him. I mean, it's not as if I had meant the words, not in the way he was thinking; I totally didn't—well, maybe I meant them a little, but he was completely overreacting. It was almost physically painful, like my heart was actually being squeezed hard, twisted in a vise. It released and then crushed in agony again. I brought my hand to my heart pressing against the pain. I felt an echoing, a reminder of something that had happened long ago, something I had experienced before but that I never had thought twice about. He let out a puff of air, avoiding my gaze. He stared at Steve, still bent over my body like it was fascinating, like he hadn't seen it seventy times before.

The pain in my chest returned and I gasped from its intensity, folding myself in half. A clammy chill kissed my skin as the light dimmed, a black fog slipping past the corner of my vision. Pupils dilating, I glanced at Brent, his fingers flexing and unflexing, preparing for battle. He motioned for me to move closer. Still doubled over, I slid my foot closer to Brent but pain spasmed in me again and I stumbled, grabbing my chest, crumpling to the floor. I screamed in a mixture of terror and pain as a strong force grabbed my waist and yanked me away from Brent. He had been tracking the mist's movement but wheeled toward me as I was dragged away from him, still struggling against my unseen foe.

The mist swirled angrily, following behind me. I didn't understand; if the mist was still trying to capture me, then what had me? I had no idea where I was being taken, but I was more concerned for Brent who seemed unaware that the mist was drawing closer to him.

"Run!" I screamed. He stood frozen in place, watching me being pulled further from him, his hand outstretched. Each side of Brent's face stood out in stark contrast to the other. The flickering fluorescent light illuminated one half and the other was wrapped in darkness. It seemed to paint him as half hero and half villain. *Go now!* I begged hysterically.

Brent stepped toward me and I felt him trying to pull me back. Despite his strength, I continued sliding further from him, his efforts no more than a gentle tug.

My voice came out weakly, "Please, save yourself."

The sensation in my chest was increasing in frequency and pressure. It had been painful at first but faint and irregular, now it was steady and strong. The feeling again reminded me of something. And suddenly I knew; my heart was beating again. Wildly I looked at Brent. He returned my gaze in understanding; he knew, too. He dropped his arms, his shoulders and head sagged as he released me. Brent's shape was becoming lost as the world became too light and too dark at the same time.

I needed to make sure Brent was all right. I needed to know he had hadn't been captured. I shook my head violently, trying to clear my vision. Everything had lost its color. In my stomach I felt a wrenching sting as the link between Brent and I was severed. In vain I tried to feel his

fate before the darkness enveloped me.

CHAPTER 15

From far away, I heard a voice sweetly call my name, a voice I didn't recognize. My eyelids felt like they had been anchored down and it required superhuman strength to open them. For half a second, I managed to peek out at the world. A woman who I didn't know was standing beside me. After a few more attempts, I managed to keep my eyes open. A bright fluorescent light hummed above me. I didn't understand where I was, but the woman was still there. She had a kind face that housed thoughtful hazel eyes, and long hair the color of molasses. I guessed she was a doctor by the white lab coat she was wearing and the stethoscope around her neck. I blinked at her in confusion.

"Hello Yara. I'm Dr. McCubbin. Do you know why you're here?"

It sounded like an easy enough question. As my mind grasped for answers I looked around for the first time. I was in a hospital room, sterile, devoid of personality, painted a non-descript color of white with a yellowing ceiling and faded charts clinging to the walls. A tattered chair was positioned next to my bed. I had no idea how I had ended up here. My head felt heavy as I pressed against the thin pillow. I lifted my hands to wipe at my eyes only to find them connected to an IV and several other machines.

"No," I answered hoarsely, my raw throat making my voice sound scratchy. I swallowed, trying to clear the sandpaper feel, but that only made it hurt more. In fact, my whole body ached, and I rearranged myself, trying to ease the throbbing pain and suffering. It didn't help. "It hurts."

The doctor smiled at me kindly, tapping my IV. "I know. The drugs will kick in soon."

I closed my eyes, willing the drugs to work faster, taking the opportunity to try to remember why I needed to visit the hospital. I concentrated my thoughts backward, trying to replay events that had led me here. I remembered the dinner party Cherie had thrown, and then talking with Brent after it in the pool house. The idea of the pool brought a feeling of dread I was at a loss to explain.

The events seemed like a chalk drawing in a rainstorm, important details being washed away by the water, leaving behind a smudged slate. I attempted to coax my memory further, but it didn't work. Every time I concentrated, the answers danced out of view, taunting me just out of reach, yet I knew what eluded me was important and it was vital that I remember.

Panic tightened around my heart and my chest clenched. I tried to breathe deeply but my lungs refused to comply. Shallow breaths were coming too fast and I was forced to close my eyes against the suddenly spinning room. I never would have believed how terrifying it could be not to remember and understand what had happened.

"Why can't I remember?"

With all the reassurance of a soothing mother, the doctor reached out and took my hand. "Sometimes our minds protect us from things that are too painful. I think the memories might come back to you, when and if you are ready." My breathing still wouldn't slow and I was afraid I would pass out. She slipped an oxygen mask over my mouth and pulled a chair over, sitting down as she slowly inhaled. "Breathe with me." I nodded in understanding as I forced myself to follow her deep breaths. I had no idea how long it took, but finally I calmed.

"Is it okay if I do my check up on you now? Your family would like to see you." She motioned behind her.

I lifted the mask away from my face. "They're here?"

When she nodded, a smile that radiated from the depths of my soul spread across my face and warmed every inch of my being. It felt like an eternity since I had seen them. I endured her questions and poking and prodding until I was cleared for visitors.

Soon Melanie, my older sister, who must have driven hours from her college to reach me here, flanked by Cherie, and Steve, entered the room. I was surprised not to see Brent with them. The doctor gave me a knowing smile as she left. "It's remarkable that you three triplets look nothing alike."

My brow wrinkle in confusion and for a brief second I wondered how hard I had hit my head.

"They were only going to let family in," Cherie explained as she sat beside me and curled herself into an upright ball. I nodded in understanding at my "siblings". I felt the final tethers of anxiety subside. My memories would come back eventually, hopefully. All that mattered was that my loved ones surrounded me. The rest would work itself out.

Cherie's eyes were red and swollen from crying. "You're lucky you're okay. I would never have forgiven you if you had died, Yara."

I cleared my throat and flinched. "Was it really as serious as that?" The expressions on everyone's faces was the only answer I needed.

"The paramedics said if Steve hadn't given you CPR, they would have been too late," Melanie said, taking my hand as she sat beside me. She rested her chin on the bed's metal bars. Her free hand used a Kleenex to wipe away the moisture that still leaked from her eyes.

I tried to make eye contact with Steve, my hero. For a second I caught his gaze but he looked away. He seemed almost . . . haunted, leaning in the corner, his arms folded.

"It would seem that you brought me back from the dead." When I said this, my heart beat hard against my ribs, as if recognizing the significance of my words more than my mind. "Thank you."

Steve bowed majestically, seeming more like himself.

" 'Tis all in a day's work, m'lady. Know ye any more dragons that need slaying?"

Melanie's cell phone started vibrating in her purse. She checked the screen and smiled. "It's Mom and Dad. I better take this. Mom has been calling every fifteen minutes since the school called her." I watched her leave, guilt twinging inside of me for causing so much worry to my loved ones.

"Do you know what happened?" Cherie asked.

I shook my head, hoping to clear the fog in my memory. I could tell Cherie had tons of information to share but right as she opened her mouth the doctor came in.

"I'm sorry but I'm going to have to ask all of you to leave now. She needs her rest."

"Doesn't she get to come home with us?" Cherie pleaded with puppy dog eyes.

"No. We need to keep her a while longer for observation."

Cherie, to my surprise, stood up without protest. She hugged me tightly. "Don't worry," she whispered, "we'll find a way back in."

That sounded more like the Cherie I knew. As my grogginess increased I heard the doctor begin to explain what had happened to me but I couldn't understand her words as I drifted off to sleep.

* * * *

I woke with a start and my body complained. I searched my memory to see if any further clue about my accident had resurfaced, but the smudged slate was still my only answer.

"Are you awake?"

I jumped in surprise.

A small chuckle escaped Steve's throat. "Sorry to scare you."

I turned to face him and stretched out my hand to loosen my aching muscles. My hands felt stiff and inflexible under all the bandages.

Steve answered my unasked question. "You scratched your hands pretty bad trying to free yourself before I got you out of the pool."

"The pool?"

"You almost drowned, Yara," Steve said, his blue eyes exhausted.

"I did?" A flickering vision of struggling underwater flashed in my head but vanished before it could fully form. I examined my frayed nails and for a second I remembered my hand making contact with something. Try as I might, there was nothing more, and instantly the image I had conjured was lost behind the fog in my brain. I groaned in frustration.

"And you saved me?"

Steve smiled into the right side of his mouth. "Yeah."

"So you're the man of my dreams, huh?"

Steve startled upright in his chair.

I reached out and grabbed his hand with a laugh. "I

didn't mean it that way. I kept having this creepy dream about drowning and in it a guy tried to save me. That must have been you." He settled back into his chair. "Thank you, Steve. You have my best friend stamp of approval for dating Cherie."

He hung his head down, the long evening taking its toll. "What were you thinking?" He asked, seeming uncomfortable. "Swimming in that dress. Alone. It was wound tight around the drain. You almost died. Do you know what that would have done to Cherie? I almost stopped doing CPR. I thought you were gone." I could see his chin clench in defiance. "Yara, I almost gave up."

Tears puddled along my eyelashes. "But you didn't."

"Yeah, but knowing how close I came will always haunt me." He paused and he seemed to be deliberating something. "The whole thing was strange. I was with Cherie and I knew you were in trouble. I started coming toward you and then . . . it was like I was someone else or something until I was doing CPR. I can look back at myself doing those things, but I don't . . ." he trailed off, raking his fingers through his dirty blond hair.

"How did you know I was in trouble?"

"You called me." He eyed me carefully, judging my reaction.

"I called you?" I cocked my head to the side.

"In a way. I heard your voice clearly in my mind. At first I thought it was my imagination. Then you called to me again but this time you told me you were drowning. Somehow I even knew to have my pocket knife ready."

"Wow."

Steve nodded slowly and I could tell there was more. "The strange thing is, in my mind, you called me Brent." He pulled on a loose thread of the chair's mauve fabric, looping it around his finger. "I've been replaying it and I know that's what I heard."

Involuntarily, my hand raised to my mouth, covering it in surprise. "I don't know what to say."

"I guess it doesn't matter." Steve reclined deeper into his chair, unraveling the thread even more. "There's something else. The cops ruled this an accident after talking to Brent and all of us . . . but I could have sworn when I first came in I saw a set of wet footprints leading away from the pool. Were you alone in there, Yara?"

The machine next to me beeped faster as my heart began to race. The room suddenly felt ten times smaller and a cold sweat broke out across my brow. "I . . . I can't remember. I . . ."

"Calm down." Steve placed a reassuring hand on mine. "I'm sorry to just throw that at you. Sometimes my tongue gets away from me." Steve's eyes crinkled warmly as he smiled. "I'm probably wrong. I wasn't really paying atten-tion— everything was happening so fast." Steve exhaled slowly. "You didn't die tonight; that's all that matters." Steve stood up from his chair and stretched out his long arms. "I'll go tell Cherie you're awake."

I stared after him, knowing I was missing something, not sure what it was and suddenly afraid to remember.

* * * *

Considering how close I had come to an untimely death, it was surprising to see how stubbornly my normal, boring life reasserted itself. Apparently not even a hospital stay could stop the unceasing tide of homework. I was in the commons building, mentally cursing at the chart of all the homework I had to make up. I had staked out a table farthest from the wall-to-wall windows, to avoid distrac-tions. My backpack was tossed onto the chair beside me, my feet were kicked up on the one directly across from me, and my textbooks and notes were strewn across the battered tabletop.

The rasp of a throat being cleared had me looking up to a sheepish Brent. He cracked his knuckles as he watched me. I hadn't seen him in a few days, not since the night of my accident. He hadn't called or checked up on me once. My eyes narrowed and my mouth tightened in a frown.

"Can I join you?"

"Can you spare the time?" I asked acidly.

"I deserve that."

With a grunt of agreement I nodded, inviting him to sit, even removing my feet for him. He sat down and I noticed several long and painful-looking scratches on his face. His brown eyes, edged with bright green, were carefully studying me.

"What happened? Wrestle with a cat?"

He looked down with a nervous laugh. "Oh, I tried to sneak off campus and ended up crashing Coach Tait's car. I got some cuts from the glass."

"Did you end up in the E.R. too?"

Brent shook his head. "No, the nurse cleaned me up good enough."

"You tried to steal Coach Tait's car?" I whistled. "Wow, you must be in a ton of trouble."

"That's putting it mildly." He cracked his knuckles again before continuing. "You're probably wondering what I'm doing here."

"Yeah," I admitted.

"I wanted to apologize to you. I felt guilty about not seeing you in the hospital. Well, for that and leaving you alone at the pool that night. Maybe if I'd stayed . . ."

"Yeah," I mumbled, running my eraser across my

Language Arts notes.

"I was scared. I mean it isn't every night you tell a girl you love her and she says it back. Then you spill grape juice on yourself like an idiot, leave to change your clothes, and come back to find out she almost drowned. And then steal a car to see her at the hospital but get in an accident, get put on probation, and then never get the chance to visit her . . ." Brent explained, his words tumbling out of his mouth. "If I hadn't spilled my drink, then—"

My mouth gaped open. "What?"

"It's my fault," Brent explained.

"I don't remember any of that, but it wasn't your fault." I said tapping my pencil against the table.

"You don't remember any of it?"

I shook my head.

"Not even that I told you I loved you and you said it back?" He asked with a frown.

"I told you I loved you?"

Brent gave me a triumphant smile. "You did."

"Sorry, I don't remember," I admitted quietly.

Brent's face fell but his eyes had a gleam of joy in them. "Oh, what do you remember?"

I thought carefully, feeling an importance to his question I didn't understand. "I . . . remember talking to you about your brother appearing at the party but that . . . that's it."

"Nothing else?"

"No," I sighed sadly.

"Does that mean I won't get another declaration of love?"

I laughed nervously. "Not right now." I was still shocked I had forgotten such an important conversation, accident or no.

"I'll try to keep my disappointment in check," Brent grumbled under his breath.

For a second his brown eyes seemed to grow cold, the thin line of green around his iris thickening, and I tensed unexpectedly, but it was gone so quickly I was sure I had imagined it. My shoulder throbbed and I scratched at it, noticing a raised ridge on the skin. I let the collar of my shirt slip down, exposing my bare shoulder, and revealing a brutal black scar there. I could only assume it had happened in the pool, but it didn't look that new.

I looked up at Brent and found him checking out my scar with intense eyes. I pulled my shirt back together and crossed my legs. Brent shook his head like he was trying to remember what he had been saying.

"I really think you should avoid astral projecting for a while. It's too dangerous."

"Dangerous? Life and death dangerous?" The words life and death seemed more ominous than they had just a few days ago. "Why?"

He leaned forward, bringing himself close to me as he whispered in my ear, "There's something out there that worries me."

"Okay— I'm an easy sell on being careful these days."

Brent seemed satisfied with my answer and pulled out a notebook from his backpack. "You missed a very important lab while you were in the hospital. Coach Tait said he'd be willing to have you come after school and make it up." He gave me a smile that didn't quite reach his eyes as he went over his notes with me.

*　　*　　*　　*

"You know it's cruel of our teachers to have you make up all of your missed assignments," Cherie said, throwing herself dramatically on her bed. "How am I supposed to have any fun while you're up to your eyeballs in homework?"

"Well, you have Steve."

Cherie blushed. "Yes. I suppose I do. Still, it isn't the same. You've been studying nonstop for days. I miss you."

"I'm almost caught up."

"I know." She sat up on her bed and glanced at me for a minute. "Do you still not remember anything that happened?"

"No," I answered, shaking my head. "I keep hoping it will come back. Every once in a while I think I remember something, but then it disappears."

Cherie shrugged, disappointed. I closed my eyes once more trying to focus all of my collective power on remembering. Still nothing. Anger and frustration rose inside of me. It was building so strong that I felt for a moment that it might overpower me. I opened my eyes, stood up and began pacing around the confines of our small room. I stopped in front of my chest of drawers and directed my pent up anger at my mirror. I dropped my arm and pointed at my image. "Remember!" I commanded myself. I didn't remember anything, but I did jump back as my mirror shattered.

Both Cherie and I screamed. I looked at the broken mirror and wondered if I had done that. What exactly happened to me when I almost drowned? Had I come back different? A chill ran down my spine. Maybe I really was better off not knowing.

Cherie grabbed me hard and spun me around. "What was that?"

"I have no idea." My fingers and toes started tingling and I was afraid I was going to project. Breathing deeply, I slowed my heart.

"Did you throw something at it?" I shook my head and tried to break free of Cherie's grasp. Her fingers closed even more firmly around my arm. "How did you do that?"

"I don't know," I said honestly.

Cherie looked at me like she didn't know me. "I didn't know Wakers could do that."

"I'm not sure they can."

"Then how did you do it? Can you do it again?"

I stared at the shards of glass sprinkling my chest of drawers and considered my answer. It reminded me of how Brent had manipulated the wind and moved things from a distance. He had told me that with practice I could do it too. But this had felt so controlled, like part of me knew what I was doing, like I had been doing for it a long time. "I'm not sure how I did it, but it didn't feel like a fluke. I think I could do it again."

The radio in the room suddenly snapped itself on so loud that Cherie and I both pressed our palms to our ears to protect them. The old song "Can't Stop Dreaming of You" filled the room while Cherie grabbed for the volume knob. I watched her spin the dial but the song continued, eardrum-busting loud. The crooner's voice was clear and sweet.

You promised me undying love
That always you'd be mine,
But now you're loving someone else
And leaving me behind.
I put my trust in you, my love,
But life's not what it seems.
Your love for me I thought was real
Lived only in my dreams

I could almost feel the words inside me, calling to me like a siren's song, begging me to listen. It brought back memories of Brent. But it was more than that. Wasn't it? My mind replayed the words of the verse and my heart broke. The next verse though put a feeling of foreboding in my chest.

I wish that you could understand
And see, and know, and feel
He cannot love you as I do,
He cannot be as real.
I hope that you will listen, dear,
To the message that I send,
'Cause if you choose to stay with him
He'll only hurt you in the end.

When the verse ended, the radio snapped itself off. I knew instinctively the song was connected to my accident. There was some clandestine message in the lyrics I was meant to decipher. I had no idea how or why, but I suddenly knew that someone needed me.

The next afternoon, I picked up my backpack, intending to study at the library— but some sort of internal compass guided me toward the garden that Brent had taken me to the night of the dance. Despite only having been there once, my feet easily found the way.

I settled myself inside the gazebo, feeling at home, safe and loved, more than I had at any time since the night I had almost drowned. Ever since my accident I had felt lonely, like I had lost something that night, some part of me. Being here, that feeling shrank.

Scratching an itch on my collarbone, I remembered my necklace was still in the plastic bag the hospital had put it in. Fishing my pencil out of my notebook, I began another round of homework catch-up. After half an hour, my back ached from bending over my book and my head throbbed from conjugating Spanish verbs.

"Knock, knock," Brent called, rapping his knuckles on the wooden post.

"Hey, Brent."

"I was going to ask if you wanted to study for the Bio exam together," he said, pointing to the textbook in his hand.

"Oh. Um, sure." I chewed on my bottom lip. "How did you know I was here?"

Brent ducked his head, seeming suddenly shy. "I saw you head into the groves, and followed when I had a chance."

"Any particular reason?"

"I'm pretty sure you know why," he said, leaning against the gazebo and giving me a confident smile.

My books slipped off my lap and clattered onto the wooden floor. He knelt beside me as I bent to pick them up, and his pant leg pulled up, revealing a black cloud-shaped scar. I'd seen one like it before and yet I couldn't place it. I was so focused on the scar, I almost missed him leaning in close, staring at my lips. *He's going to kiss me.* My palms were suddenly clammy. His new cologne surrounded me, a fusion of spearmint, ginger, and another scent that made me queasy. The troubling underlying odor smelled like . . . chlorine. A riptide of wrongness pulled me back from Brent's parted lips.

SMACK.

Something whacked me in the forehead, knocking me off balance, landing me on my butt, as an orange rolled past my feet. Feeling dizzy from the blow, I glanced up and saw a blurry Brent in double vision. I closed my eyes, rubbing them with my fists as I shook my head, trying to dislodge the visual abnormality, but when I opened them again they were both still there: one Brent inside the gazebo kneeling next to me and the other standing just over his left shoulder in the groves, mouthing angrily, "He isn't me."

In a mind-numbing, earth-tilting, stomach-heaving rush, everything I had forgotten came back. My fingers splayed over my temples and my head fell forward as I absorbed the fact that I had been murdered, Brent and I had been trapped on campus, and I had been brought back to life while the mist had been chasing Brent. My body went cold, black dots danced in front of my eyes, and my fingers tingled.

A strong arm went around my shoulders and I flinched. "Are you okay? What happened?"

He was an imposter— not Brent, but Thomas. He had killed me once already and here I was, alone in his embrace. I bit down hard on my lip hoping that would stop my hands from shaking. A sliver of wood impaled itself into my hand as I scooted away from Thomas, freeing myself. Teetering to my feet I leaned against the wooden railing of the gazebo, my eyes sliding toward where Brent had retreated into the trees.

Thomas came up behind me and placed his hands on my hips, resting his chin on my shoulder.

"You look like you've seen a ghost," he whispered into my ear. It could have been an off-hand statement, but there was an undercurrent of suspicion in it that sprouted panic in my gut.

My toes curled hard, fighting to keep me standing. I wheeled toward him and leaned heavily against the wood behind me. It was beyond important that I didn't let him know my memory had returned. I had to convince him I still believed he was Brent. More than just my life depended on it.

Stretching up on my toes I planted a very chaste kiss on his lips that tasted sickly of chlorine. My stomach rolled, wanting to heave as I threw my arms around him, holding him tight.

"I do want to study for Bio with you, but I forgot I have a study group. I better get back to my room so I can get my notes."

"I'll walk you back," he said, grinning and taking my hand in his. The pressure of his palm stabbed the sliver deeper into my skin, drawing blood.

*　*　*　*

Brent was waiting for me in my room. The difference between Thomas masquerading in Brent's body and Brent himself was undeniable. Thomas might be just as good looking when he was pretending to be Brent, but he was a poor, sloppy version of him. He lacked, and couldn't fake, the part of Brent that truly made him so appealing, so . . . beautiful: his essence. Brent was more than handsome— he had a warmth and goodness in his soul that couldn't be duplicated.

I closed the door and paused, holding tight to the door-knob as I leaned back against it, my feet shuffling beneath me. Brent lounged against the window, his thumbs tucked into his pant pockets. I closed my eyes and breathed in the comforting musky smell of him, his scent pushing me past my momentary shyness, I ran toward him to throw my arms around him but missed. Actually, I didn't so much miss as fall through him, headfirst into my desk, my body quaking with the cold the whole way.

"Are you okay?" He laughed quietly, looking over his shoulder at the heap of me.

"Ow!" I said, rubbing my head where it had made

contact with the corner of the desk. "I should have known that would happen," I grumbled. I stood up, wiping my hands and holding them up as proof that I was undamaged. "Nothing harmed but my pride."

"Still throwing yourself at me I see."

"At least I wasn't trying to hit you." I wrapped my arms around myself. "Are you always so cold?"

"You know, you really shouldn't be touching me in such an intimate manner. I might get the wrong idea." Brent dropped down to the edge of my mattress and his eyes swept over our room, stopping occasionally to study a poster or picture.

"Right, I'll try not to defile your innocent spirit anymore," I said with a grin.

"Thank you. I wouldn't want my reputation tarnished."

I laughed and sat down next to Brent, positioning myself to face him, bringing my pillow across my lap. "I guess I'm a full-fledged Waker now, because I can totally see and hear you."

"I was getting worried. I've been trying to contact you since your accident but you couldn't see me. I turned on the radio to our song and everything. What happened?"

"I got my memory back. I guess you should have pelted me with an orange earlier."

We exchanged grins. Curiously, I reached out and tried to touch his face, feeling nothing more than cold air. He placed his hand over mine, tickling my fingers with a soft frosty breeze. "I can almost feel you. Or rather, I can feel a chill, letting me know where you should be." My spine sagged with my heart and the corners of his lips twitched south. "This is unacceptable." I left my body, grabbed him, and hugged him fiercely. "That's better."

A laugh rumbled through him as held me close. "Did

you really think you could get rid of me so easily?"

I burrowed my face into the crook of his neck, breathing in his citrusy, musky scent, as his arms tightened around my waist.

"Could you please get back in your body, though?" He asked, pulling back without releasing me. "It's making me nervous."

"I want to be able to touch you, to make sure you're real." He pinched me and I scowled at him, making him laugh again as he shooed me back toward my body. I reentered, shivering at the rush of cold that trampled through me.

"Put on your necklace too, please." He said, pointing toward the plastic bag on my chest of drawers. "And never take it off again,"

With an apologetic smile I pulled it from the bag and clasped it around my neck. I became conscious of his intense brown eyes focusing on me. A blush spread across my face that deepened till I thought my cheeks might sunburn from the inside out. When he finally looked away, I chanced a look in his direction, letting my eyes caress his features. I noticed the corners of his mouth curve up and I knew that he had caught me, like a child with her hand in the cookie jar.

"I missed you."

Brent laughed without a trace of mirth. "Funny, I was thinking you had forgotten me."

Not wanting to meet his eyes I dropped my gaze and studied the sunlight whispering through the window, gliding across the carpet. "I had, but some part of me remembered. My last thought before I woke up in the hospital was worry for you. I was afraid Thomas had captured you."

Brent raked his fingers through his hair a few times,

standing up suddenly and pacing around my small room. "You kissed him."

"I did it to save my life, you idiot." I stood up, my hands on my hips, shoulders squared. "Yours, too."

"I know," he said, frowning, his fingernails hovering close to his lips, trying to fight the urge.

I tried to not smile at him. "You're not jealous, are you?"

Brent forced a chuckle. "No."

"For your information," I said, wagging my finger at him, "I was leaning away from him before you hit me with that orange. I wasn't going to kiss him."

Brent had the decency to look a little bit repentant. "I didn't know that until the last second." Brent gave in and started chewing on one of his nails again. "How did you know it wasn't me?"

"I didn't. I just knew something was wrong." I kicked off my shoes and tucked my feet under me as I sat down on Cherie's bed, across from Brent.

"I guess that's something," he said.

"He has the scar on his ankle that you got from the mist."

"Interesting."

My neighbor in the room beside mine turned on her radio so loud it shook the wall. Brent plugged his ears at her off-key vocal accompaniment of the emo lyrics floating into the room. "It's even worse without your body."

"Why is he trying to romance me?" I asked over the music, trying to get back on topic.

"Besides the fact that you're beautiful?"

My head snapped toward him. "What?"

Brent had the look of an escaping prisoner caught in the searchlight. "Nothing. He's just trying to keep an eye on you, making sure you don't remember anything."

My heart bounced merrily in my chest and I leaned toward Brent. In turn he bent toward me, elbows on his knees. "It's weird to see you wearing something besides that formal dress."

"Is it?"

Brent nodded. "Yeah. I'm beyond jealous that you just took off your shoes."

I stretched out my socked feet and wiggled my toes. "It does feel good. Those heels were killer."

Brent's eyes lingered on my toes with envy, then traveled slowly up my body to my face. "You were right from the start. Things could be fixed."

"We haven't fixed everything yet, though," I said, my voice tinged with disappointment. "How are we going to get your body back?"

Brent shrugged. "It doesn't matter."

I grabbed his hand or would have if it didn't slide right through mine. I projected again so I could hold his hand. "It does matter. It matters a lot."

He didn't answer right away and I held my breath looking up at my popcorn ceiling. Brent's emotions started to leak out in a chilly gust of wind that twirled around us, sending my curls flying around my face.

"Keeping you safe from Thomas is more important than getting my body back." He paused for a second tucking a few of the loose strands of my hair behind my ears, letting his hand trail softly down my neck to my shoulder. My body hummed like a well-played cello where he touched me. He leaned in closer and I found myself lost in the fire of his dark eyes. I felt the small gap of air separating us blistering with things unsaid, of chances missed. I couldn't breathe as he closed the space separating us, my heartbeat a frantic rhythm. The moment was perfect, as if scripted for a movie, and I strained to hear a smooth jazz swirl around us, the romantic music that informed the audience that the girl and the handsome boy were about to kiss. My eyes fluttered closed.

I waited hopefully, expectantly but was caught off guard by the friendly kiss planted on my cheek. The jazz screeched to a halt on a sour note and my eyes snapped open as I abruptly pulled back. The electrically-charged atmosphere effectively sputtered and died as if a bucketful of ice water had been thrown over it.

"Probably not the best idea," he said, his eyes still smoldering as he retreated to the window ledge. Did he mean the near kiss or getting his body back? Confused, I let my hair fall in front of my beet-red face to veil it from him, while hunching my shoulders.

"Me coming back to life is only the opening act," I said, trying desperately not to seem flustered. "The grand finale will be getting your body back, defeating Thomas, and freeing the others. We just need a good plan."

Brent's eyes sparkled with a devilish glint. "I have a few ideas."

CHAPTER 16

"That isn't a plan!" I yelled at Brent as I followed him into the tree line. He had dropped the bomb that he planned to just leave things the way they were, and then retreated out the window. Still being cautious, I had slid back into my body before storming after him. He had been waiting for me, but when I got close enough for him to hear my angry comments, he started walking again.

"Yes, it is," he answered over his shoulder vanishing behind a row of trees.

"Letting him get away with it?" I tried to say but the words tangled in my throat.

"It's the safest—"

"I don't care about tha—"

"I know you've got a lot of passion and courage, but you're not using your head."

I stopped dead in my tracks. "Really? Calling me stupid is your way to get me to agree with you?"

"No, I'm just hoping you'll stop for a moment and understand that I don't want you to risk dying again. If he gets even the smallest inkling of you not trusting him, he'll act."

"You really think he's going to just leave me alone?"

"No," Brent finally admitted, yanking at his collar,

trying to loosen it. "That doesn't mean you should put yourself in harm's way, though."

"Brent," I started, trying to sound reasonable. "How can you expect me to just leave things? He's going to keep coming after us and we're going to have to keep fighting him off. Haven't you heard the best defense is a good offense?"

"Yara, please remember, for the last few months I've watched you die before my eyes every single night and I was powerless to do anything about it." He laced his fingers together behind his head, his Adam's apple wobbling as he cleared his throat. "Please don't risk letting that happen again. You said you were willing to die for me," Brent reminded me, his voice barely a whisper. "Why shouldn't I be allowed to make the same sacrifice for you?"

"The circumstances are totally different," I argued. "I was already dead."

"So am I," Brent threw back at me.

"No, you're just bodily challenged."

Brent snickered for a second, his shoulders shaking. "Make it as PC as you want, but I'm dead. I will not let you do anything that would put you in danger."

"Is that so?" My eyebrows drew together and my eyes narrowed at him. "You can't stop me."

He held up his finger telling me to be quiet. "I'm warning you, if you try something stupid—"

"Are you threatening me?" I asked, throwing my hands in the air. "If you think you can tell me what to do—"

He gave me a menacing look. "I *will* stop you by *any* means necessary."

I collected my anger, hugging it tight to me, pretending it was gone. "You're right," I said opening my eyes wide, trying to appear and sound innocent. "It's stupid of me to mess with this. I'll let it go."

"Yeah right" Brent said, eyeing me suspiciously. "I don't trust you for a second."

"What? Why?" I sputtered, my anger unfurling around me.

He rolled his eyes at my question like it wasn't worth the air to answer it. "I don't trust you because I know you." Brent brought his fingers to his lips and shushed me. "Someone's coming."

The soft fall of footsteps drawing near to us had me holding my breath, my heart beating rapidly. The tension melted quickly when a vaguely familiar boy with strawberry blond hair and big gray eyes turned the corner. I was pretty sure I had a class with him, but I couldn't remember which one.

"Hey, Yara," he said with a slight southern drawl. "You gave me start. I thought I was alone."

"Hey . . ." I trailed off lamely, not having any idea of his name.

His cheeks grew two red spots. "Dallin."

"Right, Dallin," I gushed, hoping my enthusiasm would make up for my name ignorance.

He dropped his gaze to study his shoes. "We have Calculus together."

"Oh right. How did you do on that test?"

"I failed it." He sighed. "Rumor has it you got the highest grade."

I nodded, kicking the dirt. "Yeah."

Dallin took off the school uniform's pullover sweater and tossed it over his arm. Brent sighed in envy.

"I was actually hoping you might be willing to tutor me."

"Oh man, this is painful to watch." Brent broke out in laughter. "You do realize he's trying to ask you out, right?"

I glared at Brent before answering. "Sure."

"You better warn him about your habit of using that book as a weapon," Brent said.

"Only on you," I said under my breath.

"Only me what?" Dallin asked, not catching all of my words.

"I don't usually tutor people but I'll make an exception only for you," I lied easily.

Brent openly gaped at me. "Do you have any idea how that just sounded?"

Dallin drew himself up taller. "Great. Maybe tomorrow, right after school?"

"Sure? In the commons building?"

"Yep," he said. He took a deep breath, his cheeks puffing out. "Are you seeing Brent?"

I coughed back a laugh but my eyes still danced as I looked at Brent. "Not in the way you're thinking."

"I figured," Dallin said. "You know, with him not into the long term dating thing."

"Really?" My eyebrows raised under my bangs.

Brent's face had gone pale and he was shaking his head furiously. A strong wind picked up and lifted the russet colored curls off Dallin's face. "Yeah, something of a reputation."

"Huh."

"Anyway, since you aren't dating him, I was wondering if you wanted to go with me to the homecoming dance next weekend."

My eyeballs threatened to pop from their sockets. "Sure."

The air started whipping around us, lifting leaves and pebbles that were directed at Dallin, pelting him. My skirt and hair waved in the gusts and I shielded my eyes as small rock a bounced off of Dallin and flew toward me.

"Great." Dallin smiled broadly, lifting his forearm to protect his face. "I better go. See you in math."

As Dallin got further away from me, the air settled to a soft breeze that whispered along my skin. Rocks, leaves, and twigs dropped to the ground, and I sneezed as the excess dust tickled my nose.

"He just asked you out right in front of me," Brent complained.

I bit my tongue until it hurt, trying to stay the laughter threatening to stampede out of my mouth. Finally I said, "You do know he couldn't see you, right?"

Brent scowled. "Yeah, but how did he know I wasn't planning on asking you?"

"It sounds like your reputation preceded you," I said, my bitterness drizzling over my words. I drew circles in the dirt with the toe of my shoe.

"I never liked Dallin." Brent ground his teeth together while levitating a rock in front of him.

"So, no comment on him saying you get around, huh?"

Brent rubbed the back of his neck, and his lips moved but no sound came out, like he was practicing a speech. "I plead the fifth." He tried to smile but it didn't quite work.

My heart seemed to shatter into a thousand pieces in my chest. The broken shards punctured my lungs, making it impossible to breathe. I swallowed hard, the fragments of my heart dusting my toes.

"Oh . . ." I tried to play it off like it didn't matter that I was just another bee in his swarm of girls. Every interaction we had shared changed in my mind, now seeming less significant.

Turning a little unsteadily, pretending to get a closer look at the orange trees, I grabbed onto a branch for support from the emotional below the belt blow, peeling off a piece of loose bark. I rested my head against the tree and inhaled the citrusy scent of the blossoms. I rubbed the rough bark between my fingers absentmindedly. A chipmunk scampered along the ground further into the groves and I wanted to join him in his retreat. The life of a chipmunk suddenly seemed oddly enticing.

"Are you okay?" Brent asked, circling around so he could see me.

I forced a bright smile on my face. "Yep."

"About what he said . . ." Brent started, looking into the groves.

"Nothing I didn't already guess." I laughed, pulling a leaf off the tree and twirling it between my fingers.

"Oh," Brent said, hurt clouding his eyes, turning then more amber then brown.

An uncomfortable silence separated us as solidly as a brick wall.

"So about my plan . . ." I started.

"There is no plan. Let's get this straight, Yara. I. Forbid. You. To. Do. Anything." Fury blazed in Brent's eyes and I almost cowered at its intensity. "Promise me."

As grade school as it may have been, I crossed my fingers behind my back and promised, "I won't do anything dangerous or stupid."

* * * *

That evening when Cherie walked into our room I almost pounced on her. "Come on, we're hiking to the nearest bus stop, we're going to town."

"Sounds fun," she responded with a smile. "Why?"

I cast a nervous look around our room. "Can't talk to you about it here."

Cherie was a far more trusting soul than I was and she

simply shrugged, grabbed her wallet, and strolled into the hallway, telling me to lead the way. We cut through the groves, shaving off a half-mile, until we found the nearest bus stop. Cherie had this escape route drawn up before we ever stepped onto campus in the fall. I didn't tell her anything until we were sitting in front of the old world inspired fountain by the movie theater at the outdoor mall, drinking our fruit smoothies.

"So I got my memory back today," I confessed, gnawing on the end of my straw.

She wheeled toward me, putting her smoothie down on the stone ledge. "It must be something major for you to tell me here," she commented, her eyebrows arching.

I nodded, grasping the Styrofoam cup tightly. "Yeah." I bit my lip, trying to figure out the best way to start, and decided just to dive right in. I confided in her about Brent's ability to astral project, and then filled her in on everything∫from the party, to my death, coming back to life and concluded with my conversation with Brent today. By the time I had finished, Cherie had kicked off her shoes and was lying face up on the lip of the fountain, her hands tucked in the small of her back, her ankles crossed, and her mouth gaping open.

"I can't wrap my mind around this. You died?" She questioned numbly.

"Yeah, but you saved me. I've always loved your perfume." I sat with my legs crossed, making sure my skirt hung over my knees.

"Brent's dead? Someone else is walking around in his body?" Cherie shuddered. "I can't even stand letting people borrow my socks." Cherie was silent for a minute, letting everything digest. "So they can't get us here . . . off campus." I shook my head. "You think that he's collecting souls or whatever so he can be strong enough to leave?"

I lifted my shoulders. "That's my best guess."

"So what's your plan?" She asked.

"I'm not exactly sure."

"Well, I have some ideas." She pulled her hands out from under the small of her back and angled her head so she could observe the people milling around the various stores. "We need to get some of that licorice stuff. I'm guessing it's not like the candy we get from the store?"

"The stuff Thomas gave me was a purple powder. It probably has some other stuff mixed in." The pounding of the fountain filled in the calculated silence we had both fallen into. "I can probably get what we need from my sister. And Vovó would know where to get a recipe."

The door of the ice-cream store swung open, letting out the sound of the happy jingle its employees sang each time they received a tip. Some girls from our old school walked out, carrying their frozen treats. Cherie turned her head and I let my hair veil my face, both of us hiding from our former peers. I wasn't up to making small talk with people I didn't really care about.

"Yeah," Cherie continued once the girls had passed. "Call in the reinforcements; we're seriously outclassed right now. Too bad we can't get Brent's help, since he's determined to keep you safe. No worries though. We can work around him." Cherie was always good at making plans and I could see the gleam in her eye letting me know she had already started to formulate one. "You'll have to call your sister from here so we can talk without being overheard. We can use the computers at the coffee place to email your grandma. Why is she in another country right now?" Cherie asked rhetorically with a sigh. "Let's go visit our old friends over there and see if we can use their phones." She gave a little wave to the girls. "By the way, I think this week Steve and I are going to have a huge fight."

* * * *

"Fine!" Cherie yelled at Steve the following week. Classes had just let out for the day and the halls were emptying into the quad as students made their way home. Cherie stood directly in the flow of traffic.

"You're making a scene," Steve fumed, motioning toward the crowd surrounding them. He reached out and grabbed her elbow. "Let's go talk about this someplace else."

Cherie ripped her arm from his grasp and stuck her chin in the air. "I don't care who sees this. Let everyone know. It'll save the gossips some work. We. Are. Over." Cherie turned abruptly and stalked across the quad toward me at our prearranged meeting place. I draped my arm around her shoulder, leading her back to our room.

"I think that was one of my best performances ever." She giggled once our door swung shut.

"How did you get Steve to agree to that?"

Cherie waggled her eyebrows. "I can be persuasive."

"No details," I said, covering my ears.

"I told him the truth," Cherie said, throwing herself dramatically on her bed.

"You told him?"

Cherie nodded, burrowing her head into her goose-down pillow. "Of course."

"He believed you?"

"Why do you sound so surprised?"

"Because . . . most people simply wouldn't," I said, reaching over and flicking my desk lamp on.

"He's known something was off with Brent. They have been best friends for a long time. And Steve is refreshingly open-minded." She hefted herself up, reaching onto her

~ 266 ~

chest of drawers and grabbing a piece of gum, folding it into her mouth. "Don't worry, I took him off campus to fill him in on the plan." Cherie blew her gum into a bubble that popped, adhering itself to her face. "How did your tutoring go?"

I had met with Dallin twice so far and found that I really liked him. We didn't get much tutoring done as we kept getting sidetracked with conversation. "Good," I said. "He's really nice. He's horrible at calculus, though. It's going to take a lot work to get him caught up."

Cherie picked the gum off her chin and opened her mouth, presumably to ask another question but was interrupted by the phone ringing. She picked it up on the first ring.

"Steve, you were perfect," she gushed into the receiver. "No, you're not allowed to ask someone else to the dance." She laughed. "I can't believe she already asked you. What a relationship vulture!" Cherie didn't seem the least bit threatened by her competitor for Steve's affections. "Yeah, now you have to go hang out with Brent. Yeah, start tonight."

I tuned out their conversation, hoisting my books out of my backpack. It had been a strenuous week of letting a suspicious Thomas know I had accepted an offer from Dallin to the homecoming dance, and avoiding Brent because I couldn't lie to him very well, trying to practice my telekinetic moves on the sly, and also meeting with my sister. She had provided the materials we needed, as well as instructions from Vovó. My whole family was overjoyed that I had accepted my Wakerness, feeling confident that I could handle this. I may have fudged a few of the more worrisome details in order to give them that impression.

With a silent groan, I started on my homework. I had a handwritten rough draft of an essay on *The Catcher in the*

Rye when our window slid open, the curtains fluttering in the nippy air.

"Want to tell me what you've been up to?" Brent demanded, sitting on the window's ledge.

My heart jumped somewhere near my tonsils. "Homework," I answered turning away from him, pretending to still be studying.

"That requires you to leave campus?"

"Yep, needed some books from the public library for a research paper."

"Cut the crap, Yara," Brent said with an angry edge to his voice. "I know you're up to something. I want to know what it is."

"I'm not up to anything, Brent."

"Ooh, is he here?" Cherie asked, rising to her knees. I inclined my head and Cherie's smile grew. "Hey, Steve, can I call you back? Uh-huh . . . yeah, me too. Talk to you soon."

Brent slapped his hand against his leg. "What did you tell her?"

"Don't turn this into a thing, Brent. I told her everything."

"Hey, I have a right to know," Cherie argued in the direction I was looking. She casually dropped her pillow over the vials of mixed powder my sister had sent us that were currently littering her desk.

"You expect me to believe you told Cherie everything, you both left campus more than once, you've been avoiding me, she just staged a fight with Steve, and none of that means you're up to something dangerous?"

"I think you're imagining things," I lied, tapping my pencil against my desk. I hadn't counted on him being so sneaky, sly, or observant.

"What's he imagining?" Cherie asked, blowing another bubble.

"He thinks we're up to something." I said, recounting his list of our suspicious behavior.

"Wow, major ego?" Cherie smacked her gum again. "I like pretend drama, I think it adds to the passion of relationships. And if you must know, we snuck off campus because . . . Yara needed a new sexy dress for her hot date this week." I marveled at Cherie's ability to lie on her feet and carry on a conversation with a ghost she couldn't see.

Brent's cheeks actually turned pink. "Oh . . . I should have figured that . . ."

"And she isn't avoiding you she's been keeping busy to keep Thomas from being suspicious. Well, and she's been busy flirting with Dallin," Cherie said, winking at me.

I wished myself invisible so I wouldn't feel the harsh pressure of Brent's eyes on me.

"So you've been busy flirting with a guy you just barely met instead of trying to help me?" Brent demanded, standing up, our curtains undulating in the sudden gusts of air his anger was causing.

"Yes, I've been doing exactly what I promised. I'm letting everything drop," I said. Strands of my hair whipped against my cheeks and I pushed it off my face, glaring at Brent.

"So everything we went through meant nothing? You're just going to leave me like this?" The ferocity of Brent's gale made our door rattle on its hinges. His hands were clenched into tight fists by his side, his brown eyes darkening until they were almost black.

"Of course it meant something. I'm just keeping my promise to you, Brent," I fibbed, the lie catching in my throat like extra chunky peanut butter. "Isn't that what you wanted?"

"Is everything okay in there?" A voice asked outside our room.

"Uh . . ." Cherie said, scrambling to open the door. "Yeah everything's fine."

"Yes," Brent conceded, his strong breezes still blowing. One caught the door and it opened wide, slamming against the wall behind it. "I don't want you in danger, but I didn't think you'd give up so easily either." Brent ducked his chin, but not before I saw the profound sadness swimming in his eyes.

"I didn't give up easily, Brent." I gathered my tangled hair in my hands. Our posters and pictures snapped and quivered in the gusts.

"Who are you talking to?" Debbie, from my social dance class asked, standing next to Cherie at the threshold of my room, her hair twirling around her.

"Do you mind? This is a private conversation," I snapped, turning back to Brent.

A small smile etched his face.

"What's so funny?"

He just shook his head, the air suddenly still, letting my hair rain down around my shoulders.

"She knows there's no one there, right?" Debbie asked Cherie.

The words I had been forming died on my lips, I felt the blood retreat from my face and my head felt like an anvil had just been dropped on it. If this had happened a few months ago, shame would have been burning inside me. The fire in my gut now was a different kind of flame.

I spun toward Debbie, eyes blazing. "Of course there's someone there." I pointed directly at Brent. "He needs my help and you're interfering. You can't see him because he's a ghost and you're not a Waker." Her mouth slacked open along with Brent's and Cherie's. I shooed her away with a dismissive wave of my hand. "Now run along and tell everyone about the crazy girl." I turned back to Brent. "Oh, don't think I'm done with you."

Brent looked positively staggered and dropped back down to the window ledge. He tucked his chin to his chest, hiding his face from me. I lowered myself next to him, smoothing my skirt. Cherie was still trying to close the door on our visitor who was now peppering her with questions.

"I really am glad you're not getting more tangled up in this mess," Brent admitted with a small voice. "I really don't want you involved in it. I guess part of me was jealous."

"That makes sense; I would be jealous if you were the one alive," I said, crossing my ankles.

"That . . . that isn't exactly what I meant," Brent said slowly.

"Oh. My. Stiletto. Heels. You did it!" Cherie sang, rushing over to me and grabbing me in her arms, pulling me up.

"What?" I asked stumbling over her feet.

"You just admitted to a near stranger that you could see ghosts." Cherie beamed at me with a brilliant smile.

"Oh yeah. I guess I did."

"Are you okay?" Cherie asked, taking my hands in hers. She gave me a searching glance that made me uneasy.

"Why wouldn't I be?"

"You were always so nervous about developing the Waker gene and even more afraid that people might find out."

I cocked my head to the side trying to gauge my feelings. "I used to think that, didn't I? Not anymore; I'm good."

Cherie sat on her bed and tucked her legs under her. I plopped down beside her. "What does Brent think about it?"

I lifted my eyes toward him only to find he was gone. He had slipped out, and things were still strained between us. I only hoped someday he'd understand I hadn't been going on without him at all; I'd just been trying to find a way to bring him with me.

"He's gone."

Cherie sighed. "Good, because we need to talk. Your announcement to our dorm will force us to move faster than we planned." I nodded. "We have to do it tomorrow, before Thomas hears you've been seeing ghosts again."

The next evening, Cherie and I were going after Thomas to get Brent's body back and I knew he might kill me... again.

CHAPTER 17

The following afternoon, Cherie and I were in position. She was hiding behind a patch of neglected weeds just outside campus, while I was crouched against a large shrub that straddled the edge of the property. I was pressed against the prickly bush, hoping I was concealed. My hands were slick with sweat and I mentally reviewed the locations of the vials I had strategically hidden around campus. All of them had been laced with my grandma's herbal concoction. Several test runs had confirmed that even as a spirit I could remove and replace the stoppers. I dried my palms on my jeans waiting for Steve to lure Thomas, still wearing Brent's body, into our trap.

The air was still, no noise from insects or animals interrupted the twilight. Leaves clung to the trees, seeming almost afraid to fall and disturb the perfect silence. My ears strained to hear Brent's and Steve's voices through the quiet. Eventually, the tread of their walk echoed through the stillness, their conversation stabbing at the quiet. When their words floated to my ear, my throat constricted and my muscles coiled, ready to spring. I positioned myself to spy through the leaves.

"She broke my heart, man," Steve slurred, taking a swig from the bottle he carried. The smell of alcohol was overwhelming, and if I hadn't known Steve had only splashed the liquor on himself and was only pretending to be drinking it, I wouldn't have guessed it now.

I had to force myself to breathe, reminding my body how it was done. With each breath, I worried I would be too loud and give myself away. My quads began to protest my squatting, burning from the tension. I repositioned myself to my knees, giving them a rest.

"That stinks," Thomas said, smirking at Steve's heavy and clumsy footsteps.

"I don't need her, when I've got my bros, right?" Steve belched loudly and looked rather proud of himself. "Just look at what her slutty best friend did to you. She led you on this whole time and then agreed to go to the dance with that Dallin jerk." Steve smacked his lips together. "Who needs 'em? Am I right?" Steve asked. "She hurt you, man. Let my friend here help ease your pain." Steve shoved his drink toward Brent.

Thomas eyed the bottle carefully. "No thanks."

"What's wrong with you, man? All the guys have noticed you seem off. Different. I've never known you to turn down a drink," Steve said, his words bleeding together. He tripped over a rock and scratched his head when he looked back, not comprehending what had happened.

"You really can't hold your liquor, can you?"

"Course I can." Steve gave him a sloppy smile. "Whatever, if you won't help me drink away my sorrows . . . you can go." Steve clutched the bottle to his chest and leaned heavily on a tree. "Just don't expect the guys to want to party with you anytime soon."

Thomas stood there, weighing his options before extending his arm for the bottle.

"I knew I could count on you," Steve almost sobbed,

releasing his grip on the glass container.

Thomas wiped the top clean and then took a long pull of the drink. He coughed, clutching his chest. "That burns."

"Will put hair on your chest . . . and then curl it," Steve said, trying to stand up without the aid of the tree and swaying with the effort.

Thomas pushed the bottle back to Steve but Steve wouldn't take it.

"One drink? When did you turn into such a lightweight?"

Thomas frowned, but took another large gulp that ended up with him doubled over, coughing and choking. Then he shot up tall, his body rigid, the bottle falling to the ground as his spirit was ejected from Brent's body. Brent fell, stiff as an ironing board to the ground.

"Are you okay?" Steve dropped to his knees, his drunken act forgotten as he bent over Brent.

I jumped from my hiding spot and Steve spun toward me, his fist curled ready to strike.

He sheepishly dropped his hands. "Sorry." He looked again at Brent lying on the ground. "Did it work?"

"Yep." I hoped we had added enough of the licorice powder to the alcohol to keep Thomas away until I was ready for him. Steve and I hoisted Brent, carrying him across the line that marked the edge of campus. The back of my shirt clung to me, moist with perspiration that had nothing to do with physical exertion. Cherie was waiting for us and looked anxiously at Brent's limp body.

"Give him more to drink, just to be sure," I instructed, tossing the open bottle to Steve. He crouched down next to his friend and cradled Brent's head, tipping it back and pouring a few ounces into his open mouth. Steve set the bottle down and collapsed on the ground next to Brent, wiping the sweat from his face.

Cherie folded her arms behind her back as she took her post as guard. She gave me a confident smile and a small nod, letting me know she was ready. My necklace was secure around my throat and I stroked it lightly for comfort. With a deep breath that didn't stop my knees from knocking together, I stepped back across the invisible barrier and separated from my body. This was the part of the plan that worried me the most, leaving my body behind on campus, relying on my necklace to protect it.

I paused briefly to appreciate the still life photo of my friends, the determined set to Cherie's shoulders as she tried so hard to be brave, Brent, pale and helpless on the ground, and his best friend worriedly sitting beside him. I turned away, ready to act.

* * * *

My insides couldn't have been more queasy if I were about to plummet out of a plane without a parachute. Thomas was a serial killer without remorse and I was about to confront him. Every part of me was begging my spirit to flee but it was more than just my life on the line, I couldn't run away. I took a deep steadying breath, my hand on my chest as I stepped forward.

Thomas sauntered toward me. "Pretty clever, Yara," he conceded with a bob of his head. "You saved your boyfriend, but it won't do you any good." Within a split second he had thrown his arms out and began to change before my eyes, blurring, distorting, changing into a giant shadow of dark mist. Thomas was gone, and in his place was a wall of inky fog. His voice turned my marrow to ice. "What did you think would happen now?" He taunted.

The metallic taste of fear in my throat and the sulfur-like odor of cowardice glued my feet to the ground and my tongue to the roof of the mouth.

Thomas's shrill cackle strained my nerves. His black vapor circled, gathering itself until it shaped back into Thomas's form. The green of his irises kept undulating, changing color— green, brown, hazel, blue, back to green— while his dark pupils glowed with hatred directed entirely at me. His spirit was distorted, stretching at odd angles where hands and feet from the spirits trapped inside pushed out against him, trying to free themselves, his whole skin crawling with the efforts of the enslaved souls. His prisoners moved inside him and his stomach rolled and shifted. Bile churned inside me as he pushed his captives back, watching me the whole time.

"All those people you've killed . . . you've trapped . . . you keep them . . ." I shuddered unable to finish.

"Yes, I keep them with me."

"But they're fighting against you."

Thomas smirked. "Yes they do, but it's a nuisance at best. Really, after sixty years I hardly notice it anymore. They increase my power." He began circling, his eyes running up and down my body, making me feel violated. "I've been waiting a long time for a soul to make me strong enough to leave . . . to really live again." He stretched his arms out, the storm inside him still bulging grotesquely.

"What do you want to do with your power?"

"I don't crave power, only freedom, the ability to leave this cursed place."

"Some people would say it's only cursed because of you," I said before I could stop myself.

"Well, my plan was to leave, which would have made everyone happy, but now you've robbed me of my body, so after I capture you— and Brent— I'll have to kill one more Pendrell student. And that death's on you." Thomas licked his lips; a horrible grin grew across his face. "You can still come willingly you know."

"Why would I do that?" I lifted my hands in front of me and took a step away from him.

"It'll be easier for both of us if you do." Thomas cracked his knuckles.

"I'm not really interested in making it easier for you." I could feel the comforting weight of my necklace under my shirt and I resisted the urge to touch it.

He intertwined his fingers behind his back, the spirits inside him pressing out against his skin, one clearly defined hand reaching for freedom. "Still, if you choose to come with me, I'll let Brent live and I'll release you, too. After you've joined my ranks, I'll be strong enough to leave. I'll even let all these other spirits go. Pendrell will never hear from me again and neither will you. Everyone will be free."

"You'd leave Brent alone? You'd free me and your captive spirits?" I asked, understanding that a lot of good could come out of the bargain.

Thomas smiled, his white teeth gleaming. "Yes."

I took a step toward him before I realized what I was doing. "I don't believe you," I snapped, shaking my head.

He raised his hand to his chest. "I won't take that personally."

"Assuming I was crazy enough to agree to this, what would happen after you left here and freed us all?"

"I'll still need to find bodies." He held up his finger. "But they won't be boys from Pendrell. I can be more selective with who I choose."

"How would that be different than what you're doing here?"

He continued on like he hadn't heard me. His eyes were wild, his tone desperate. "I can find out what it means to be older than sixteen, go to the movies, to the beach, have a serious relationship with a girl. I can visit my parents' graves. Denny's grave," he said, his voice suddenly soft.

The name Denny brought me back to the board in Cherie's room. There was a Dennis on it; could that be Denny? "Denny? He was your best friend, wasn't he? And yet you killed him."

He bent over, placing his hands on his knees for support. There were actual tears in his eyes when he looked up at me. "I didn't mean to do that." He collapsed on the ground and reclined against a tree. "I was dying. There was so much pain, I could barely get out of bed or think straight. The only relief I felt was when I projected." He looked into the groves toward the old pool house, rubbing his hands up and down his arms, setting off a cascade of ripples. "I found Henry one night— he was trying to kill himself."

"Henry, the third victim, was trying to kill himself?" I asked despite myself.

Thomas wiped his eyes with the back of his hand. "Yes, I walked in on him weighing himself down with sandbags. He begged me not to stop him." Thomas's eyes looked lost in the past. "I jumped in to save him as he sank to the bottom and dislodged the sandbags. When I got him to the surface, he still fought me. He didn't want to be rescued. I couldn't believe it; he was throwing away what I wanted the most. I realized as he struggled against me a way to please us both. I pushed him under and held him there. I gave him what he wanted— I made sure he died. He didn't want his body anymore, so why not take it for myself? He wanted to die while I wanted to live."

"So that's how all this started?" A hawk swept past us gliding through the trees, a small rodent pinched in its beak. Goose pimples formed on my arms as I imagined Henry's rescuer turning murderer.

"If Denny hadn't walked in on us, it wouldn't have turned ugly. He just didn't understand." He dropped his head in his hands. "Denny tried to save Henry, even though it meant the cancer would kill me."

"So you decided to murder him, too?"

"Of course not," he said, his tone chilling. "He was going for help, to turn me in. I was chasing him to stop him, to explain. We struggled, I pushed him and he fell. Hard." His face showed all the horror he must have felt that night, something akin to regret swirled in his eyes. "There was so much blood. It was everywhere." He held up his hands to me, as if expecting the blood to still be there.

A pang of sympathy pulsed through me as I looked at the broken person in front of me. He didn't seem as scary to me, he seemed more like a wounded animal who needed help. I took a step toward him.

He rested his chin in his hands. "If you found that you had accidentally killed Cherie, what would you have done?" I couldn't come up with an answer, I wasn't sure if I'd be able to live with myself. Thomas sensed a minor victory and pressed on. "I didn't mean to do it. I was disgusted when I realized what I had done. Henry died because he wanted to, but Denny was an accident."

I took another step toward him but paused as I asked, "So why didn't you just stop then and turn yourself in? Why not make it right?"

"What would turning myself in have accomplished? It would have dishonored both Henry and Denny, making their deaths pointless."

"You believe that?" I scoffed, drifting a few paces back, my sweaty palms clasped together.

Thomas frowned. "I was in Henry's body. Would it have been fair to Henry's family to ruin their son's reputation by turning him in as a murderer? The other choice was going back to my own dying body, and there was no way I would do that. The only thing I could do was to stage the drowning and the fire to cover everything up. I thought that would be the end of it."

"But it wasn't. You needed a new body every two years." A chill ran down my spine as I backtracked some more.

Thomas nodded. "The body begins to rot after that. The wrong soul is in the body and the body knows it. Henry's decayed faster once his spirit had crossed over, so I knew it was best if I kept them from the light, and away from their bodies." He lifted his head from his hands.

"But after that night, you've made the choice over and over to kill someone else. How do you justify that?"

"I don't have to justify it. I do what I have to do to survive, just like you or anyone else. Besides, my best friend had already died because of me— what were the other deaths compared to his?" His voice sounded dead, past feeling. "You know, Yara, my life hasn't been easy since Denny's death. I've been a prisoner at this school for over sixty years; isn't that penance enough?"

"No, because you keep killing people!"

He glared at me in a way that made the hair on the back of my neck stand up. "It doesn't matter. After tonight I'll have enough strength to break open my cell. I just needed the right key, Yara, and that's you. If you want the deaths to stop, the souls freed, and Brent's life restored, now is your chance. Are you willing to join me?" He held out his hand and his fingers started to stretch longer as they reached toward me.

"No!" I took a step back.

His face was incredulous. "Even after you've heard my story? Even now that you understand what I've gone through? Even after you've heard what you'd be getting in exchange?" He huffed and shook his head as if I was the most incomprehensible person he had ever met. "Don't you see I'm not the bad guy?" The corners of his mouth pinched together as he waited for my response that never came. "Fine. Do this the hard way. Nothing personal," he added casually. "I actually like you, but that doesn't change anything. You're strong enough for my purpose now, so this is how it has to be."

Gone was his repentant self; he had morphed back into a madman. He didn't move but a cloudy arm of darkness stretched from his shoulder, reaching for me, gloom emoting from his very fingertips. Instinct took over and I slithered backward. A second ghostly hand extended itself, then a third. I flicked my wrists frantically trying to keep them away, to stop the advancing limbs that were scrabbling toward me. But I wasn't strong enough; they barely even rippled at my counterattacks.

My confidence crumbled, realizing that my best defense wasn't even close to being strong enough. Calling Brent for help wasn't an option, because I refused to endanger him in any way. This was a rescue mission; I wasn't about to let the tide turn and become a damsel in distress. I only had to distract Thomas long enough for Brent to get his body back. Of course, I thought ironically, it would have helped if Brent had any idea his body was now Thomas-free.

I spun around blindly, running away into the orderly rows of trees. There was no place to hide from Thomas here; only the messy disorganization of the ivy and eucalyptus trees would offer me any protection.

I ran full tilt toward them. My hair flew behind me, my sneaker-shod feet zooming across the irrigated paths. Smells of blossoms, rot, and nature rushed through me as

I pushed my spirit as hard as I could. Thomas was behind me, catching up yet not overtaking me, almost like he was enjoying the hunt.

A gust of wind knocked me to my knees, robbing my lungs of air. I spun, crouched in a defensive position only to see Thomas getting to his feet, too, stretching one of his ghostly tentacles out to Brent, who stood amid the shower of wind that had knocked Thomas back. Thomas planted his feet and spread himself out, letting part of himself become the mist while his own shape remained. The mist twisted around Brent, trapping him in.

Thomas reached out another arm to grab Brent and without thinking I sprinted toward Thomas's spirit and catapulted onto his back, my small fists clawing at him. He jerked frantically, trying to toss me from him, but I clung on, refusing to let him get to Brent. Every part of me was a weapon. My fingers dug into him, my heels kicked at him, my arms squeezed him hard, like a python. I was even whacking him with my chin in the soft skin at the bottom of his neck, my necklace swinging with the motion.

There was an ear-shattering explosion when the charm of my necklace glanced off of his cheek. Howling in pain he collapsed onto all fours. His image shattered and scattered from under me, and several of the trapped souls leaked from him. As soon as they were free from his hold, the brilliant bright light of eternity materialized, beckoning the newly-freed entities to it.

"No!" Thomas yelled, trying to regain the hold he once had on them, but his link had been severed. The souls hovered near the light for a few moments, then vanished into its warm depths when its rays reached them. Happiness and goodness peeked through the gloom before Thomas pulled himself back together, clutching his remaining captives.

His usual olive coloring had grayed; losing those spirits had cost him strength.

I was still sprawled on the ground mesmerized by what had just had happened. Brent pulled me to my feet.

"We've got to go get our bodies while he's still weak."

"I may not be as strong as I was, but I'm still stronger than you," Thomas spit out. The earth protested beneath me as Thomas gathered all his power to him, preparing to fight.

My feet were awkward and kept tripping as I followed Brent's lead. I clutched Brent's hand so tight our skin felt molded together. The darkness behind us was tipping the earth, twisting the ground, rolling the dirt.

Cherie stood at the edge of campus, a frozen sentry guarding our soulless bodies. We were only feet from her when a friendly voice called to Brent.

"Brent, please don't run from me."

Brent dropped my hand as his body spiraled around.

"Neal?" He exclaimed.

"Brent," I begged, "we have to keep going." The undeniable déjà vu of the moment made me dizzy. "Remember my dream?"

Brent's body was stiff but he shook his head for a moment trying to clear his fuzzy mind before his eyes glassed over, appearing vacant.

"Neal needs me," he explained, his voice hollow, pointing toward his brother who now stood out amongst the spirits that made up the mist.

"That's right, Brent." Neal smiled with his mouth, but it never reached his brown eyes. "Come to me." He extended his finger, motioning for Brent to move closer.

"I can't leave her," Brent explained, gesturing toward me.

Neal beckoned Brent closer. "That's alright. You can bring her with you."

Brent smiled at me like this was the obvious solution as he pulled me to him. My already racing pulse quickened when the memory of my nightmare flashed in my mind, another nightmare coming true. Struggling against his strong embrace did no good; he simply hoisted me off the ground, dragging me forward. Neal and Thomas smiled at Brent encouragingly the closer we got, Neal murmuring persuasively about how much he missed him, his deadly siren song luring him in.

"Brent, we need you to take her necklace off and give it to us," Neal said in a cooing, honey-smooth voice.

Without hesitating, Brent reached out, yanking my necklace hard enough for the chain to snap, the broken pieces of it plinking onto the hard, dry earth. Something inside me splintered at Brent's betrayal and I crumbled as my vision blurred.

Thomas was going to make me part of his mindless army. I was going to join ranks with the other souls he had captured. I lay prostrate on the unforgiving earth, my hands flat in front of me. I could feel a steady rhythmic pulsing against my palm and realized my hand had come to rest over one of the fallen beads. Several things clicked together in my mind as the warm bead beat against my skin. I remembered the floral plant buds inside the necklace were meant to protect pure spirits from evil ones and how contact with it had weakened Thomas. As I lay atop the scattered pieces, the seedling of an idea formed in my mind. I kept my head down, resting on my forearms, while my fingers began stealthily gathering up the broken bits of my necklace.

"Stand her up," Thomas ordered Brent, who roughly set me on my feet.

Thomas's look of triumph was more than I could bear and I dropped my chin in submission. There was a loud ringing in my ears, a pounding against my skull and goose pimples rising on my skin as the darkness of the mist pressed in on me. The tinny taste of fear coated my tongue and my sweat-soaked fingers trembled.

Thomas opened his mouth to speak and I dove at him, pushing him backward, with me on top of him. His jaw hung slack in surprise and I took my chance, shoving the necklace fragments into his mouth. With every ounce of strength I had, I forced his mouth shut while slapping my other hand over his lips, not allowing him to spit them out.

The smell of singed hair and flesh permeated the air as he sizzled from the inside out. Writhing under my weight, Thomas threw his head back and the green of his eyes rolled up, leaving an empty white space staring at me. His fist smacked across my jaw and my head swung to the side as hot pain seared my face. Brent was beside me in an instant, catching Thomas's hands, pinning them above his head.

Thomas's chest collapsed into a dark crater where souls erupted free with a wet slurping sound that made me cringe. Released spirits hovered around him, shapeless and lost, confused at their sudden freedom after decades of imprisonment. With blinding brilliance, the white light reappeared, its rays shimmering enticingly toward the newly freed souls.

"*No!*" Thomas screamed from between my fingers as one of his former minions took a step toward the light. He struggled in a desperate attempt to regain control, but he was too weakened by the pankurem plant concealed within the beads trapped in his mouth. One by one, the boys stepped into the light, and were tucked into its embrace, the light restoring their frame from vapor into the young men they had once been, the blank expressions replaced by looks of pure joy.

As each spirit vanished, Thomas's inhuman screams became more horrible. Thomas was transforming as well. Far from the threatening monster he had been only minutes before, he now lay stripped, reduced, and pathetic. Despite all that he had done, the murder and enslavement of dozens of young men, my heart twisted with pity and tears slid down my face as I listened to his pleas for mercy.

"It burns," he cried. "Please stop! I swear never to take another body again!" On and on his promises went as he begged and bargained, promising me he would change his ways if I would just show him compassion.

His desperate pleas tugged at my heartstrings. I wanted to believe that people could change, and for a moment my hands loosened as I contemplated showing him leniency. Sensing what I was doing, however, Brent forced them back with a firm shake of his head.

"Yara, we have to finish it. There are some still trapped," he said, softly but firmly, his eye shining with the same agony that my heart felt. Brent kept his trembling hand over mine, lending me support, as the remaining victims of the curse were sucked from Thomas. He now lay panting on the ground, a withered old man with thin hair, seeming too weak to even stand.

When the last spirit wrenched itself from his control, I pushed away from Thomas, shaking, disgusted and emotionally scarred. My stomach curdled and I dry-heaved, leaving an acidic taste in my mouth that I tried to wipe away with the back of my hand.

I was still trembling and needed Brent's arms around me. Looking around frantically, I thought for a horrible moment he had gone into the light with the other spirits.

I soon found him, though, standing a ways off with his brother. He and Neal were huddled together hugging and talking quietly to each other. Sensing me watching them, they both looked my way and Neal gave me a smile that was a twin of Brent's charismatic grin. He leaned toward Brent and whispered something before turning back to me with one last smile. He hugged Brent before walking straight into the light.

With the last soul in its embrace, the light quietly shrunk to a small pinpoint, then vanished, leaving me blinking in the dark night. There were no stars in the sky but I could see Brent perfectly as he stared silently at the spot where his brother been, his eyes glistening. He angled away from me and I pretended not to notice him rubbing the tears from his eyes.

"Brent?" I called timidly, wanting to offer support but not force it.

My voice seemed to snap him back into the moment. He straightened, rolled his shoulders a few times as he composed himself, then turned to examine the remnants of Thomas, who was still curled up pathetically. Thomas's eyes swung toward Brent, his expression wild as he watched Brent advance. When Brent was only a few feet away, Thomas suddenly roared, his face becoming crimson, and he morphed into a thin veil of fog.

Brent was prepared for this; his arms were thrown wide, conjuring a miniature cyclone out of the formerly still air. Thomas, weakened as he was, couldn't fight back, even in his fog form, and his essence was trapped in the circular frenzy.

"You got him!" I shouted.

Brent shook his head. "Maybe, but I'm not sure what to do with him."

"I know where to put him." I lifted my finger and one of my herb-laced vials that had been hidden in the nook of a tree floated toward me. "In here."

I coaxed the stopper out of the glass and held it out for Brent who smiled in satisfaction. "If that isn't poetic justice, I don't know what is," he said, pointing his finger toward his small twister and guiding Thomas's fog toward the bottle.

Like a genie forced into its lamp, Thomas was funneled into his glass prison. Brent put the cork cap into place and made the vial levitate in the air. He walked completely around it, inspecting it

Thomas's hatred radiated from the bottle like poisonous venom. His inky consciousness glittered lethally in the fading light. The smoke swirled and twisted like tentacles until finally Thomas's face appeared, warped in a grotesque haunting grimace as he pushed against his glass prison, trying to escape, the vial barely rattling.

Brent and I may not have been able to read each other's minds anymore, but he could still tell from my expression what I was thinking. "It's over, Yara. We won."

I gulped; I had the overwhelming sensation that what we had done wasn't enough. I'm not sure what I had expected, maybe a fairy tale ending where a magic wand fixed everything, including all the darkness we had been through.

But this was no fairy tale. Nothing could bring back the thirty boys that had died. Nothing could take away the grief that had torn their family's hearts into shreds. Experiences like this, I realized, are wounds that never quite healed; they stayed with you and no amount of justice would erase the scar.

"Yara? Are you okay?" Brent asked, touching my

shoulder gently. "So . . . your grandma's necklace, huh?" I nodded. "Who knew?'

"She did."

"Yeah, she did." Brent smiled. "She's sort of my new hero."

"Mine, too."

I shook off my previously morbid thoughts and turned to him with a wan smile. He rocked back and forth on his feet as he chewed on one of his nails, contemplating me. We just stared at each other, there not being words profound enough to encompass what we had just done. It had changed us. I felt different, like I had gained something, but been robbed of something as well. In Brent's eyes, there was a deeper maturity, a travel-worn wisdom and depth that flecked the brown of his eyes. It made him more rugged, more beautiful but at the same time it gave me a pang of sorrow to see.

"I guess we should get back to our bodies," he offered.

"Yeah," I agreed shuffling from foot to foot.

Cherie still stood on the edge of campus, frozen in time, her face showing the traces of fear she had been bravely trying to hide. Steve sat beside Brent's vacant body. I dove back into my body, the familiar icy chill snapping over me as time started moving forward at a snail's pace. Cherie and Steve began moving, each blink and action slow, like a stop-motion movie. Our times were still out of sync as I crossed the campus divide and grabbed Brent's body under his armpits. Drag marks cut across the rocky path as I brought him across the barrier line. Brent reconnected with a luxurious sigh, like sinking into a warm bath.

"We did it," I whispered to Cherie.

Steve sat upright, looking around in confusion before leaping at Brent and catching him in a chokehold in case I had failed.

Cherie jumped to see me no longer by her side but in front of her dusting myself off. "How? Oh . . . is it over?" Cherie asked. "Just like that? Did it work?" She sent a suspicious look to Brent who was yelling at Steve to let him go.

"Yeah, it's really Brent now." I answered, fingering my throat where my necklace should have been. The real necklace had snapped with its spirit-twin.

Steve released Brent with an apologetic grin and swatted him on the back with a manly grunt.

"Ugh." Brent smacked his lips. "What did you give me to drink?"

"A vile concoction of whiskey laced with black licorice and Brazilian herbs," Cherie said. "Yara's grandma said alcohol was the best way to dissolve and mask the flavor of the herbs." Then Cherie launched into the details of our plan, from her fight with Steve to the clandestine meetings with my sister.

"I knew I couldn't trust you to not do anything stupid," Brent said half-heartedly. "I think he stretched out my body, it feels different," he complained lifting his arms and stretching his legs. "It wasn't meant to house thirty souls."

Cherie then threw her arms around my neck, hurling questions at me. She finally noticed my monosyllabic responses and got the message I wasn't ready to talk. She rather conspicuously tugged Steve away, leaving Brent and me alone.

A heavy silence hung in the air but I didn't feel the need to speak. I picked up the scattered pieces of my necklace, carefully rubbing them across my palm, wiping the dirt from them, and stuffing them in my pocket. Brent grasped the vial in his quivering hands, his head bent.

"You saved my life again," he said, his voice cracking.

"I'll never be out of your debt now."

"It wasn't me. We did it," I corrected.

"I'm beyond grateful, Yara, but you weren't supposed to take that sort of risk for me. I didn't want you to." He stood in front of me, his eyes still overly red from crying. He tucked a lock of my hair behind my ear then let his hand rest on my cheek, his thumb fanning softly across my face. His Adam's apple bobbed as he swallowed. "What would I have done if you were killed permanently this time? Why would you do that?"

"You already know why," I said, looking away and stepping back. I remembered too clearly how he had reacted to my declaration of love and how he had shied away from our potential kiss in my room. I was a smart enough and had enough pride not to want to repeat those experiences. I shrugged. "It was the right thing to do."

The scarlet clouds on the horizon reminded me of blood. I pivoted away from them, shivering and taking a few steps into the groves. Brent caught my wrist and I curved toward him.

His rich brown eyes were dark, solid, no trace of jade; it was fully him. He looked like he wanted to say something but his jaw tensed and instead he let his hand travel from my elbow to my hand, the strong pulse from his fingers like a balm to my injured soul. I raised our entwined hands and placed them over the steady thumping of his heart a twin of the rhythm in my own chest. I pressed my head to his chest letting the steady pace of his heart and his citrusy, musky scent envelop me, lull me into a place of security. A place safe enough that I didn't have to pretend I was okay. I failed to sniff back the tears that began to leak from me.

I should have been happy. I should have been relieved. I should have felt like celebrating, but I didn't feel any of those things. I felt weak, fragile and helpless because all I could do was cry.

Brent put his arm around me whispering, "I know." I wasn't sure if he was agreeing with the fact that we had conquered Thomas, if he knew the real reason I had risked so much to save him, or if he understood why I was crying. I decided it didn't matter. All that mattered was that he was holding me.

CHAPTER 18

A few days later, Cherie and I were in our room doing a complex pre-homecoming dance grooming ritual. All it really involved was snacking and getting ready with greater care than normal. Beauty supplies were strewn across our floor and cluttering our desks.

"So what did he do with the vial? Bury it?" Cherie asked.

"No, he bought a small padded safe for his room. He's afraid to let it out of his sight."

"Well, I don't blame him." Cherie shuddered. "So Brent was pretending to be hypnotized by the mist?" She asked before taking another big bite of her green apple.

"He said when I reminded him of my dream, he came up with a plan. That's why he didn't give them the necklace, but broke it, spilling the beads. He trusted me to know how to use them." I removed the cotton from between my toes. I held out my foot, wiggling my toes as I examined the pale pink color.

"Why did I miss all the fun?" She complained, twisting the stem of the apple before it snapped off.

"You had the important job of guarding our bodies."

Cherie guffawed at me and ended with a snort. "Lot of good I was, being frozen in time and all." She tossed her apple core and the broken stem into her trashcan. "So even though Brent's alive, you're still going to the dance tonight with Dallin, huh?"

I plugged in my curling iron and laid it on my desk on top of a ratty blue hand towel. "Yeah, and Brent's going with Sara. Thomas had asked her."

"Oh." Cherie cleaned her hands with a wipe and threw it in the trash. She patted her hands dry on her jeans and then took her blonde hair and piled it on top of her head, twisting so she could observe herself from every angle. Grabbing one of the bobby pins on her desk, she stuck it into the curls then grabbed some more, putting a them in her mouth.

"Why didn't you both dump your dates and go together?" Cherie asked around the bobby pins pressed between her lips.

"Dallin doesn't deserve that." I guided the curling iron down a section of my hair. "Besides, Brent didn't ask me to the dance. He seemed overjoyed that he gets to go with Sara." I tried to swallow down the bitterness in my voice but it got caught in my throat by a lump of rejection. "I mean, sure, I risked my life to save him, you know. No big deal. So glad I saved him so he could date other girls."

"Let's not forget that you agreed to go with Dallin after Brent had protected you from the mist all those times." Cherie coaxed a curl into place with her finger then made it stay with another pin. "And he was also willing to give up getting his own life back and freeing his brother to keep you from harm."

"That was different . . ." I said defensively.

"Maybe not to him," Cherie pointed out with a shrug.

My now-beating heart sunk like an anchor to my knees as I considered her words.

Dallin and I had danced four songs in a row when my feet protested and I begged him to sit a few out. He guided me toward the bleachers in the gym. Silver and black material was draped from the top of the room, forming a false ceiling, and then cascaded down, paneling the walls. White lights twinkled from the potted trees, large silver clocks adorned the walls and small clocks made up the center-pieces of the black-linened tables.

"Want something to drink?"

My gaze slide to the refreshment table, which seemed miles away on a path lined with hot coals. "That would require me to move," I whined.

Dallin gave me a dangerous grin. "I'm more than willing to get it, but it will require payment."

"Fine, I'll answer all of your Calculus questions for you on Monday."

"Just as I had hoped," he said, his voice tinged with disappointment at my non-flirty answer. I liked Dallin, enough not to lead him on until I knew the 'Brent door' had been slammed shut and deadbolted. "I'll be back."

Dallin retreated down the stairs while my eyes found Brent and Sara dancing in the crowd. Judging by the mutual smiles, they appeared to be having a great time. I forced myself to look away, concentrating on the pale pink patterns on the delicate fabric of my dress, my fingers tracing the lines and twirls there. The song ended and a new one started. I continued to study my dress, pretending it was fascinating.

"Did your date dump you?" Brent asked.

My vertebrae cracked because my head popped up so fast. He towered above me, looking mouth-watering in his black suit.

"No, he went to get me something to drink."

"Oh, I was afraid I was going to have to be a gentleman and offer you a pity dance." Brent eased himself down beside me.

"Nope, you don't have to be a gentleman," I said lightly, wiping my suddenly sweaty palms on my dress.

Brent leaned in close, his minty breath tickling my cheek. "Good to know I don't have to be a gentleman with you."

"Ha, ha," I said sarcastically, but not moving away from him, and pretending my pulse hadn't sped off like a NASCAR driver. "Where's your date?"

"She's . . . in the bathroom, I think." Brent swiveled his head toward the dance. "Having fun with Dallin?" Brent asked dryly.

"Yeah," I said through gritted teeth. "How's Sara?"

"Great." Brent studied his nails and I could almost see the longing to chew on them flicker in his eyes. "So, I was wondering if you still wanted to get training to control your projecting."

"Well, I only did it that once without meaning to . . . well, and the time Thomas spiked my drink."

"I keep forgetting what a natural you are. You really don't need my help." Brent slumped, resting his elbows on the bench behind him.

"You have lots of other things you could teach me." I said quickly. "Training would be good."

"Yeah, it will be like old times," Brent said, nodding his head, something akin to a smile playing on his lips.

"Hey, Brent," Dallin said uneasily, noting how close we were sitting. I quickly put some space between us, and Brent shook his head in obvious amusement. My cheeks burned as I took the water Dallin offered me.

Brent gave me an ironic look, his eyebrows arching slightly. "I'm surprised you still accept drinks from guys."

I discreetly stepped on his toe. "It's a matter of knowing who to trust."

"I was just about to ask your date to dance," Brent explained to Dallin, standing up and extending his hand toward me with a million watt smile. I nervously gulped, my eyes shifting between Brent and Dallin.

"No, thanks. I'm feeling dehydrated," I answered, lifting my cup of water to my mouth. "Maybe later."

A crease formed between Brent's brows that gave me more satisfaction than it should have. I had a feeling he wasn't used to being turned down.

"Later," he agreed, flashing a smile toward Dallin. With that he walked away, asking the first girl he passed to dance. Without meaning to, I found myself staring after him. Dallin sat beside me and followed my gaze to Brent.

"What was that?"

"Nothing, really."

"If you say so," Dallin said, not sounding quite sure he believed me. After sipping our mutual drinks we made our way back to the crowd, dancing every song.

*   *   *   *

"That was fun," Dallin said as we approached the double doors of my dorm. He'd hardly said anything since we'd left the bleachers. I think our encounter with Brent had dampened his spirits.

"Thank you for a great evening," I replied, pausing before opening the door. I gave him a friendly hug and bid him a good night, then retreated into my dorm foyer.

I had pulled out my room key from my purse and pushed the button for the elevator when a familiar voice called, "Want to go for a walk?"

I missed a step and wobbled on my heels to find Brent sitting in our lobby resting in one of the plush leather armchairs, his feet irreverently kicked up on the coffee table. His hands were clasped behind his head, the picture of ease.

I bit my lip, tucking a curl behind my ear. "That'd be great."

He casually looped a thumb through his belt loop as he stood, then opened the lobby door for me. The contrast in temperature between the lobby and the early winter weather outside seemed more dramatic than it had a moment before. Brent noticed my shiver and offered me his suit jacket. He helped me into it and I tried not to be too obvious as I snuggled into it gratefully, inhaling the citrusy musk of his cologne that made my knees momentarily buckle. Tucking my hands into the pockets of his jacket, I strolled beside Brent, his gait slow and leisurely, like there was nowhere else he wanted to be but by my side.

Billowy lavender and indigo clouds covered the moon, creating an artistic landscape. The subdued light and flower-perfumed air created a romantic setting as we walked the well-worn paths of Pendrell. Conversations unsaid and experiences shared followed us like shadows, but we didn't speak. There was an undemanding easiness in our silence, but it also crackled with insistent possibilities.

When we approached the commons building, Brent pointed toward it with a jerk of his head, his eyebrows raised in a question. I nodded and followed him to its outdoor courtyard, now deserted. We huddled near the wood-burning fireplace, settling into metal chairs placed near its edges. Even though the night air was chilly, something, made me uncomfortably warm, so I slipped Brent's jacket off my shoulders and draped it over the back of my chair.

I rested my head on the metallic backrest and stared up into the stars; there seemed to be thousands tonight. I wondered how many other people were watching them along with us. A shooting star shot across the twinkling canvas and, closing my eyes, I made a wish on it. The fire crackled and sparked, the heady smell of wood smoke hung in the air. It was a perfect moment. Sitting beside Brent, studying the stars, not feeling the need for words had my heart almost bruising my ribs with its intense thudding, but it was also achingly familiar, comfortable.

After a while, Brent shifted in his chair, and then rearranged himself. I turned my head toward him, allowing myself to admire how extraordinarily handsome he was in the blue shades of moonlight with his gorgeous features cast in dim shadows. It reminded me of a face similar to his that had lived in darkness for several years.

"What did Neal say to you before he went into the light?"

"What you'd expect: words of love and thanks. He also asked that I let my parents know what happened." Brent gave me a little wink. "Oh, and that my girlfriend was hot."

"You'll have to introduce me to her someday," I teased, resting my elbow on the arm of the chair and tucking my hand under my chin, watching Brent.

"I'll set it up," Brent said, stretching his legs out in front of him. "It's so weird to not know your every thought."

"I know," I agreed. "What are you thinking?"

He used one of his fingers to lift my chin, forcing me to look at him. "You look incredible tonight. In fact, you look so delectable that it's hard to keep my thoughts gentlemanly."

My cheeks burned and I started to protest, shaking my head adamantly, unable to accept the compliment and waved my hand at him dismissively. I gently pulled back, his fingers tentatively released my chin. I let out an un-ladylike snort. "Fine, don't answer."

He raised his eyebrow in response. "Don't believe me? I can prove it." He then took a moment to let his eyes slowly wander over me in an embarrassingly intimate and appreciative manner that made me shiver slightly. Brent tilted toward me with a wicked smile, accompanied by a newly-formed desire for me in his eye, that I refused to believe was real.

"Oh, shut up, Brent," I said, angry at myself for almost falling for his smooth words and sexy eyes.

"Don't ask questions you don't want answers to." He chuckled, reclining back again.

"Only if you stop saying things you don't mean," I retorted, trying to force my voice to sound light as fluff.

Brent rose from his chair and strode to the window of the commons building looking into the building's game room, his shoulder resting against the brick. His reflection in the window mirrored his amused grin. "This coming from the girl who took advantage of my weakened state and, while I was sleeping, moved so close to me she practically forced herself into my arms."

"Oh, please. You're the one whose arms were wrapped around me," I argued out of habit, folding my arms with a scowl.

Brent's warm breath touched the clear windows, steaming them slightly. "You're also the one who kissed me while in my previously mentioned weakened state. Then you claimed to not mean it. Tell me, do you take responsibility for any of your actions?"

I jumped out of my chair, one of my hands on my hip, the other wagging at Brent as I walked toward him. "It was an accident," I snapped. "Not to mention, you kissed me first."

Brent looked almost bored with the conversation and gave me an exaggerated yawn before answering. "That was to stop your meltdown. It didn't count as a kiss."

"Right," I fumed, my index finger poking him in the chest. "So we're even then. My kiss didn't count because it was an accident and yours didn't count because it was strictly for medical purposes. Neither of them counted as kisses."

"Would you have wanted them to?" Brent demanded suddenly, bending his neck so he whispered it in my ear. His mouth gently grazed my earlobe, his breath caressing my neck. He lifted my finger that was still digging in between his ribs and circled his own around it, then slid his hand down until our fingers were intertwined. My insides melted into a sticky Yara-puddle of romantic goop.

Sandpaper lined my throat. I opened my mouth, intent on making some snippy comment. "I . . . I mean . . . you. . ." My traitorous brain allowed words to abandon me, leaving me stuttering and flushing like an idiot.

"I thought so." Brent pulled back and examined my face with a smug smile that made my racing pulse skitter to a stop.

"Why, you . . . of course I—"

Brent cut me off in the most unexpected way. He took me in his arms where I gave a feeble token struggle. He held me tightly, both our hearts beating loudly in a harmonious rhythm, before he pulled back enough for his supple, soft lips to find mine. The whole atmosphere around us changed. The air felt thicker, full of something new, exciting but scary, and smelled sweet like vanilla.

Emotions boiled inside me as my joints turned into

jelly, my heart went up in cinders and even my pinky toe swooned. Joy can be overwhelming, too, I found, as I projected without meaning to. To my amazement Brent must have felt it too, because his spirit followed mine; we both had left our bodies in the same instant. In the back of my mind, I was aware that the trees around us swayed at the sudden gale of wind circling us, my hair lifted and wound around Brent's head, chairs rattled, loose stones shuddered, trash cans tipped and their contents spilled across the ground before becoming airborne, even the fire roared louder. When we finally pulled apart, the area around us was littered with debris, broken branches, toppled objects and Brent's hair spiked unevenly, though that might have been from running my fingers through it.

"That was . . ." I trailed off trying to find the proper adjective.

"Long overdue?"

"Long overdue? You're the one who got skittish when I mentioned how I felt and backed away when we almost kissed."

"You call me on all my crap, don't you?" He laughed throwing his head back. "That's one of the things I love about you," he said. His fingers skimmed up my shoulders until they cradled my neck and my whole body tingling.

"Love?" I couldn't meet his gaze so I studied his strong chin instead.

The veins on his neck pulsed, the muscles in his shoulders tensed and he cleared his throat. "Yeah, love, Yara." His fingers traced the contours of my jaw and I leaned into his touch. "What Dallin said was true . . . I did date around a lot, but with you it's been different— it's been different from the beginning. I don't want anyone else. I haven't wanted anyone else since I met you."

His chocolate brown eyes, filled with passion and vulnerability, were like black holes trapping me in their gravitational pull.

"I don't either."

A brilliant smile flashed on his face and his shoulders loosened. He looked around at the tipped table, strewn garbage, fallen leaves, and general chaos of the usually tidy quad. "Impressive."

"I think we can do better," I said, resting my head on his chest, where his heart beat strong and sure, matching the cadence of my own.

"There's always room for improvement," Brent agreed with a promising grin. "It just might take a lot of practice. I'm something of a perfectionist."

The wind picked up intensity as Brent's lips found mine, and I decided our training sessions were going to be a lot of fun.

ACKNOWLEDGMENTS

I would like to thank and acknowledge:

My husband, for all his help, support, love, mad grammar skills and not judging me for writing in my pajamas, even into the afternoon.

My kids, for giving me hugs and kisses when I got discouraged.

Mom and Dad, for always believing in me and helping me in any way they could.

My Grandpa Gene and Grandma Doris, who inspired so much of this story.

Maddy, my first reader, for reading every draft and letting me know what didn't work.

The irreplaceable Alma, for doing the cover design, letting me know when a guy wouldn't say what I'd written, giving me several verbal kicks in the butt and admitting she hated my first prologue.

Melonie, for helping me write some great one-liners, helping skeleton scenes grow flesh, and all the hours spent brainstorming with me.

Anna Genoese, my talented editor, who also has fantastic taste in television shows.

Renee, for helping me figure out how to get rid of the second Evan.

Andy, for asking, "Does her name have to be Abby?" and helping me define a music genre.

Jodi Meadows, for taking the time to explain how to show, not tell.

My big sister Melanie, for showing me that writing a book was possible.

My big brothers Steve and Brent, who are (were) the world's best brothers.

Marietta Zacker, for asking if I needed a second Evan.

Suzie Townsend, for giving me some great feedback , and for giving me hope even while saying no.

Heather, for being a proofreader, and when needed, a critic.

Michelle (Honey), for helping edit the many versions of my book.

Cherie, for liking Brent's lazy grin, being a beta-reader and all her positive energy.

Ashley, for her expert feedback and suggestions for several key scenes.

For all my other friends who were my readers and editors: Christy, Laurie, Erica, Nicole, Jody Lynn, Cali (my long lost twin), Christina (Peak) and Jill.

A big Thank You to Gillian, David and Chris for inspiring me in the first place.

And last, but in no way least, I want to thank Kamilla Quast for believing in my book enough to pick it up and take a chance on me.